THE TREASURE DEL DIABLO

John T. Wayne

THE GASLIGHT BOYS (series)

THE NEW STANDARD IN WESTERN FOLKLORE!

THE TREASURE DEL DIABLO

John T. Wayne

THE GASLIGHT BOYS (series)

THE NEW STANDARD IN WESTERN FOLKLORE!

Mockingbird Lane Press

The Treasure del Diablo
Copyright © 2017 John T. Wayne

Mockingbird Lane Press—Maynard, Arkansas

ISBN: 978-1-6353524-1-2

Library of Congress Control Number: Information in publication data.

0 9 8 7 6 5 4 3 2 1

www.mockingbirdlanepress.com
Graphic art cover: Jamie Johnson

Map on front cover by: David Rumsey Map Collection, www.davidrumsey.com.

Always store your riches where no one can get at them.
Not even the devil!

THE GASLIGHT BOYS

From 1861 – 1865 a storm rolled through our nation and in its wake left behind a path of death and destruction. Over 100,000 children lost everything they had come to know including both parents. This tragedy took place during the Civil War and sadly for years after; during a period known as Reconstruction. What became of those children? How were they instrumental in shaping the future of our society? These questions are answered in my series of books called, "The Gaslight Boys." Charles Dickens is credited with being the original Gaslight Boy, but there were many other Gaslight Children created by the war. The Gaslight Boys series brings to life the hardships, the conditions and individual struggles buried and /or forgotten by time.

These are the stories of the young men and women who grew up to become great in their own right, men and women of the great society. Some of them became great, some became outlaws, and some died short of the chance. The Gaslight Boy novels are their stories.

John T. Wayne

Author's Note

In a unique moment of providence, I came across the origins of the term Federal as in: Federal Government. In an unrestricted essay dated 1673 we see in the true concept of the worship of God; the Eucharist was called "a Federal Banquet." I was stricken by the use of the term Federal in such a manner not at all referenced by our churches or government today. The term Federal then was first recorded in American English as a covenant, explicitly between God and mankind. This discovery brings an entirely new sense of understanding to the term Federal Union.

The Founding Fathers chose the term Federal for our form of government specifically because they wanted to remind themselves each and every day of the rest of their lives they had just signed a contract with God Almighty. They in turn pledged their lives, their families and their sacred honor to defend this sacred contract which they delivered, and many of them paid with their lives. This Federal Contract then has been signed, sealed and delivered, in American Blood. The Founding Fathers upheld their end of the covenant and now today God is still upholding his end of that agreement.

The term Federal was first recorded in English about 1660 when the settlers began to refer to the 13 colonies as The Federal Union. This then was the origin of the Federal Contract between God and America. I for one am not ashamed to claim my inheritance.

God Bless America!

For my friend U.S. Army Major: Ron Miller who was the Helicopter Safety Officer in the movie, The Green Beret.

---Tailwinds!

Chapter 1

Man and horse struggled to get a foothold in the shifting silica of the rust colored dune planting each step clumsily in the scorching desert sand, their faces wrapped with cloth to keep the smallest of irritating dust particles from clogging their nostrils. Atop the crest the man pulled rein bringing his horse to a stop. Scanning the horizon he saw no deliverance from the searing waves of heat, only another burning hot dune and another, and on the horizon a thousand more. Rolling hills made of wind-blown sand distinguished the path to the east and south. To the north and west rested a few jagged escarpments of rock and more sand pocked the horizon to infinity. The stallion folded its legs, first his front then his rear, couching on top of the dune with the indifference of dying.

Het up with his luck, the unfortunate horseman yanked hard on the reins, but the horse refused to respond. Reaching behind his neck the young man pulled a razor sharp bowie knife from its sheath and sank the weapon to the hilt in the hind quarters of the non-responsive sorrel. Blood oozed deep red as he withdrew the blade but nary a twitch offered itself in response by the condemned beast. Bobby Joe Riggins understood with clarity the fate befalling his last remaining animal and he was a man who could tell you a thing or two about how to lose a complete pack train of burros. Starving for nourishment and water, the sorrel's body simply stopped

1

working; like a steam engine out of fuel, having no more coal from which to draw its energy. He had witnessed exhaustion such as this recently for he had lost a dozen burros in like manner the past few days, sometimes surrounded by life-giving foliage which they ignored, lacking the will or the energy to eat.

Disturbed by recent developments, the young man thrust his knife back into place after wiping the blood off on the rump of the dying animal. It was time to rest anyway. The sun was high and fierce, small gusts of wind whipped around in swirls and a hot summer day was marching steadfastly into the early afternoon hours where temperatures would easily reach one hundred seventeen degrees in the shade. Yet there was no shade on the land south of the border; not with the sun so high overhead. Bobby Joe Riggins, as was his adopted name, wished he was anywhere else on earth, but wishing would not change his current situation.

"Maddening. The entire chain of events was maddening. Why didn't you stop sooner?"

The accusation and subsequent question was spoken in the tattle-tail silence which shrouded the treasure hunter's thinking.

Removing his blanket roll, he fastened one end to the saddle which still adorned his ill-fated beast. Slowly he relieved it of the undue burden, leaving only the saddle, an item he couldn't carry anyway. Pulling his pistol from the well-worn holster, he stuck the muzzle into the horse's ear and squeezed the trigger. The gun barked its unmistakable orders and inch by inch the animal lowered a lifeless head until the entire carcass rested firmly on the scorching desert sand indicating the horse had been all but dead when he pulled the trigger.

"Well that was a wasted bullet," he muttered.

Stretching out his blanket, he tucked two corners under each end of the saddle and attached the two remaining corners to the ends of his rifle and shotgun barrels, placing them at just the right angle in the sand, keeping the blanket stretched away from the horse yet high enough for him to crawl under the makeshift lean-to for shade. Because there was a slight breeze, he waited a few minutes, allowing the sand in the newly shaded area a chance to cool down a bit. It was likely the occasional gusts were a fleeting thing, yet under current circumstances every advantage needed to be exploited.

Ultimately crawling under his blanket next to the unwitting carcass, he collapsed beside the expired beast and leaned back against his sacrificed saddle to rest. Painstakingly, the bewildered adventurer gathered his personal effects about him, and then repositioned his hat on his head. Feeling the slight breeze in his hair as he did so caused him to change his mind and remove the hat altogether. Closing his eyes he contemplated exactly how this trip evolved into such a disastrous chain of events.

Three weeks ago he left El Paso and headed due south with two stout horses and a dozen slow moving burros, crossing the border late at night, unobserved by man or beast. The first two weeks he rode straight south avoiding any contact with humans, friendly or otherwise. Then, when he was near Chihuahua, he skirted the settlement and turned due east heading directly into the heart of the Desert del Diablo better known as "The Devil's Land."

Now after a week's travel into this scorching God-forsaken country, he knew why the territory south of the border was so appropriately named.

He should have turned back before now; he should have, but he wanted to at least see the gold bars, maybe hold some of the plunder in his hands or even bring a little of the high grade bullion home with him. Only his unquenched desire to secure something of the treasure pushed him to go on this long, and now he would pay for such a foolish decision. The burros dying on their feet were the first sign something was awry and any reasonable man would have taken the hint, but when gold fever takes over the decision-making process, calm and reason are usually the first things that vanish.

He understood his error now and he also recognized, with an alarming finality, the precarious situation he placed himself in. A new game was afoot. His very survival hung in the balance. He thought back to the story he had been told about the gold being elusive, gold taken by Cortez when he marched north from Mexico City after he subdued the native Aztec's of the southwest. The gold had been stolen again and again over the last three hundred years only to be stolen one more time. Finally found and acquired by emperor Maximilian of Mexico in 1856 the gold was stolen from his grasp by his own soldiers. Now it was resting in a Spanish water tower in a ghost town in Mexico and he had the map. Anyone could have found it by now, for it had been twenty years, but there was an equal chance the gold was still there.

The legend was a perplexing thing. About every twenty years the gold made an appearance, then as suddenly as it appeared the treasure would disappear until the moniker "The Treasure del Diablo," rested on it. The Devil's treasure. Men who touched it seemed to die, yet he'd not touched the bullion just yet. He didn't believe in the old superstitious tales anyway. It would take more than the handling of gold to prove him wrong. He was bent on proving those tales false and returning home with the treasure.

He knew the desert well enough to respect what God had created as most thoughtful folks did. You could stack all of the odds in your favor, plan your route with precision timing, pray for a safe trip and wait until all of the stars were perfectly aligned, yet the possibility of calamity remained. A mistake in navigation, a canteen, a water bag that sprung a leak or a perfectly healthy animal going lame, could leave you stranded in the worst possible circumstances. Not to mention having to deal with unreasonable and inhospitable Indians.

Life had presented dire circumstances to the young man before, and he knew the only way to survive was to keep his wits about him, not panic and carry on as best he could. He was near his destination, the ghost town of Madera, Mexico, yet the rules he operated under had changed. They were now live or die.

This was nothing new for him. There was one thing he had learned early on in life; if he was going to find some happiness he was going to have to travel a long way to get it. He knew it was a long way because from the point he had started there just wasn't any happiness to grab hold of. He was certain his mother and father had loved one another, but where had they found love? And what was necessary for them to be happy? His mind often strayed to things of the past which he had no control over, then abruptly returned to the trouble at hand. It was a pattern, but one he learned to live with. It would take life changing events to get him to think in any other manner of that much he was certain.

He just parted with the only mode of transportation he had, short of walking. His only alternative was to survive, well, it wasn't his only alternative, but he never liked to give credence to the other possibility. Any chance of recovering the hidden gold of Cortez was lost for the time being. Bobby Joe Riggins, the treasure hunter, had to find the nearest water hole and fast. Finding water would require every ounce of energy and intelligence he could muster.

The Desert del Diablo was his new enemy. A dried-up, sun baked stretch of earth and wind-blown sand dunes spotted here and there with jagged rock. A desolate land traveled by few and survived by less, a land that swallowed up and buried its own dead.

After several hours of waiting under his makeshift shelter, the sun began to relent, taking with it the hottest part of the day. He took stock of his possessions and began to wonder how many items he could carry without being overburdened. The last thing any sane man wanted was to suffer the identical fate that condemned the horse. He decided if he was able to survive, next time he would fetch some good old Missouri mules. They could maintain a better pace than burros, thus keeping up with the lead horse without struggling. Looking back it was obvious why the burros died. The pack animals hadn't been able to keep pace with the horses. As each one of the burros expired, he shifted their burden to others, and in so doing, he sealed their fate.

Taking stock, he noticed his gear amounted to far more than he could carry, even without the weight of the saddle. Everything would have to be abandoned, everything except for his rifle, canteen, compass, and the rawhide map showing the location of the hidden gold, along with the only sources of local water.

Opening saddlebags, he retrieved the last piece of jerked beef and noted with disdain how woefully inept his prepared rations had been. On his next expedition, he would more than double the food rations or he risked repeating the mistake he already made. If growing up on the streets of St. Louis had taught him anything, it was to make a mistake was all right, providing you learned from the error, and the miscalculation hadn't cost your precious life. A wise fellow wouldn't make a habit of repeating such monumental blunders.

Lifting the detailed map from his bag, he studied his surroundings, and marked what he believed to be his position on the hand-me-down parchment. After checking his position again, he scrutinized the scribbling and stared at the fading sun in dismay. If his calculations were correct, he missed the only water source he was likely to find in this barren wilderness and was now south of Sacred Springs by a good ten miles. Worse, was the fact the water hole was only an occasional supply which might be dried up unless there had been recent rains. Only a few ounces of the life-giving fluid remained in his canteen, and thinking of the water convinced him to taste it before anything else happened.

"Ten miles. If I get out of this I might be the luckiest man alive," he muttered.

He'd been on his own for a while now. Life had been pitching him to and fro since birth. Now as a young adult, things seemed to be no better. He wanted an easy life, he wanted things to go his way for once, he wanted love, but loneliness was always at the door.

Reluctantly he stood and stretched. Gathering his essentials, he placed his bowie knife, an extension of himself, around the nape of his neck. Stepping out in a predetermined direction, he headed due north where he suspected there would be fresh water at Sacred Springs. Sacred Springs was located right smack dab in the middle of the Desert del Diablo! He wondered at the irony of such names as he began to stretch a leg with a good distance eating pace.

For several hours, he walked while the evening waned, often switching his rifle from left hand to right and then back, not wanting to exhaust either arm, though ultimately exhaustion began to overtake him. As the devil's vale overtook the evening, a full moon rose, lighting his way on such a peaceful night, sending a mysterious glow across the landscape of blackened desert rock and soft sand, casting everything in black and white. Stooping, he paused to pick up a small pebble then dropped it in his mouth, slowly swishing it from side to side in an attempt to get his saliva flowing again. Disgusted with the recent turn of events, he continued to hike due north, wondering how he'd misread the map to begin with, a bungle that caused him to miss the only water hole for miles. With nothing else to consider for the moment he thought about the gold. It eluded him, just like in the stories he heard of old. Would no one ever get to spend the treasure?

From the moment he'd been born in the post office in Hermann, Missouri, to this very minute, nothing had transpired as he'd wished. True, he never shrank from trying, but no matter what he undertook things had a way of turning sour. Nothing in his life was off limits. Often he succumbed to the belief he'd been cursed, one of those generational curses that follow a man all the way to his grave, but somehow time after time he would shake off the feeling of doom and continue on in the hope he would someday find success. Often as not, this little flame of hope was all he had.

His father had been the postmaster in Hermann, hence the reason he'd entered this world in the new post office that had been built in 1840. He was also aware his father died on the Missouri River in a boating accident late at night, leaving him fatherless at the age of three months. All Bobby Joe knew was the untimely death had something to do with the unloading of mail from the *Omaha*, the steamboat that transported goods up and down the Mississippi, Missouri and Ohio Rivers. The *Omaha*, a steamer, whose landing he never missed when the boat docked on the wharf in St. Louis.

Just six months after his father's death, his mother died in a struggle to deliver another baby into the world, leaving him with no parents at all. Whether or not the child lived was an issue he was never able to resolve. So many times when he was growing up, he'd dreamed of having a brother or sister, someone close to share his experiences with, but alas it was a dream that never materialized, for he was now a grown man of twenty-three.

Of the few trips he made back to Hermann, the only thing he'd discovered was the post office where he'd been born still stood on the hillside overlooking the river and Hermann landing. There was no road to the east as the hillside that anchored the post office ascended steeply. From there the street followed the river westward to another hill that held the courthouse. In between was any number of local businesses, a winery, a blacksmith, two stables and a mercantile.

Anyone who might have known anything of his past couldn't remember the details of his mother's death or they'd moved away. A fire in the courthouse destroyed records that might have given him the answer he was looking for. He gave up his effort to uncover family history. All he had was a birth name of Westmoreland, information he acquired from Captain Grimes senior of the *Omaha* and if he died in this God-forsaken land, he would never know anything else.

In 1861 he lost his adopted parents to an earthquake on the New Madrid fault-line, the same fault-line that caused the Mississippi River to run backwards for more than twenty-four hours in 1811, and create what was now known as Reelfoot Lake in Tennessee. Twice orphaned, he headed for St. Louis, and within a year, the Civil War. The Federals wasted no time in securing the state of Missouri with their forces, but Missouri ran strong with Confederate blood. The Yankee's might have controlled the ports and landings, but southern folks learned quickly how to get around such heavy handed tactics.

Captain Grimes was a well-respected riverboat pilot, and along with Mark Twain, was summoned to pilot a boat for the Yankee fleet just before the onset of war.

However, the captain and his friend had other plans, and Grimes ran the Yankee blockades on the Mississippi River to deliver mail to the Confederate troops, most of whom were homesick for news of their families. Bobby Joe grew to know both father and son personally, for he'd been summoned many times to deliver mail to Grimes outside of town at Lemay Ferry.

For lack of a better alternative, the ladies of St. Louis began sewing reverse pockets into their petticoats to hold an allotment of mail. Most of the time, Bobby Joe would not have eaten but for the grateful matrons who insisted on feeding the orphaned youngster living on the street. After the war started though, things took a grim turn, for there were hundreds and then thousands of orphans showing up on the streets, and living under the gaslights. It was a dark time for children of all ages. Many were abused, many died for lack of adequate shelter and many of them were taken advantage of for a morsel to eat.

Some of the boys were known to swear, thinking their language made them appear tough, but after a while, it occurred to him that this was a mere cover-up. Their weakness exposed, he never gave thought to joining them for it did expose a certain weakness, but they themselves couldn't see or understand it. The boys who resorted to such language did so to cover up the fact they were afraid. Whether afraid of the future, their daily existence or what life had done to them he never knew.

He might have been all right except for the war between the North and South. The trouble was, picking sides in a so-called neutral state like Missouri could get a man, or a boy for that matter, killed and when the war had started he was only a boy. For nearly five years he tiptoed around St. Louis trying to keep his hair while making neither side mad. By then the place was overrun with orphans. The girls got the orphanages, thus the boys got the streets and a nickname: "The Gaslight Boys." He became one of the many youngsters who worked the riverfront for a way to survive. Truth be known, he wished he was back there now.

He left St. Louis shortly after the war, figuring to make his mark out west. Young Bobby Joe saw the true workings of reconstruction and wanted no part of the affair. The war had not affected the western states, not much anyway, so he made a decision to move on and headed west. The problem was every bad man in the country seemed to have the same idea. Folks like Catfish John, Wild Bill Dolin, Bat Masterson, and others migrated west after the war and this fact made life difficult at best for everyone else. Men young and old tiptoed with caution or got their fool heads blown off. That was the reality of the times.

Throughout his difficulties and upbringing, it was several years before he'd any idea of his real birth name, yet he learned to accept the name he'd been given by the Riggins'. They had been a good God-fearing family, yet what had their faith gotten them? It seemed to him, death and destruction had no particulars and played no favorites, the Grim Reaper was quite adept at taking the good right along with the bad. Now everything seemed far away, separated by distance, tribulation and the sands of too much time.

Repeatedly, he resisted the temptation to divert around hills and dunes. He navigated by dead reckoning, for even the slightest of errors could cost him his life, and indeed may have already done so. The empty canteen became a burden as was his rifle, only he couldn't release them. If he lost either one his life, or what he had left, wouldn't be worth a plugged nickel. The moon continued to glow bright directly overhead, illuminating his path, yet his feet seemed to drag a little more with each step. He plodded on.

Slowly his calm deserted him. He set his strength and experience against an unfamiliar land, the harsh and fiendish environment of the Desert del Diablo. He realized, at this instant, death was close, closer than it had ever been. Only then did he lose his ability to suppress his fear. Shadows swirled about him, but how? The shadows should not be moving, but they were darting by, first on the left, and then on the right. With all the soberness of a dying man, he realized there shouldn't be any shadows at all.

He tried to swallow but his throat was a mass of raw and swollen membranes that produced untold agony with the attempt. His eyes, dry from lack of water, continued to scan the desert floor searching for any evidence that might betray the whereabouts of that precious life-giving liquid, but he recognized nothing. No animal tracks, no plant life, nothing! His eyes blurred losing their ability to focus. It was time to stop. To continue when he could no longer see was foolish. Exhaustion consumed every muscle, every fiber of his being and would lead him astray. He dropped his...no! They were gone! Tumbling to the sand he searched frantically for his rifle and canteen. He could only pray the sun would awaken him. He knew very well what would happen if he failed to rise with the first light of dawn.

Chapter 2

Randy Bean was a gun for hire, a trade he'd learned at the hands of the Federal Government during the Civil War years earlier. Dean Reynolds had paid him to do a job and do the job he would, yet for Randy there was no mistaking the fact Dean was not the top dog. There was no question he was taking orders from someone else, of this, Randy was quite certain. As certain as he was, he had no idea who the real ramrod might be. As a killer for hire he could care less where the money came from, but he did like to know who was pulling the strings in an organization. Dean Reynolds was obviously a front man and the displaced rancher was being used like a plough horse with no inkling of his true station in life. Jack said as much and Jack Fuller was his best friend. They'd ridden together since before the Civil War when they were growing up in Knob Lick and now they worked for the same man.

He spent the afternoon waiting for his prey and now the wait was over. There could be no doubt as to the identity of the lone rider. Black and white paint, black and white vest, crossed cartridge belts, and two tied down pistols, it was without doubt, Pablo Mendoza the man he'd been waiting on.

In his mind only a fool would travel across such country as this adorned like a polished rodeo rider on parade. He smiled to himself and unsheathed his buffalo gun. All that shiny hardware could be spotted from miles

15

and in Indian Territory, no less. Dean said the young man would be flashy, but Randy never expected this.

Watching through his Civil War field glasses, the ones he had kept when the war was over, he observed the man's behavior and waited. When he stopped to get a drink, and squatted down to fill his canteen that would be the time. Checking the position of the long range sight, he pulled the precision weapon around beside him and checked his load then put the butt of the rifle to his shoulder and took aim. His target was over three hundred yards away, but he wasn't worried. He knew what he was capable of.

He never gave thought to the lives he took, not since the first man he'd killed during the Civil War. The first killing had been especially hard on him, but now he was numb to the act. He only thought of the next one, his next easy payday. He'd learned early the value of a sharp-shooter during the war when he'd been directly assigned to kill Confederate officers during battle. It was his only job, and he was good at it. Killing pay was much better than troop pay or punching cows. When the war ended, he felt a certain loss, his services weren't needed. Like so many before him, when the war ended, he was a human train wreck with no inkling of how to transition back, so when the opportunity presented itself for him to continue his sharp-shooting abilities, he jumped at the chance without considering the fact it would make him an outlaw by proxy.

The problem with becoming a criminal is giving up freedom, even if it's a little at a time.

Bean never thought of such things, although true. He never thought much about anything beyond the next target or the next job. Had he done so, he would likely have gone mad. He watched closely as Mendoza reached for his canteen and stepped into the pool. He knelt down filling the canteen that was covered in cow hide.

Exhaling, he held his breath, hesitated a second, then carefully squeezed the trigger on his sharps fifty. The buffalo gun boomed and the young man jerked sharply, then fell face first into Sacred Springs, the only water hole within fifty miles.

He wasn't finished. Picking up his field glasses he watched the body floating face down for nearly a half hour. Only when he was completely satisfied the rider was, in fact dead, did he gather up his belongings and head for home leaving the body where it lay.

An experienced gun for hire, he had his own unique way of fulfilling an assignment. He never took anything off a dead man for fear the man's possessions might implicate him at a later date. He always made certain his mission was accomplished by the use of field glasses just as he'd done on the battlefield. To ride up to a wounded man was a good way to get killed and he had no intention of becoming an unlikely victim. He'd seen the scenario played out before by other men in other places who were not as careful and it was never prudent to be found standing over the dead body regardless of the circumstances.

It was a long ride back to Sonora, but he was up to the rigors of travel with another notch to carve on his rifle butt, another successful mission behind him. He was careful to never get involved in the circumstances of a particular case. Taking sides in any matter only muddied up the waters. No one needed to tell him, something he knew from experience, in which he was almost hung. The circumstances meant nothing, only the money. Outlaws didn't make friends, which is the way he preferred his life. Truth be known, he could do without company altogether as he found most relationships repugnant. Jack Fuller, a man he'd known since he was twelve years old, was his only friend in the world, yet he kept to himself most of the time and didn't take well to people in general. He did, however, like to talk right after a killing, not because he needed to share the experience with them, that would be foolish, but because company helped him to forget about what he'd done. Of course, that's to be expected when making a living killing others.

As he picked up his things and rode away, he suddenly encountered one aspect with this killing that he wasn't ready for, one thing to which he hadn't given a single thought. The job took place so far from any known civilization it would take him nearly three weeks to return to Nogales on the border. Very much an unwelcome thought as he would more than likely continue to review the killing in his mind, one he wanted to forget. His way was to forget what he'd done by immediately spending time with others, though he was, for the most part, a loner. Conversation and company, along with a few stiff drinks usually made him feel better. Although he never discussed his killings or missions as he preferred to call them, the company of a good woman was able to help him forget.

Nothing out of the ordinary would happen this time he told himself. It was just this unholy land, this "Devil's Land!" Too many old and frightful stories were told and spread by old-timers who actually knew something of the place from years gone by, yet what did they know?

Although certain none of the old tales he'd heard were true, he reviewed the stories one by one in his mind as he swiftly guided his horse back toward the border. There were Indians to watch for and he would need the remaining water holes. His attention needed to be placed squarely on the task at hand, the thing that would do him the most good, and his surroundings. This far south a man could have his scalp lifted by any number of Kiowa, Apache, Pima or Comanche, just to name a few.

He rode with caution, and he rode with purpose, guiding his horse with utmost care, yet his trip became unsettling. He was far from any conversation and would be for weeks. Once he made Nogales at the border he could stop and have a drink or two and maybe talk a little with Red, if the bartender was still around. He had a few old friends along the border, and some of them would likely be at the cantina in Nogales.

Topping out on a small rise at the edge of the sand dunes he rode his horse out of the barren landscape and into a jagged, rough country, an area covered with high rock formations, tumbleweeds, and small dry sagebrush. Although he now rode on sand, it was no longer deep and his horse didn't sink ten inches with each step taken. Travel would be much easier and faster now.

Five miles to the north and west he found the trickle of water he was looking for. Pima Springs was a little known water hole which thrust itself out of the land in an unlikely place surrounded by nothing. The only hint water existed was green vegetation on the rock bottom shelf, something you couldn't see until you were actually within a stone's throw of the location. Here is where he bedded down for the night and let his horse trail loose. The animal would not stray from a good water source or the little vegetation available for foraging at the spring.

He was determined not to think of the man he'd killed, yet as though haunted by the vaquero, he could think of nothing else. Throughout the night he tossed and turned, immersed in nightmares about the murder of Pablo Mendoza, who came for him in his sleep. Constantly he dodged the horse and rider, running for cover, only to be discovered again and again as if there was no sanctuary from the dead man's ghost.

Long before sunup he was in his saddle and riding, completely worn out by relentless nightmares. Awake, he could control his thoughts, or so he believed. Still, he watched his back trail and thought of little else.

With an aggravating conscience, he questioned himself. Why was this one so different? Why was this one haunting him so? Never before had he encountered these kinds of nightmares or disturbing thoughts. One by one he recounted the horror of each tale he'd heard, all of them tales and images of gore, destruction and waste.

The trouble with becoming an outlaw is, although all physical evidence can be erased, and although the crime itself might be gotten away with, there's absolutely nothing that can be done about the trail left in one's own mind. He cursed himself for the thoughts he was having. Was there no end to such punishment? Not a soul was around to point out the folly of his actions, yet his mind was working overtime to make him feel remorse.

Spurring his horse, he picked up his pace for Arizona, disliking every aspect of the desert in which he was traveling and the time necessary to return to Sonora.

Wind gathered down the long hills whispering softly at first, but then it gathered its wings and howled in earnest. He noted the sudden change by watching as the bones of a nearby human skeleton were uncovered. He paused long enough to tie his neckerchief about his face.

"Confounded devil," he muttered from behind his bandana. The wind was going to hound him again today. Why couldn't the devil just leave him be? Every time he killed a man, the wind came howling. Always the wind reared its ugly head as if demons were riding on pitch black iniquity, hell bent on seeking him out, searching for the killer of innocent men.

Chapter 3

Cold...Bobby Joe was shivering cold! Unconsciously he tried to burrow deeper into the soft desert sand but his efforts were futile as warmth avoided him like the plague. Breathing...someone was very close to him and breathing heavily. An all too cool gust of wind blew sand into his face and open mouth. As the wind gust died away he opened his eyes for a moment. His vision was nothing but a blur and it took him several minutes to gain any kind of usable focus and rub the sand from his eyes. Water, he needed water. Tilting his head upward he stared in disbelief into the unlikely nostrils of a horse standing over him. Then he remembered where he was and what was happening.

"Great," he managed while spitting sand. "Now I'm hallucinating."

Closing his eyes for a moment, he hoped the hallucination would go away, but the strange animal remained. He could in fact hear the horse breathing louder now. Then the horse nudged his right arm, as if to say, "It's time for you to get up." Again he blinked his eyes to clear his vision and opened them to see his improbable antagonist standing over him, reins trailing. Did hallucinations include sound and touch, or were they only driven by sight alone? It was a question he didn't know the answer to, but wished he did.

Rolling to his feet, he brushed himself off with his weather-beaten old hat and slowly straightened. Every bone and joint in his body cried out in pain. The horse nudged him in the back shoving him forward a few steps. He came close to losing his balance and tumbling to the ground.

"Would you quit it?" he challenged as he spun around to address his illusion face to face. "Who are you? Why are you bothering me?"

The horse stared as if to say, "You are supposed to be in the saddle by now, let's go!"

Turning his back on the unwelcome illusion, Bobby Joe walked away from the animal, but he could hear the horse's hooves on the sand behind him with each step the animal took. When he turned back around, the creature was still there, observing him with now wary eyes.

Either his senses had completely deserted him or he beheld a miracle. Knowing he'd killed all his animals riding after the gold, he was now staring at one that was unbelievable, a black and white paint like he'd never seen before. The animal stood a good seventeen hands tall. This horse was as big as the Clydesdales he'd seen running around St. Louis, only more muscular, if such a thing was possible. He had seen many paints before, but none of them could hold a candle to this one when it came to size, strength and stamina.

A rifle rested naturally in the scabbard, the saddlebags were fastened securely behind the saddle and the animal gave all appearances of being fresh. The big horse also could have belonged to a Spanish Vaquero as the saddle and bags were studded with silver. Cautiously, he stepped toward the horse, which did not move, and grabbed up the trailing reins. Surprisingly the horse stood fast while he struggled up, which took some effort. He had never known such soreness as when he pulled his pain wracked body into the saddle of the unknown stallion. Considering his condition and the size of the stallion he did all right while the horse remained still for the task.

Once in the saddle he knew he was no longer imagining things and he began to examine the issue of the unlikely animal. Who could own such a magnificent animal, and where was the owner? Why was the animal so fresh? Was this horse the devil's own mount? Maybe this was the ride that was supposed to deliver him to the gates of hell. It would be just like the devil to trick him. He was about to slide from the saddle when an idea occurred to him. He gave the horse several easy commands and the animal followed them all. It could not possibly be the devil's own ride he concluded, but a lost horse.

What had happened to allow a horse of this magnitude to wander off on its own accord saddled and ready for riding? Instinctively he scanned the horizon for tracks, yet the only ones he could see were his own and those of the horse. At once he back tracked the paint. In his mind there were only two answers to explain such a horse being here at this moment and in such immaculate condition, neither of them bore a good sign. If the animal's owner was still alive, back tracking the stallion was the only way to find him.

The first thing he saw as he steered the horse on its back trail was the sun bleached skeleton of a dead man pushing up through the sand surrounded by a few short blades of grass. As he continued, he witnessed other skeletons, then a wagon wheel protruding three quarters from the drifting sand, still attached to the turned over wagon. Then as he persisted, he saw even more skeletons, one after another as if lining the path to hell itself, only none of these bleached bones bore any indication of what he was searching for. All he saw so far was the remains of people and animals long dead, their bones bleached pure white by the sun and the elements, yet he was searching for someone who still lived, or only recently deceased.

Three miles further along he found what he was looking for, but his presence wouldn't be of any consequence to the man. The Spanish dude was face down with a bullet in his back, his life's blood spilled into the only water hole for many miles, Sacred Springs!

The man, unmistakably a Spanish vaquero wore chaps, spurs, and an unusual black and white vest which matched his horse. The man lay face down in the only water source Bobby Joe was going to find this side of Sunday. The gun belt around his waist sported two ivory handled pistols. His black and white cowhide covered canteen floated in the water beside him. His shirt was deep blue and his pants were denim, and the boots appeared almost new.

Stepping down from the big paint, he surveyed the area. An outcropping of rocks about three hundred yards to the north seemed to be the only cover large enough to conceal anyone who might be waiting in ambush, and the horse he would have to be riding. He made a mental note to head off in a northerly direction when he was done cleaning up here at the water hole. People and animals would need this water and to leave the body would contaminate it. He was the only person who could do anything to recover the fresh water. This was not an assigned duty and he would be the first to tell you he was no goody two shoes, but being the only water hole for many miles in any direction meant someone had to clean up the mess the killer had left behind.

Alas, the habits of western men. Nothing needed to be said most times and yet any western man could look at his surroundings, study on a situation and let the earth do most of the talking for him. No words need be spoken and yet a conversation was taking place just the same, a conversation just like the one Bobby Joe was now engaged in.

The man's tracks revealed plainly where he'd squatted down to fill his canteen. The deep gouges his boot toes left on impact, the bullet carrying the unsuspecting target out into the pool with its momentum. No doubt the rifle had been a big one, for at three hundred yards the bullet would have been slowing down, yet such a firearm still had enough impact to bury the man face down in the shallow pool of water. He studied the situation a bit longer and then took a look at his distant surroundings.

Walking over to the water's edge he stepped into the edge of the pool and retrieved the dead man's canteen. Still three quarters full he turned it up and poured a swig into his parched mouth. His tongue was still swollen from yesterday, but with water it would recover. Not knowing if the canteen was contaminated he spit it out after swishing the liquid around in his mouth for several seconds. He tasted no blood, but then he never expected to in his current condition. Pouring a dab on his left hand he judged the water to be fresh and took a good swallow. Letting the first drink he'd had in nearly two days sink in, he tilted the canteen back to his mouth and drank deeply, then capped the remainder and set the water aside.

Wading deeper into the pool he straddled the lifeless fellow a few moments then flipped the carcass over. His condition was such that he was unable to accept what he saw and he stumbled backward over the dead body landing in a heap on his rear, sitting in the shallow pool of blood tainted water.

Except for the mustache and goatee, Bobby Joe could have been staring at himself. Looking more closely he decided the fellow was the same build and about the same age, yet the man was obviously of Spanish descent. The vaquero's complexion was a bit darker, but the sun could darken the skin enough to make the difference he supposed. He had the sensation of looking in a mirror.

He never knew if he had a brother or sister and would likely never know, yet he wanted to believe it so. Could the man before him be his brother? Impossible! He dismissed the question as soon as the thought came to him. If he had a brother the man would not be of Spanish descent, yet he could not look at the man before him and not consider him a brother for the resemblance between them was that uncanny.

No tenderfoot would be riding alone in such a place nor carrying the kind of weaponry this man had on him. The horse, the guns, his clothes, even his Spanish saddle and lariat were all indicators of his prominence in society. There was the horse. How could anyone discount such a fine specimen of horse flesh? No, the dead man was someone who would shoot your hide off if you slighted him in some way, Bobby Joe was certain of it.

The two cartridge belts crisscrossing his chest did nothing to distract from the Spanish vaquero's unmistakable style. Bobby Joe was sure that when this man rode anywhere he rode with respect for others and would command respect in turn. The man before him was no tenderfoot, yet he had been murdered with ease. Obviously, he'd not been expecting anything of the kind or for someone to sneak up on him.

Carefully he unbuckled the man's gun belt and lifted a pair of ivory handled Russian .44's from the blood tainted pool. The guns were an amazing piece of artwork. The steel was coated and forged in plating. He'd never seen the likes of them. They looked almost as if they were gold plated. Draping them across the horse he went back and dragged the body out of the water. Once he had the man stripped and the clothes lying across the mount to dry, he began to dig a new pool next to the existing one. Shoveling the sand from the new location, he tossed sand into the existing pool to help speed the flow of water through the natural sand filter. As the water began to flow into the new hole, it came in clean from twenty feet away, yet a lot of the water was just underneath the surface and would fill the new hole now the sand was dug down.

For two hours he worked, and was pleased when finished. Likely, the old water hole was forever buried; yet the new main pool remained close enough to maintain similar depth and proportions. When enough time had elapsed, the water below the surface would filter in providing fresh drinking water for both him and the horse. Had the dead man not been carrying a hand shovel, Bobby Joe would never have been able to transfer the pool and save the water for whomever or whatever came along behind him.

With the rider's own rope he dragged the look alike corpse well away from the water hole and buried the man.

When finished, he paused for a moment and said a few words, more for himself than for the dead man, and mostly a statement of thanks. For without the dead man's horse, gear and clothes, he would himself be dead or very near so.

Walking the horse back to water, he let him have his fill, then drank himself and topped off his new canteen. Slowly he began to don the dead man clothes and gear. His own clothes were torn, shredded from travel and unrecognizable. Knowing the dead man wouldn't begrudge him what he needed, Bobby Joe dressed in a very unfamiliar manner. In admiration of the dead vaquero he gave thanks as he slid into the new duds.

Taking a new blue shirt from the saddle bags he put it on and tucked his old one away. Once he was fully dressed in the dead man's outfit, he noted the only difference between them was a two month growth of beard instead of a neatly trimmed mustache and goatee.

Only a couple of items remained and he strapped on the ivory carved pistols with reverence knowing the last man who wore them was now dead. At the outset the guns hung naturally and easily on his hips. The mule skin boots were a perfect fit, though still damp. Having scrubbed the blood from the back of the vest, he slipped it on. Then he strapped on the crossed cartridge belts full of ammo and settled them into place. Mounting up, he sat his new found horse surrounded by another man's style and life's work. Lifting the man's black sombrero from the saddle horn he placed the large Mexican umbrella on his head and pulled the leather string tight. Although the sombrero seemed tight at the first it would stretch once he'd worn it awhile.

Looking around once more he tried to figure just what had happened here. Murder. A man had ridden in completely unsuspecting, dismounted to fill his canteen and took a shot in the back from a distance. He was then left for dead. The killer, whoever he was had been sure of himself. Otherwise, he would have ridden up to make sure the job was complete, or would he have? He was not in the killing business so he pondered over his assumption for a few moments and concluded he really didn't have a clue.

It was mid-day and he needed to rest. The digging had left him exhausted but the water hole was no place to rest or relax. Indians, wild animals and anyone else who happened along would need the remaining water. Although the chance of someone else being in this God forsaken desert at this exact time and place was unlikely, but you just never knew. By his count three men had been here in the last day so he felt it best if he were somewhere else should anyone else make an appearance on the scene.

Nudging his new horse, he headed due north for the outcropping of rocks he'd seen earlier. As he rode around the back side of the formation he found exactly what he'd expected to find. The spot where the killer had waited, and what was considered real evidence. An expended shell casing from a Sharps .50 buffalo gun lay near the base of the rocks. The man hadn't even wiped out his boot prints. Sitting the paint he studied the situation further. Someone had wanted the vaquero dead, but why? He'd been riding from the east, a detail of which Bobby Joe was certain, but where had the vaquero been riding to? Stepping down from the horse he picked up the shell casing and sifted through the sand for more evidence that might aid him in identifying the killer. He found nothing. Turning, he put his foot in the stirrup, but halted instead. The killer had been waiting in yesterday afternoon's shade. In another hour the area where Bobby Joe stood would be completely shaded and he would be able to wait out the heat of the day in the coolest spot he was likely to find this side of the border.

Removing the blanket roll, he made ready his bed, then removing the saddle that had been on the horse too long already, he rubbed him down. He could wait. The heat of the day would soon be on them and would make riding much too uncomfortable and too risky. The fact he wasn't feeding the buzzards right now was no fault of his own.

Leaning back against his newly acquired saddle he opened the saddlebags to see what he had. He was rewarded on one side with stores of food. The other side contained a letter, another shirt, extra socks, another pair of jeans, and seventeen twenty dollar gold coins. Fresh minted gold coins are something an outlaw might be caught with, which would explain such a magnificent horse, as outlaws often preferred the strongest and fastest animal they could find as a good horse might mean the difference between life and death. It could also help explain the man's untimely demise, yet had he been a wanted man, surely the killer would have returned the body as evidence to collect a reward.

No, this was murder plain and simple. Besides this horse was such a looker no outlaw alive would ride him for fear of being too easily identified. An outlaw would prefer to lay low and inconspicuous. This man had been shot in the back from three hundred yards and left for dead. Murdered, but why?

Opening the letter Bobby Joe discovered a more practical motive.

Pablo,

Your uncle Don Pablo Mendoza is dead. He was thrown from his horse last week and never regained consciousness, circumstances continue to remain suspicious. He died this morning at sunup. Later today we learned he left everything to you. Although adopted, you are the only family he has left. You are to come at once to claim your inheritance.

"Adopted?" Bobby Joe asked out loud. The man he'd found dead was adopted?

The home ranch is approximately one hundred and fifty thousand acres, about seven thousand head of cattle, the ranch compound, two large holding corrals, four barns and six line camps. All is yours if you can reach the ranch within six months of your uncle's death. If you do not claim your inheritance by August, 14th of this year it will go to the next of kin.

Senor Reynolds believed he would inherit, but he did not know about you and has become a very dangerous man not at all worthy of being the ranch's new owner. He may have already killed several men, although I cannot prove my suspicions at this time. He may do the unexpected as he was present for the reading of your uncle's will, so be careful. Things are in good shape for now, but your neighbors to the east and west smell free range. If Reynolds takes over much blood will be shed unnecessarily, so come quickly.

Jeb Blackwell
Sonora, Arizona Territory

The letter had been addressed to Pablo Mendoza of Laredo, Texas and dated February, 14th 1876. The man had left Laredo, Texas on the border of Mexico and was no doubt riding to Sonora, Arizona to claim his inheritance. Someone made certain Pablo would never arrive. As Bobby Joe put the letter away he found a razor and a small mirror Pablo had used to keep his goatee trimmed. Why not shave? Why not trim his beard into a goatee? He was already wearing the dead man's clothes and guns. Why not?

As Bobby Joe trimmed his beard he fantasized about what such a ranch would be like; to own such a layout. How must a man feel to have so many men at his beck and call, to be the actual decision maker of such a spread? Then he remembered the shock of finding the man shot in the back and realized he could never do anything but go after the hired killer. Suddenly, as he finished trimming his new goatee he regretted having shaved with such a deliberate thought as to take over the ranch of the dead man, but then wouldn't Pablo Mendoza showing up anyway be the most effective way to flush out the killer? Could he ride in as if the killing had never happened and claim the inheritance? Of course! That was the answer.

He looked at himself in the mirror and took stock. Sooner or later a man has to own up. He can go on being contented or evading a problem so long, but there comes a time when he asks himself, "What have I done with my life?" and often as not the answer he is forced to give is an unhappy one. He remembered who he was and the thought was unsettling for he should be somebody by now. The last seven years he'd devoted to hard work, yet it had been work he accomplished for another man at a ranch up Montana way, backbreaking hard work, but he had learned cattle and how to use a gun.

It seemed he had always been treated as better left alone by others who were more fortunate than him. When would he be considered an equal by other men? When would they look him in the eye and not look down on the orphaned young man? Had it not been for the Civil War he might have been all right, but the war had orphaned a lot of children.

He put the shaving gear away and noticed a secret compartment on the inside of the saddlebags. It looked as though it was designed to carry important letters or documents. Searching the small fold he found a copy of the will, a bill of sale for the horse, and a detailed map of the ranch along with some newspaper clippings from Sonora, clippings of murders that had gone unsolved. Reading the clips, he decided the killer had migrated south, far south of the border. Every killing was detailed and done in the same manner as the killing of Pablo Mendoza. Was this what Jeb had meant when he said to be careful? Pablo had gotten careless.

Putting the papers away he lay back and covered his head with his new umbrella style hat. He tried to visualize the ranch and its holdings. Just the thought of such a cattle ranch was tranquilizing. What kind of man would it take to ramrod such a large outfit? How comforting it would be to ride into town and have everyone believe you were untouchable? What a dream, but such a dream would never happen to a gun hand, not a young man who could hardly speak a lick of Spanish. To have such a fantasy was delusional.

In the last seven years he'd pushed cattle all over the northwest, but never had he ventured this far south. Never in the desert had he herded cattle but how much different could the environment be? He had paid his dues all over the west, and what did he have to show for it? Nothing. Nothing but another man's horse and rig. Even the gold he'd been riding after belonged to someone else. The fact he had anything at all to help him return to civilization with was no fault of his own. Such a development had a way of making a man wonder just who he was and where he was headed.

Many were the times he'd longed for a better life and through all his efforts he'd come up empty-handed. Sitting there thinking as he was prone to do of late, he determined to make a change in his life. Far too many times he'd collected his pay and ridden to town with the other cowboys, drank, played, and fought only to recuperate on Sunday and start all over again on Monday, dead broke.

That's why he'd ridden after the gold. Now as he thought about things consciously for the first time he knew his station in life had been the reason all along. He was sick and tired of his fellow man treating him as "better left alone." He would do what he had set out to do. He would recover the stolen gold shipment from its twenty year resting place and buy his own spread. But first he had a murder to report, and he would have to replenish his supplies. One would require money, both would require time.

Remembering the murder, he wondered just what he could do. All he could think was ride to the ranch or send a wire to inform Jeb of the circumstances of Pablo's demise, or was it? He had the dead man's horse, his clothes, his guns, the will, a map of the ranch and having trimmed his beard to a goatee, he was the spitting image of the man himself. If in fact the killer wanted to prevent Pablo from claiming his inheritance, what would happen if Pablo arrived anyway? With everything he had in his possession, there was nothing to stop him from replacing the dead man, although his knowledge of the Spanish language would be a problem. Besides, what better way to flush out the killer? Although alike in appearance, the language and mannerisms would be totally different. Were those differences enough to tip his hand to the people who had not seen him for years, or at all? There was no mention in the letter that anyone at the ranch had ever seen or met Pablo Mendoza and the letter had been written in English. There was the fact he was a dead ringer for the man he'd buried, and he needed a stake. Going after the gold left him flat broke.

He would have done things different, in fact he'd set out to do just that and where had his decisions gotten him?

"That's a sobering thought," he mumbled to himself.

All he had to his name was a twenty year old map that belonged to a dead man, along with another man's rig. Regardless of the circumstances, no man deserved to be shot in the back and left for the buzzards, not even this fellow Pablo Mendoza. Ultimately, Bobby Joe realized if he didn't go after the killer himself, the scoundrel would get off scott free. Chances are no one else would care. If the dead man were ever found, who would identify him? How long would that be? Bobby Joe looked around and realized this part of the Desert del Diablo was full of bleached white skeletons that would never be identified.

The killer's tracks would be wiped out by the elements long before anyone knew Pablo was dead, yet judging from the ones he'd found, the killer could only be a day or so ahead, and would not be expecting any type of pursuit. Such a crystal clear revelation convinced him to track the killer down. Any chance of recovering the gold was lost until he could return with another pack train. After twenty years in an abandoned Spanish water tower, who could say if the gold was still there? Anyone could have discovered it by now. His mission was plain and simple—go after the killer.

Saddling the horse as the sun drifted low in the western sky; he mounted up and studied his surroundings, making sure he hadn't missed anything. Turning slowly he headed out, following the killer's trail. The paint felt good beneath him and a fine horse he was. Bobby Joe had never experienced a smoother gate. The new clothes were comfortable and so were the guns at his side. He still had his knife, as always the weapon hung around his neck between his shoulders. It was great to be alive to breathe fresh air drifting slowly over the cooling desert sand, yet someone took those things from Pablo Mendoza. He was going to find out who was behind the killing. The best way was to assume the man's identity and show up at the ranch in time to claim the inheritance.

Of course he would be a moving target unless he could catch up to the assassin before he reached Sonora. Then again, he might be a moving target even after he caught up.

There was no evidence to point directly at Dean Reynolds, only speculation. According to the letter, the man had reason enough, but was he smart enough to disassociate himself from the killings? How shrewd of a man was he? Ride the man down. That was the answer, and if it was Reynolds then so much the better. All the information Bobby Joe possessed gave no mention of the fact anyone at the ranch had ever seen Pablo before now except for maybe his uncle, and Uncle Don Pablo Mendoza was dead.

Turning his mount unexpectedly he tracked himself back to the point where he lost his own rifle, shotgun, and canteen. It would never do to leave a loaded rifle lying about and the extra canteen was something he could still use. Any stray Indian could make use of such a weapon and he had no intention of becoming a victim of his own carelessness.

Eventually a full moon illuminated the soft white desert floor just as it had the night before, but now he was mounted. The horizon looked like the reverse of daylight, but there was still plenty of light to see by. The traveling temperature was cooler, much cooler. His old trail was prominent and easy to follow. The big paint was stepping out at an easy distance eating gait. The horse felt good beneath him, and he was thankful to be alive.

He devoted another hour to retrieving his rifle and canteen along with his shotgun, then rode back by the water hole to quench his thirst, filling the canteens and letting the paint drink. Once again he rode to the outcropping of rocks off to the north, skirted them, and picked up the killer's trail, guiding the horse at a steady but easy pace.

As he rode away from the water hole he saw more signs of the dead, remembering the name of the desert in which he was riding. The "Desert del Diablo," what a place! How many people had died within a stone's throw of water or only a few miles away? The evidence seemed to indicate there had been many. But for the untimely demise of Pablo Mendoza, he too, would be pushing up daisies as they say back in Missouri and sometimes in Montana.

Missouri. He was hell and gone from St. Louis, Missouri or anything to do with the boys back home, the ones he'd grown up with down on the wharf. The Gaslight Boys. What would they think if they could see him now? How many of them tended cattle in Montana or ridden the outlaw trail? Who among them would have even attempted to make the ride deep into Mexico to recover the stolen gold shipment? What had they done? Who had they become? What kind of men were they now?

Who among them had ever shot a mountain lion or rode after rustlers when the herd was threatened by them? How many of them could lay claim to being an expert marksman with a rifle or a pistol, let alone both? How many of them were married, had children and were raising families of their own? Their numbers had been staggering. There were thousands upon thousands of children living on the streets of St. Louis during and immediately after the Civil War, so much so they'd started putting them on trains and taking them farther west looking for homes or anyone to raise them. Orphan trains they were called. They came out of New York, St. Louis and New Orleans that could not have possibly supported so many orphaned children on their own.

The term cowboy had not even existed prior to the war when cattlemen were called cow punchers, wranglers and drovers. The migration of so many youngsters west to find a job that would allow them to eat, had been the origin of the term cowboy because they were nothing more than orphaned young boys. Bobby Joe had been one of them. Now, years later they had grown into real men, but the term cowboy had stuck to them like glue.

As he rode into the night he heard something. Finally he decided it was the wind. The wind they called el Juicio, and he brought the horse to a stop. The el Juicio wind confused him, for he'd never understood it. He was not a superstitious person, but he suspected el Juicio did things to people. The Spanish wind brought judgment. The gust would start slow and quiet, then build until it was out of control. It would build until there would be brawls in saloons and cantinas, and gunfights in the streets. It lasted for days, weeks, and sometimes months, but it always changed folk's behavior. Women would stop cooking just to start a fight with their husbands, and men would die.

He sat the horse listening to the el Juicio for a moment. It teased at his shirt sleeves as it whispered in his ear and caused his sombrero brim to flap. A shiver twitched down his spine. The wind was talking to him, every fear he'd ever possessed suddenly came to the forefront of his mind, but he shook them off. He could almost hear his mother's voice, a voice long dead, riding on the wind, saying to him, "Be careful my son, the Devil is on the loose."

Chapter 4

The killer knew the country in which he was riding, he knew the location of water holes, where to ride undercover, how to pace his horse. He made good efforts to leave no tracks whenever possible by putting some kind of cloth over the hooves of his mount and taking to the rocky terrain as often as possible. While a horse would sink to some degree in sand, rocks were altogether different. Obviously the man was no tenderfoot. He could not possibly know he was being shadowed, yet he was taking every precaution available to him while putting as much distance as possible between himself and the murder scene. The fact he was doing so without putting his horse or himself in any significant danger was of no comfort to Bobby Joe.

"I reckon this is going to be a saw-tooth kind of ride partner," Bobby spoke to his newfound companion and while the horse did not exactly understand, he twitched his ears in agreement.

For three days he trailed the killer and for three days he lost ground. The man was good. Although on a smaller horse, it looked as though Bobby Joe would never catch him this side of the border.

"Spooky," he said to his new stallion as it seemed to fit the situation he now found himself in, "we're following an old he coon on a sure-footed horse. If we're going to catch him this side of Sunday we'd better get a move on."

Touching Spanish spurs to the paint, rider and horse headed across the valley floor at a gallop. The dawn of a new day was on them and the killer would be stopping at his pre-determined water holes until he learned Bobby Joe was treading his heels. Unless the assassin stopped to rest, he figured to be roughly a day and a half behind by now. The paint had an easy distance-eating gait and thirty minutes later they found the next water hole, a small rock basin still holding water from a recent rain, a basin right at the bottom of a long ridge.

Stepping down he allowed his horse a good drink from the remaining water then pulled him back and tied him to a cactus before he could drink too much. Some men preferred to drink from a water hole first while others preferred to let their horses. He was of the latter opinion in that he believed in a horse's loyalty. If you took care of a horse, he was obliged to take care of you, yet there were times when you could not let a horse drink until the animal had cooled down sufficiently. If the horse came second, it usually had no reason to be loyal. Loyalty was the same with people he thought. He believed the man with a loyal horse was always a few steps ahead when he found himself in a fix or any kind of tight spot.

The killer had been here and not long ago. Tracks were everywhere and disturbingly fresh. No doubt the man had chosen this place to rest up for a day. The most recent tracks were only a few hours old. Bobby Joe had intended to rest as he preferred to ride at night when traveling was easier, but he was closing the gap, and decided to ride on. He stood a good chance of overtaking the lone rider within a few hours.

Letting the stallion drink deeply one more time he topped off his canteens and mounted up. Riding out of a good camp was hard to do for he needed rest as did the horse, but the killer was close at hand and any advantage was to be used to its utmost potential. He would ride as far as the cool morning air would allow and then he would rest. There was no sanity in riding such a magnificent stallion to his death.

Randy Bean was distraught. He was absolutely certain he'd shot and killed the outlandishly dressed vaquero only a few days ago. He'd left the horse behind simply because such a horse would stand out in any crowd, and people would no doubt ask questions. Questions no killer would dare answer.

Now he was either seeing things or he was being pursued by the same man he'd killed back at Sacred Springs. As the sun rose in the east from his position atop the low lying desert mesa, Randy observed the horse and rider as they shadowed his tracks. Through the lens of his ever present field glasses he could see he was being trailed. It was incomprehensible the vaquero could even be alive, let alone track the man who pulled the trigger, yet it seemed to be exactly what was unfolding before his eyes.

Bobby Joe Riggins drew up at the crest of a small hill and studied the tracks on the ground before him. The killer could only be an hour or so ahead. From where he sat watching on the crest, the desert floor opened before him as a wide and distant cauldron with heat waves dancing excitedly over the rough valley floor. Sparse vegetation dotted the landscape in front of him, yet even in the Desert del Diablo there was life if you knew where to look. A man could find the substance necessary for survival if he slowed down long enough to observe his surroundings. If not, he might become part of those very surroundings by hastening his own death, a lesson he'd learned from his own recent experience.

The killer's tracks faded off into the distance before him, but there was no sign of the assassin. Looking around, he saw the mesa from which he was being watched and suspected as much. Immediately he turned at a right angle and eased his horse down into a draw where he could not be observed by anyone lying in wait. He wanted to track down the killer, and bring a man to justice. The idea was to get the killer, not to become a victim. He'd hunted men before, but this kind of hunt was different. This man was a professional killer who could drop him at three hundred yards.

From what he'd seen there was little chance a man could get on top of the mesa, but he also knew he was looking at only one side of the steep cliff. Although he was a good distance away, he didn't want to be observed, if in fact, the killer was up there.

He navigated the wash as far as he could before it emptied out onto a huge dry lake bed near the north side of the mesa. From what he now saw, a man could ride his horse right up the back side with little or no trouble. As he sat his mount at the end of the wash he saw both horse and rider making their way down the steep slope directly in front of him. Nudging the paint he eased back into the wash, only allowing enough room for him to watch the descending rider.

Bobby watched the assassin as he reached the valley floor and took off across the terrain at full gallop. He'd decided to travel post haste, although the sun had appeared and the heat of the day would soon be on them. This change of habit, Bobby Joe observed, was a good sign he'd been spotted for the man had been riding only at night, if simply to take advantage of the cooler temperatures. A killer such as the one he now followed would not want to be trapped on top of a mesa with nowhere to hide.

There was little doubt in his mind he'd been seen; consequently matters were now complicated. The Sacred Springs killer would be looking to ambush him the first chance he got. To go after him now was more risk than Bobby Joe was willing to chance. The only thing he could do that made any sense whatsoever was to let the murderer run. Riding all night had left both him and Spooky worn to a frazzle. They needed rest, and soon.

What made no sense was to explore the mesa. It wouldn't tell him anything he didn't already know. While the morning was still cool he would continue his pursuit. He would ride as far as he could while searching for shelter somewhere away from the sun. An hour or two more wouldn't hurt them, and the effort would keep the killer that much closer. The killer could ride all day if he wanted, but he would have to stop when the sun became too hot.

Nudging his horse he headed off in the same direction as Pablo's killer, laying back just enough to ensure he did not become a victim. The back-shooter and his horse were in sight for a short time only as the gunman had obviously decided to quicken his pace.

A man can see a lot more trail than just what appears on the ground if he sets his mind to studying. Although he had little to go on, he had a distinct feeling the last thing the killer had expected was for someone to be following him. Although Bobby Joe had trimmed his beard to match Pablo's, donned the man's clothes and weapons and was riding his horse, the magnitude of what he was doing to the killer never occurred to him. As of yet he still considered himself plain old Bobby Joe Riggins, not thinking he would claim the dead man's identity until he showed up at the ranch and staked his claim in person.

In his mind, the change of identity was yet to happen. But he reconsidered this. The killer saw only Pablo Mendoza, the man he'd just assassinated. If that was the case, it was wearing on the killer's mind. He was being hunted by the very man he'd dry-gulched a few days ago. It was unfathomable, yet Bobby Joe could read that sign as well and knew this was what was happening to the man ahead of him.

He chuckled as he realized the killer's plight, but then he remembered who he was following. If he was such a cold-blooded murderer, wouldn't he wait then ambush whoever was tracking him?

As soon as he asked the question he knew exactly what the killer planned for the day. This man had pulled off about as cold-blooded a killing as Bobby Joe had ever seen, one shot directly in the back and dead center. With budding clarity, he realized the same fate awaited him unless he changed course immediately.

Alarmed by his sudden proximity, he rode cautiously, constantly scanning the terrain for any cover where a sniper might lay in ambush. The desert opened up before him, spreading out as one big mass of sand. The land leveled off as the mesa faded into the distance behind.

He had a panoramic view of what lay before him, yet the killer and his horse were gone. Without conscience thought he dismounted and led the horse into a nearby ravine suspecting the killer might have him in his sights that very moment or be setting up such a move.

Randy Bean was coming unhinged. He had the perfect ambush set up and just as he was setting the long range site on his buffalo gun the target disappeared taking the treasured horse with him, cloaked by the ever threatening desert. The rider had only been about two hundred yards away, a sitting duck. Now both he and the prized stallion were nowhere to be found. The ghost vanished into thin air as if reading his mind. Could such a thing be possible? No one could read someone else's mind. Still, remembering he was in the "Desert del Diablo" he grumbled to no one in particular and pulled away from the edge of the wash.

Sliding his buffalo gun into its sheath, he stepped into his worn leather saddle with disgust. Guiding his horse he ambled down the wash and once again struck out for Sonora. He rolled a smoke as he attempted to realign his disturbed thought patterns to more acceptable answers, but all solutions eluded him. He was distressed to say the least. All indications pointed to the fact he was being pursued by the same man he'd killed only a day or so before. Without a doubt it was the same horse, the same saddle, and the same man. Yet, that was impossible. He had watched the body through his field glasses for no less than ten minutes after he's shot him and he'd known where the bullet had gone. The way his victim landed face down in the pool of water left no doubt.

Pablo Mendoza was dead before he made his final splash at Sacred Springs, yet Randy had confirmed his kill to be absolutely positive. Being thorough as only he was capable, there could be no doubt as to the demise of Pablo Mendoza. Now for reasons unknown to him, he was being followed by the very man he'd shot dead. What was it the old timer had said back in Nogales? "The Desert del Diablo has haunted the souls of many men."

"Get a grip!" he told himself as he rode north. "Those old stories are just that—old stories," although as he rode his thoughts were disrupted. He was gripped by terror and fear and with no explanation that would allow him to ride easy in the saddle. Even if the bullet hadn't killed Pablo instantly, the man would have drowned in the pool of water as he lay sprawled, face down, unmoving. No one could survive with is face in a pool of water for thirty minutes without moving unless they were already dead.

Looking back he knew the kill was confirmed in just ten minutes. He'd spent the next twenty arguing with himself over whether or not to take the man's horse. In the end he chose to err on the side of caution and leave the animal at Sacred Springs, a decision he now regretted. He'd only made the argument in the first place because the horse had been so magnificent, but now he was convinced he'd made the wrong decision. If he'd brought the horse along, he would not be haunted by it.

Thinking once again how positive he was of hitting his target, he put spurs to his horse deciding the best thing he could do was get out of the area. The realization he'd most certainly killed the young vaquero did nothing to relieve his anxiety. He'd been witness to skeletons lining the paths he took no matter what direction he rode. Some were Indians, some were Mexicans and some were no doubt white men, yet all were unmistakably dead men. Over time vultures had picked the bones clean, but the fact remained they were human bones. Recalling his undesirable nightmares, he picked up his stride with renewed determination and headed for Nogales on the border. There he would be close to Sonora, almost home. The sooner he was out of this God forsaken country the better off he'd be.

It was time to rest and time to plan. Bobby Joe closed the distance on the killer unexpectedly and in doing so the man was now alerted to his presence. A showdown out here in the wilderness was possible, and he welcomed such odds. One against one was better than he'd ever encountered in such a situation, but the killer of Pablo could just as easily have no taste in his mouth for a face to face confrontation.

Several hours later as he rested easily in the washed out ravine he now occupied, he heard a slight rasping sound that seemed to emanate from around the bend ahead of him. Was the killer closing in? Anything was possible as the man had disappeared from view. He listened intently to what he thought was a human wheezing as if struggling hard for air. Could this be the killer laying a trap? No doubt the man would be tricky, and for this reason he waited, listening. Thirty minutes passed yet there was little change in the sound.

Mounting his borrowed stallion, he turned in the opposite direction and rode out of the wash, heading back in the direction from which he'd heard the sound. If he was riding into a trap he wanted to be out in the open, not pinned down in a ravine, yet he had to reenter it from the other side. He'd heard tell of Indians playing tricks like this in order to get you in close, and although he doubted there were any Indians in the immediate area, the killer might know of such a trick. A man capable of doing what the killer had done might know many ways to lure his prey to within range. If it was Indians, there would no doubt be more than one.

Six shooters ready, he cautiously nudged his horse over the edge of the draw into the ravine. When he was close enough to once again hear the wheezing sound he reined in. Dismounting he drew one of Pablo's pistols, then he eased closer to the bend to have a look see. There, behind a small cluster of rocks was a wounded man covered in blood with at least three arrows protruding from his body. Convinced this was no Indian trick, Bobby Joe holstered his pistol and scrambled down to the man. He looked to be a Comanchero, part of the outlaw Comanche tribe, and mortally wounded. He would do what he could for the man for who knew what a man's limitations were? Maybe the man would live if he had the right help.

Scrambling back to the paint he gathered the reins and led the animal to where the wounded man lay in the bottom of the dry stream bed. Hastily he spread out the blanket roll on the ground and moved the delirious man onto the softer bedding. Examining the man's wounds, it was obvious he'd put up a respectable fight and dragged himself to cover, breaking off the arrow shafts so he could move with greater ease. Looking around, Bobby Joe saw all the evidence he needed to decipher what had taken place here.

This man had been attacked by a small party of ranging Indians, but had fought them to a standstill, getting himself to cover. No doubt the Indians were still out there waiting to move in and finish him off. They would wait until the man was dead, then ride back in and lift his scalp with no resistance. They had his horse and whatever else he might have had, but would they know the wounded man was no longer alone? If the Indians were still in the area, and Bobby Joe could bank on it, they would know. He holstered his pistol.

Indian arrows were a contrary thing, depending on the brave who made them. Some were made to go in with ease, but designed to stay in once they'd penetrated. Others were designed to be removed and used again at a later time. Looking at the broken arrows, Bobby Joe had no idea which ones he was dealing with, but the broken fragments had to be removed regardless. Laying one of his canteens close by, holding his old worn shirt in his left hand, he gripped the first arrow and jerked the shank free, knowing the arrow would come out with less pain if jerked out quickly. The man gave no sound to suggest he had any idea what was happening to him. He pulled out the other two with no more response than the first.

"If you were a horse, I'd shoot you where you lay," he mumbled.

"If I were a horse," the man said, his voice faint and raspy, "I'd expect it, Amigo."

Bobby Joe looked into the eyes aglow with life of the wounded man for the first time. He grimaced, but transitioned into a penetrating smile.

"They have me, and now they have you, senor."

Bobby Joe recognized the three deeper shadows on the side of the ravine in front of him, and knew instantly what the man meant, but Bobby Joe was no pushover, and the Indians had never seen a fast draw. Palming both pistols and throwing himself to one side while twisting around in a one-eighty he threw himself against the wall of dirt and fired both pistols, not stopping until all three bodies lay sprawled at the bottom of the ravine. He emptied the guns, then immediately reloaded. The guns were still warm from the action when he dropped them back into their black leather holsters. The bodies of the three Indian braves were losing their warmth faster than the guns he'd had used to shoot them.

"You are one cool handed amigo. You take me home now, no?"

Picking up the canteen he helped the man to drink and then laid his head back down.

"I'll gather their horses. I won't be long."

"No hurry, amigo, no more Indians left."

"Keep your gun handy. I was tracking a killer when I found you."

"I've no bullets, amigo."

"Boy, they did have you didn't they?"

Bobby Joe pulled six bullets from his belt and loaded the man's gun then stepped into the saddle, riding after the Indian stock. He was back in fifteen minutes with three unsaddled ponies and the man's own horse. The Comanchero opened his eyes when he rode down into the ravine.

"I found your horse. Can you ride?"

"You get me up in the saddle, I'll ride," the man said.

Helping the man up, Bobby Joe gathered his blanket roll and canteen then struggled to help the wounded man. Once he had him astride his own horse, Bobby Joe mounted. He tied the Indian ponies together and attached them on the left side of his saddle, then took the reins of the wounded man's horse and rode out. So far his day had been anything but restful, but then this was nothing new. Someone else was always creating unwanted circumstances in his life. Would things ever change?

The Comanchero was game, the epitome of tough. Not only did he make the ride, he was conscious the entire time. He was talkative, appreciative, and at times downright funny. At times he spoke in a Spanish dialect and Bobby Joe didn't even pretend to understand what he was saying. Then other times he would gather his wits about him and realizing the man he rode with spoke only English, he would speak in English, although it was often broken.

It was a four day ride to where the man lived and in four days Bobby Joe found himself liking the outlaw. A Comanchero was a border outlaw, the worst kind if he knew anything about them, but Bobby Joe had also earned the man's respect.

Miguel sat in a rocking chair on the front porch of an old cabin which he called home. In reality, it was a safe haven for Comancheros. He looked over at his friend who had brought him in and wondered, for he had never seen the like.

"Amigo, you saved me and for that I owe you."

"It was nothing. I would have had to kill those Indians sooner or later."

"In all of my days, I have never seen anyone handle guns like you. Not one of my men can hold a candle to you, senor."

Bobby continued to work with his reins and knife, repairing a spot that was giving him trouble of late. "I don't need any thanks, just friendship."

"Those guns you carry must have been a gift from nobility," Miguel said.

"They were a gift."

"You must be someone, somebody, no?"

Bobby Joe thought about what the man said. He was nobody, had never been anyone of consequence. He wanted to be somebody, to be someone and maybe the letter and the will he carried would give him that chance, but he'd never amounted to more than the average cow hand.

"In another time, another place I would be killing you for such weapons, but you have disarmed me. I cannot take from the man who saved my life."

Miguel was a leader of men, and most of those men were out looking for their boss man when the two rode into the hideout. He received their stares and some of the scoundrels would have tried to kill him then and there if not for the order given by Miguel to belay such action. Today, several men were lazing about in the shade of the front porch.

"You men think me fast," Miguel said to the crowd of tough men gathered around their leader. "I used to believe so. Leave this one alone," Miguel warned before he was helped up from his chair and eased himself inside.

Bobby Joe witnessed the instructions Miguel gave his men; all that had been necessary. The second day while sitting in camp watching over his charge, Bobby Joe lounged on the front porch chair watching two of the Comancheros practice drawing their guns on each other. The same two men had been staring at him wantonly at times and arguing amongst themselves as if they just had to know how fast he was.

After thirty minutes of this type amusement; for this type of gunplay was all amusement in his view, he walked over and stood facing the men. Quickly taking their guns he made sure they were in fact empty, then emptied his own in front of them as witnesses and took about ten paces away, spun and drew. As expected he caught both men flat-footed and unprepared. Facing them, he holstered his guns and motioned for them to draw on him. As realization struck home, the outlaws grabbed for their guns, but both stopped short as they were staring into both barrels of Bobby Joe's already drawn weapons.

Casually, he reloaded and dropped his weapons back into their holsters. He then deliberately turned his back on them and returned to his chair on the front porch. There was no way he could have told them they were way too slow, he'd had to show them and the stares and glares he'd been getting earlier in the day had now turned to astonishment then respect, or was it fear? Either way he felt safer. He tried to remember everything he'd heard about these renegades.

The Comanchero have little to no name recognition in the formal history books of our time and almost none in former times, but the Comanchero was no myth. They were hunters who traded with Indians. They fed many tribes in exchange for loot taken from the wagon trains of the white man. Most times their plunder was taken from the dead bodies of the pioneers heading west into untamed lands. From time to time when live prisoners were taken they were often as not sold into slavery in Mexico.

Comancheros were not generally known to raid a wagon train unless it drifted south of the border which almost never occurred. They had a tendency to keep to the south from fear of being hunted by American law. When they did ride north they rode to trade with the looting tribes; and in this way they were able to claim they had nothing to do with the killing and looting which had taken place north of the border.

In time however, the Comanchero began to raid across the border and take cattle, women, and anything they could carry back into Mexico. Originally Mexican buffalo hunters, the men developed a brisk trade with the Comanche Indians to include women and children taken from the white settlers. They were experts at butchering and drying the meat they killed, and in packing the jerked beef, a well-known staple below the border and a big influence in what was to happen later on.

With an established trade, the Comanchero eventually developed a liking for the underdog red man. Soon the Comanche redirected their trade to a type of war trade. No longer contented with jerked beef, their requests grew to included scalps, horses, weapons, cattle, and anything a local rancher would consider necessary for survival, including his woman. The Comanchero were named appropriately as over time they became dyed in the wool half-breeds sympathizing with the plight of the southwest American Indian, often times giving them refuge below the border.

These were the men with whom Bobby Joe stayed and shared meals. When he rode out of the Comanchero compound, he had friends, and he had a blood brother in Miguel who wasn't fully recovered, but out of danger and getting better by the day. The bad men below and along the border were keenly aware of the fact Pablo Mendoza was a man for them to leave alone for he'd told them who he was and no man among them believed themselves capable of beating the vaquero in a fast draw. Only Miguel knew him to be Bobby Joe Riggins. This was something he couldn't quite grasp, yet Bobby Joe was trying to set up the identity change he knew was coming.

Before he left for Sonora, Bobby Joe put the doubts of the Comancheros to rest. Although he had shown them he was a mucho fast hombre, they hadn't seen him hit a target of any kind. They wondered if he could hit the broad side of a barn. A childish disagreement once again developed between the men and soon the grounds were in an uproar. Although he could not speak fluent Spanish, he understood a good deal. During the disturbance, he saw a coyote some two hundred yards away, looking down on them from a large boulder. While the men argued over whether or not he could shoot straight, he once again got out of his rocking chair and stepped out into the yard. As silence fell, he palmed his gun and fired directly over their heads causing several of the men to duck in reaction. Then realizing he was up to something other than shooting them, they regained their composure and what little nerve they had left.

He holstered his weapon walked over to his stallion and saddled Spooky up. He rode out of camp with the men staring after him, none of them yet realizing his purpose, for they hadn't seen the animal. Ten minutes later he rode back into camp and dropped the dead coyote at their feet. Unsaddling his horse he resumed his perch on the front porch and watched the men in abject amusement as they came to the only conclusion possible. There had been only one shot, and the coyote had been freshly killed. One and all now understood.

The following morning the man known to the Comanchero band as Pablo Mendoza rode out for Sonora. He wasted too much time, but he'd not wanted to leave the compound without being sure Miguel was well. He took Miguel into his confidence as the two men seemed to understand and respect one another. Only Miguel knew what he was wrestling with, only Miguel could sympathize with his Sonora based problem. Miguel agreed he should ride to the ranch and claim the inheritance in order to flush the killer out. It had been Miguel who insisted he use the name of Pablo Mendoza when in camp, for all knew and respected Don Pablo Mendoza the senior.

Bobby Joe thought about things as he rode toward the border. There are times in life when a man makes his plans and nothing goes right and there are times when he fails to plan anything, yet everything seems to turn out perfect. Choosing friends can be like that. The ones you choose are usually the worst for you and then life brings along just the right characters, the ones you need at the time you need them and they are usually someone you would never have given the time of day had you a choice in the matter.

For two weeks Bobby Joe had postponed the inevitable, two weeks in which he had picked up more

Spanish words and gotten to know the Comanchero. They were hard men with little patience for tenderfoots. They rode hard, played hard, and died hard, but they were men to ride with. Several times Comanche Indians had visited the compound. During those times the men would drink and fight until they passed out from their festivities. Gun play happened a few times, but Bobby Joe defused the situations almost immediately so no one got hurt and Miguel lost no men. This last item was greatly appreciated by Miguel.

Bobby Joe stayed on long enough to see the man through the worst of his recovery then headed for Sonora. He was running out of time to stake his claim and past the time to find the killer of Pablo Mendoza. No one else would do it. No one else would even know about the killing, except Miguel.

Chapter 5

A cool morning mist spread itself across the ranch known as the Slash M, the early rays of sunshine struggling to force their way through the thin layer of fog. A lone lizard perched on a shaded stone with drowsy satisfaction under the single cactus near the center of the courtyard scarcely noticed when the stranger on his studded horse entered through the front gate on the opposite hill. Many unanticipated strangers had visited the Slash M of late and the insecurity that extended itself across the Slash M range hatched no effect on the slothful creature.

The ranch and its surrounding buildings were more beautiful than Bobby Joe could ever have imagined in his young fertile mind. His experience with ranches led to no pie in the sky dream which compared to the one he was seeing. A ranch was, at best, a solid built home for the family and a bunk house with a barn or two, and the line camps that were most times one room log cabins. Considering the horse and outfit he'd recently inherited he should have known what he would find to be a grand estate; a castle although he'd never seen one. He had a working knowledge of their grandeur and to him this was nothing less than a castle. The only thing missing were the knights in shining armor.

Bobby Joe wondered just what he was doing. A rough and tumble ranch he could claim, but this was a king's ransom the likes of which he'd never envisioned possible on the frontier. Pablo's uncle had built an unprecedented empire. Don Pablo Mendoza had carved a castle of stone and rock from the surrounding hills. The Spanish influence was unmistakable and obvious, yet the place was set up for defense against any attack be it from Indians or anyone else. The ranch house itself was built from carved stone and adobe brick in the shape of a large square with a courtyard in the center. An unmistakable Spanish water tower was centered in the courtyard with a large barn on the west end. Outside the structure were two larger barns also made of adobe brick and a large corral. The landscaping someone had done about the place spoke of a woman's touch and only served to make the setting more striking and intimidating for the man who was about to stake a claim that was not his.

He came in search of a killer. To smoke him out would require claiming an inheritance that rightfully belonged to Pablo Mendoza, or had until the man had been murdered. He thought it unfortunate the only way he could flush out the killer was to lay claim to such a vast estate, and convince the killer he had missed his target down in Mexico. Everything Bobby Joe noticed bespoke excellence and stateliness, from the iron chiseled hinges on the doors and gates to the horses loafing in the corral.

When gathering the horses south of the border after finding Miguel wounded and presumably dying, he'd found where the killer laid in wait for him in another attempt to ambush him. On finding the spot, he thought Miguel had saved his life as well, though he said nothing of this to the leader of the Comanchero. For his entire visit, the main subject had been his inherited task. Miguel alone knew of the burden he had for the dead man who saved his life.

Bobby Joe never expected to become a blood brother to Miguel, yet the man insisted he do so. Bobby Joe had more help than he knew what to do with only he didn't understand this fact yet. He'd discussed his actual plans with the Comanchero for he'd felt it necessary to involve Miguel's mind and get it off thoughts of his wounds. It didn't hurt to have another opinion on the matter either. This was a lone venture, just as going after the gold had been a lone venture, yet he felt he could trust Miguel. The gold! He had been so consumed with the murder of Pablo Mendoza and helping Miguel he'd completely forgotten about the treasure.

A vast and attractive estate lay before him with an accommodating well-fixed lifestyle which Pablo Mendoza would have died for, had in fact, died for. Now the entire estate would likely go to Dean Reynolds unless he himself took the name of Pablo Mendoza and claimed the inheritance. Today was the last day he could do that according to the will, August 14, 1876. It had been exactly six months since the death of Uncle Don Pablo Mendoza who'd died on Valentine's Day.

An old Mexican sat on the front porch swing observing the rider from a distance. Even before the old lizard named Tipper began to stir, the weathered old man turned his head and spoke toward the screen door.

"A rider is coming, senorita," he said in Spanish.

Short high-heeled footsteps drummed across the marble foyer from within the depths of the house, stopping just as they reached the double front doors, one of which was open.

"Is it Senor Reynolds?" a feminine voice inquired in Spanish from within the home.

"I—no—I—you look and see." the old timer spoke again in Spanish.

Stepping through the doorway the distressed but well-dressed young lady started toward the old man so she could see through the courtyard entrance at the far end of the front porch. Unexpectedly she stopped, frozen in mid-stride. The unmistakable rider wore a black and white vest and rode a large black and white paint; although he was still too far away for her to make out his features. The way he sat his saddle and the vest, there could be no other like it. She had made the vest especially for him in Laredo as a wedding gift.

"It's Pablo!" she shrieked. Turning swiftly the overwrought young bride ran back into the house to freshen up, to look her absolute best for her husband when he arrived.

A few minutes later the lone rider ambled through the courtyard entrance and guided his horse toward the corral on the southwest end of the complex. Pio Martinez eyed the young rider with curiosity as the big man, all of six feet three began to unsaddle the top-notch stallion.

Oddly enough, the man did not seem to be in much of a hurry such as a man who hadn't seen his wife in nearly six months should be. Then again, who was to say what a man should be like after making such a journey as this one had just completed. The new Pablo hadn't stopped to introduce himself and kept his eyes averted. It was a strange thing, yet explainable in times such as these. A man such as Pablo need not explain anything to anyone. He was entitled to act as he pleased, yet why hadn't the vaquero stopped by the porch and introduced himself, he wondered?

Pio rose from his perch when he caught glimpse of something else. Three familiar men on horseback roared past the front gate on the distant hill side and were covering the distance to the ranch compound at an all-out run, working their horses into a sweaty lather. Pablo was rubbing down his stallion in the barn and would be out of sight of the three horsemen when they entered the courtyard. Recognizing the situation and his place as foreman, Pio settled back into his comfortable perch on the front porch swing to wait. There was no sense letting the circumstances become a complete disadvantage. To alert Pablo now would only get him killed. If he remained where he was Pablo could enter the situation from behind and as a result would have the drop on these unwelcome guests.

In no time the three riders raced into the courtyard pulling their horses to a stop so hard two of them reared up in protest. The largest of the three men slid from his saddle as if he'd been doing so all his life, and while the horse was still in the air he covered the remaining few feet to the stairs, bounded up them as if his feet were on hot coals and squared off in front of the lounging ranch foreman.

"It's mine!" Dean Reynolds commanded confidently. "Today was your last chance. By sundown I want you to take all of your belongings, your ranch hands and anything else that doesn't belong to me and get off my ranch."

Pio never blinked an eye, nor did he allow Dean's words to rattle him. Pio Martinez sat and waited for what he knew must happen.

"Didn't you hear me, you greaser? I said its mine! Start packing!"

Bobby Joe couldn't help overhear the instructions Dean shouted from across the courtyard and the young gunman knew without asking who the new arrivals were. The long, tall drink of water from Montana had not planned his arrival in quite this manner, yet a challenge had been issued that would require Pablo to stake his claim now rather than later. There was no further choice in the matter, no time to mull it over. Pablo Mendoza would have to declare his identity and do so without hesitation. The fact Pablo's killer was one of the three riders made no difference. He would have to claim the inheritance for Pablo here and now in order to preserve the lifestyle of those who lived here. Dean Reynolds had just made it perfectly clear they were not welcome to stay a moment longer.

As Dean and Pio engaged one another in stares, the unmistakable sound of spurs jingling emanated in the courtyard somewhere in the silence that followed Dean's challenge. His two friends still sitting their horses also noted the sound behind them.

Turning his head ever so slowly and looking over his shoulder, Randy Bean knew the approaching gentleman without mistake. Dean Reynolds and Jack Fuller also turned to look, but it was Randy who turned ghost white. Tormented, confused, and panic stricken the man eased his horse away from the once dead vaquero.

He'd reported to Dean the job in Mexico was completed only after thoroughly convincing himself he'd been hallucinating on the ride home. Now the man he supposedly killed, the man he'd reported as dead, was here to claim his inheritance as if nothing had happened.

Pablo's presence at this exact time was physically impossible. The attendance of Pablo Mendoza was all wrong yet the unnerving event was taking place anyway. An involuntary chill raced down Randy's spine. Sweat appeared on his forehead, trickling underneath his hat brim and down his white face. His own spirit seemed on the verge of leaving his body when spurring his horse, Randy Bean left the courtyard at a dead run. Once outside the main compound he continued to run the stallion until he gained a safe distance, then brought his horse to a stop and turned to look back.

Bobby Joe Riggins was no fool in situations such as this. He stopped just short of the two remaining horses, keeping the other horseman in front of him and in a cross fire should the situation turn to gun play. He had no idea the man before him was Jack Fuller, although he was certain the man who'd just ridden out was Pablo's killer. He'd carefully positioned himself in such a way as to be able to draw on both men at once if necessary.

"Who are you?" Dean asked.

"Maybe I should be asking the questions, you're on my property."

"You are Pablo Mendoza?" Reynolds was incredulous.

"I am," Bobby Joe said, the lie sticking only a little in his throat.

Reynolds studied him for a moment. "You don't sound like any Mexican to me."

After a short silence, Bobby Joe knew what he had to do. "It seems you are completely mistaken in your expectations of me, Mr. Reynolds. Yes, I know who you are. Furthermore, I've arrived in time, and your plans to own this ranch have failed. I should also warn you I intend to stay and run my ranch the way it should be run. Any attempt by you or your men to sabotage my ownership, disrupt our work, or to subvert the ranch operation in any way will be met with a swift and thorough reprisal. I believe you've already made one attempt on my life, and as you can see your hired gun missed. So if you really want me dead just drag iron mister. I'm no longer in the mood for playing games."

At that moment the petite young bride of Pablo Mendoza, who'd been in the house, stepped through the open door and started to spring for her husband, not recognizing the danger. Bobby Joe took his eyes off of Reynolds for a split second and Dean Reynolds took advantage of the sudden distraction. He went for his gun.

Dean's right hand had clasped the butt of his revolver when he let go as if he'd grabbed a red hot branding iron. His abrupt change of motion was the only thing that saved him for he was staring down the business end of two heavily decorated Russian .44's, one covering him, the other covering the man on the horse.

"I would suggest you get back on your horse and ride, until you are off Slash M land."

The young lady stopped in her tracks and slowly the old Mexican raised himself from his seat on the front porch swing, removed his pistol from his waistband, cocked the hammer and rested the cold steel barrel on the back of Dean Reynolds' neck. An unmistakable death-like tremor sent a shiver down Dean's spine as electricity from the gun barrel lifted his hair.

"Senor Reynolds, I think you are no longer welcome on Slash M range. You ride, no?" Pio waved his gun.

"I think that's a good idea. Why don't you clear out," Bobby Joe added.

Dean walked to the edge of the front porch, each move exaggerated and slow, but Bobby Joe watched him carefully. Bobby Joe took a step forward as Dean hesitated for a second. It wouldn't be surprising if Dean didn't make a grab for the girl. Contempt flashed in his eyes as he glanced at Bobby Joe.

"I wouldn't if I were you," Bobby Joe said.

He turned and with reckless abandon Dean stomped down the stairs, grabbed a handful of mane and flung himself into the saddle of the lineback dun. Jerking the reins he wrenched the protesting animal around and sank spur. The horse whinnied an objection and fairly leapt into a dead run as if shot from a cannon. Reynolds and his horse were out of the courtyard and still picking up steam before Jack could get his horse turned and headed in the same direction. As Jack cleared the courtyard entrance, Bobby Joe watched the two outlaws meet their companion then ride off Slash M range.

Bobby Joe holstered Pablo's ivory handled revolvers and carefully headed up the front porch steps. As he reached the top, Pio extended his hand in greeting. He glanced at the girl for a moment wondering what she'd intended when she came through the door, then gave his attention to the ranch foreman.

"Senor Pablo, welcome. We have had mucho trouble," the foreman said in Spanish.

"I prefer to speak English," Bobby Joe said.

"Si senor, welcome. We have had much trouble," he repeated in English.

"What kind of trouble?" Bobby Joe asked, regretting he must, for now, let Pablo's killer ride away. He was listening, yet his eyes followed the three horsemen until they were no longer on the horizon.

"Senor Reynolds has been harassing our men, and has run many of our hands off with threats of violence and other tactics. Also, I believe he has been gathering Slash M cattle to a place suitable to only him. Somewhere on the south end of our range I think. He no steal them, but now he will steal them."

"How many head do you figure he's rounded up?" He stole another glance at the young girl.

"Two maybe three hundred of young steers at the most I think."

"If we have hands that would run from the likes of Dean Reynolds we're better off without them. They wouldn't be of any use to us if they were here, and it would mean keeping an eye on weak defense issues which we won't have the time for," pausing, he added, "We can't show any weakness, especially now that I've arrived."

The young lady winced at his words. Her actions did not go unnoticed by either the ranch foreman or Bobby Joe, yet neither of them engaged her.

"Of course, you are right Pablo."

There it was. He had made his claim and now he would be called Pablo. He would have to remember the name and it wouldn't be easy. Did the girl know something of his play, something of importance? Was she keeping important information to herself? He scowled at the idea the girl might hold an elusive piece to a daunting puzzle. Her behavior indicated she knew something, but what? He could not engage her at this time, he had to let it ride.

Conchetta Mendoza eased herself back toward the front door, yet she continued to listen as the two men discussed the ranch, its surroundings and recent events.

"Has anything else happened I should know about?" Bobby Joe asked.

"The ranch is in trouble since Don Pablo's death. Bank, how you say, freeze assets. No one is allowed to draw money from ranch accounts. It can only be drawn out by new owner, and you have not been here. My signature was always good before Don Pablo Mendoza's death, after he die, my signature no good. We have no cash for to meet payroll. Many ranch hands ride away. Am sorry, senor there was nothing I could do."

"How many hands do we have left?"

"We have five very good hands. Six when Hughe Rainwater is in the mix. He left for Prescott three weeks ago and has not yet returned."

"Should he have been back by now?" Bobby Joe asked.

"Si, he should have returned. He is a good man, one to ride the range with, senor. Dean may have tried to stop him from his mission, but he would fight for the Slash M brand all the way to the gates of hell."

"You think Dean may have tried to stop him?"

"If he found out, he would have tried. Ees very bad hombre, not too tough only bad, but if he learn he may have tried to stop Hughe."

"How bad does he want this ranch? You think he'd kill for it?"

"Si, maybe he already has."

"What exactly do you mean?"

"Senor Don Pablo Mendoza was thrown from his horse and died, this I find very hard to believe. Maybe he was getting old, but Don Pablo Mendoza could skin any bronco he got back of. And the horse he rode that day; no gentler horse in our stable. He could break horses, sun up to sun down. Never but once did I see him fall and he got right back on. Reynolds was with him at the time of the accident. Add for yourself."

"I see. Well, it was obvious I was an unwelcome sight for Mr. Reynolds."

Pio's expression revealed nothing. If he knew anything at all about the deception, he was keeping the knowledge to himself.

"You were unwelcome to them, but very welcome to us and fast, maybe the fastest pistolero I have seen," Pio said.

Bobby Joe had heard such words before from other men in other towns. He'd not wanted the reputation of being fast with a gun, but if you talked with certain people back in Wyoming and Missouri they would insist he was faster than Wild Bill, Jim Courtwright, or John Wesley Hardin. The only reason he'd acquired the skill at all was he felt such a thing might come in handy someday. So far he'd defended himself four times successfully, and hunted down a gang of rustlers, winning each gunfight with lightning speed and pinpoint accuracy. Oh yes, and he'd gunned down three hapless Indians south of the border.

He was not a braggart and didn't want a reputation as a gunfighter. Two years ago he'd spent a cold and lonely winter up in Montana at a line cabin with the only handy reading material being a Bible. He remembered reading somewhere in there that a braggart had already received his reward. Bobby Joe believed in the word, or as much as he knew of the Bible and therefore didn't talk about himself. Mostly he listened. A man with a good ear could always learn faster than a man with a big mouth. He'd learned that much living on the streets of St. Louis. He'd seen many of the latter die in senseless gunfights because they didn't know when to shut up. Pio sensed the new owner's unwillingness to talk about guns and hesitantly changed the subject.

"We still have six very good hands left on the payroll senor. The youngest and most recent may be the best of the bunch."

"What's his name?"

"Billy Bonney." Hesitating, the foreman added, "No family he says."

"Well, if Reynolds and his men haven't run him off yet, I reckon he'll do."

Just then the supple young bride stepped forward and politely intervened. "I have coffee on if you gentlemen would like to come into the kitchen."

"Sounds wonderful," Bobby Joe replied.

Without hesitation Conchetta turned back to the house and to Pio's amazement, Pablo followed her in without acknowledging his wife's presence. No hello, how are you, no hugs, kisses or anything. Pio paused trying to understand what he'd just witnessed. Pablo's total disregard for his wife's presence was unsettling for the foreman. For a man who hadn't seen his lovely young bride in several months, Pablo acted awfully peculiar. Then he thought about Conchetta. Even Conchetta was behaving in a very strange and cool manner toward the man. She was not behaving as though she were married. She'd arrived at the ranch months before with a letter of introduction, a letter penned in Pablo's own hand writing. Had it been a fraud? A moment later Pio entered the front door and settled in his usual dining room chair more than a little confused.

The new Pablo had already seated himself at the kitchen table straddling a backwards chair. Conchetta was pouring coffee into three different cups as Pio watched her suspiciously from his customary perch. The ranch foreman was in a quandary, astounded by the lack of husband-wife participation from either of them. He expected Pablo to speak Spanish, but if he did it was a second language as his English was too good for Spanish to be his primary tongue. The vaquero fit Conchetta's description perfectly, right down to the clothing, his goatee and the big irons he wore slung around his hips. She'd claimed the rider to be Pablo from a distance, yet the girl acted as if he were just a plain old house guest, a total stranger. What about the formerly blood-stained vest and the patched hole dead center of Pablo's back, for Pio had noticed a dried blood stain had been thoroughly washed and treated and the worthy patch job completed. The evidence of a bullet hole? Watching Conchetta with keen eyes, the old Mexican began to surmise that somehow the man before him was not Pablo Mendoza. How could he make sure without arousing suspicion? Without warning he happened on the answer.

"Senor, may I introduce Conchetta Castillo? She is a ward here and a very good friend of your Uncle Don Pablo Mendoza's."

Bobby Joe acknowledged her with appraising eyes and took his cup of coffee.

"My name is Pio Martinez. I have been Don Pablo Mendoza's foreman for the last fifteen years. I sent you the letter via Jeb Blackwell our local banker who holds the ranch deed."

"I am pleased to meet you both. I am R...Pablo Mendoza." Bobby Joe watched for the girl's reaction as she placed Pio's fresh cup of coffee before him on the dining room table, but he could tell nothing. It was as if her mind were somewhere else far from this room. Nothing in her manner revealed any concern. If she knew anything at all about his ruse she wasn't letting on and by the look on Pio's face his conclusion was just the opposite. He was wearing a look of genuine puzzlement. He again turned his attention to Pio because if there was anything wrong with his claim it would be best to find out now.

"Is there anything wrong?" he asked the foreman point blank.

"No senor, I am just pondering over the problems I must face as ranch foreman now you have arrived."

"Maybe I can be of some help. It would seem to me we could both benefit a great deal from one another if we can get better acquainted so I understand what you need to get the job done, and you know what to expect from me. Why don't we start there?"

Pio looked at the man with measuring eyes. This he had not expected. If the man was an imposter why should he care to manage the day to day ranch affairs? "You make plenty sense, senor. What can I tell you?"

"We could start with Dean Reynolds. Can you tell me more about him?"

"Dean killed two men in a gunfight last month, but after seeing him today, I don't know how," hesitating he added, "The two men who ride with him are Randy Bean and Jack Fuller."

Randy Bean! Good God Almighty, nothing else could have explained the situation better for Bobby Joe. Randy Bean was a killer-for-hire and he didn't come cheap. Neither would his saddle partner Jack Fuller for that matter. He'd never met either of them until today, yet he should have known them by their descriptions. In the west it was a known fact an outlaw could generally be spotted long before he was introduced to anyone simply because outlaws and their latest forays were the subject most often discussed around western campfires. An outlaw's description could precede him into an area by as much as two or three months if he was ambling along taking his time on the trail. In most cases an outlaw's description or whereabouts was only a few days or at best a couple of weeks ahead of or behind him.

His expression didn't change, but something inside his stomach tightened ever so slightly at the mention of the two killers. The fact the likes of Randy Bean and Jack Fuller were involved changed everything. Things could turn ugly without warning and may in fact have already done so. Bean was a killer of the worst kind and neither of the men cared who they shot nor when. Bean, he'd followed up from Mexico, the one who'd sent Pablo to his death for he was known to be the dry-gulch type of killer.

"Heard of them. If they're working for Dean Reynolds we'd better be prepared for the worst. Do we have any first aid supplies on hand?"

"No, senor."

"Then we'd better lay some in. What about ammunition?"

"Very little, only what we are able to carry in our guns, I think. Do you expect trouble?"

"Let's see. On one hand we have just made Dean Reynolds very mad at us and he has two of the most notorious hired killers west of the Mississippi working for him. I don't think Reynolds is smart enough to have hired those two, which means someone else is likely ramroding the situation from behind the scenes. I'm certain someone wants me dead."

By the time Pablo finished his summary, Pio's jaw was wide open. "I see your meaning plain, senor, how silly of me. We have also neighbors pushing cattle this way, hoping for more range, and we are missing cattle."

Pablo listened, then continued. "We have six ranch hands, and only five are present to cover one hundred and fifty thousand acres of land. We have no supplies and little ammunition. Why should we expect trouble?"

"Si, we are in bad shape, senior."

"The only thing that's kept the wolves at bay is the fact no one knew whether or not I would show up and no one knew what things would be like once I did. Now that I'm here I fully expect the gates of hell to open up and I don't want to be caught flat-footed." Hesitating he added, "I'm afraid once my claim is known, those who've been waiting on the sidelines to see where the pieces might fall will no longer be content to wait on the sidelines. They will test our boundaries and our resolve, and Pio I want the ranch to be ready!"

Conchetta made her way to the table with her own cup of coffee. Bobby Joe knew she was hanging on every word he and Pio said. She was, he knew, vested in what happened from here simply because of her presence.

"You are correct, senor. I had not thought beyond your arrival. I was so worried about my own future I had not thought of everything. Forgive me."

"Pio there's nothing to forgive. You kept the ranch together and in one piece. No one could have done any better. The fact we are short on good cowhands is no fault of your own. I'm quite pleased with your performance in the matters at hand."

Quite unexpectedly Pio did not consider the intruder a menace. For the first time in a long time he'd received a compliment. With Don Pablo Mendoza they used to come every now and then, but for the last few years they'd dried up altogether as a result of Don Pablo Mendoza's age. The old man had become more cantankerous as time went on. Pio realized how long it had been and how much he relished such a small compliment. It was so small a thing, yet so satisfying. Not only did he appreciate the compliment, but the impostor, if he was in fact an impostor, had thought things through very clearly. He seemed to have a working knowledge of such matters as would need attending to, and he was a pleasant sort of man with a wry smile hidden beneath his neatly trimmed facial hair.

"What should I make my first duty?" Pio asked.

"In general, or do you want me to be specific?"

"Straight up specific as you say, until we know one another better."

"All right. It's too dangerous to make a tally of the herd right now but I still want to look over the range so any decisions I make will be the right ones. I will want to meet the rest of the hands as soon as possible. The more I know about what we have to work with the better chance we have of getting through this transition alive, and Pio that's my first and foremost concern. I don't want to lose even one of the men. Is that clear?"

"Si," Pio agreed. The man before him was not just correct he was earning Pio's respect with lightning speed. The same speed he'd used earlier to dispatch the person of Dean Reynolds, but what of Conchetta? Had Pablo sent her ahead of him as was her story on her arrival, or was something else askew? The old man remained puzzled as he glanced down the table at the girl. He knew in time he would know the truth about what was happening, but he was the ranch foreman and once again had someone to take orders from. He'd not liked the last six months at all. Six months of no one to check with, six months of the bank telling him no, six months of losing hands. It was a good feeling to have the burden of the ranch operation lifted from his shoulders. Pio Martinez had for the last fifteen years been ranch foreman and he wanted to get back to what he knew. His priorities were clear and certain. He would do his job as expected. He'd always ridden for the Slash M and as far as he was concerned the brand was Senor Pablo's until otherwise disproved or specified.

"Are the men close enough to round up without too much trouble?"

"They are close. Have many cattle up close. I will have them here for noon tomorrow." Glancing once again towards Conchetta, Pio added. "Will you please show Senor Pablo to his quarters? He ride very far and is tired, I think."

"Thank you, Pio. I did ride all night not wanting to be late. I'll grab my things from the corral first." Stepping off of his chair and sliding it back under the table, Bobby Joe walked out of the room and out the front door. He'd made his claim, yet something seemed amiss.

When Pablo re-entered the house, Conchetta arose from her seat at the opposite end of the table and led him down the long hallway to the last room on the left.

Bobby Joe fell in behind the young lass, marching down the hallway step by step, and Conchetta felt chills run down her spine, for she could not turn and look at the man who had shown up in her husband's stead.

Fear of what might have become of her husband made each step along the corridor a step of fright for the young bride; the coal oil lamp cast shadows as they moved. The hair on the back of her neck stood on end as she reached down and turned the doorknob to what should have been her bedroom.

"You're room, Senor Pablo," she said. "You will find everything just as your Uncle Don Pablo kept it. Nothing has been disturbed." She knew because she'd been saving the master bedroom for herself and her husband once he arrived. She closed the door behind Bobby Joe and retreated back down the hallway into the night, trembling as she walked from the man she had just escorted to the master bedroom, and who might well in fact, be responsible for her husband's death. Where was her Pablo?"

Moments later the Spanish conversation taking place at the kitchen table was low and to the point. "How did you know he wasn't Pablo?" Conchetta asked.

"If he is Pablo, if he is not Pablo, I do not know. I only know the two of you have not met. You are unfamiliar with one another."

"Whatever do you mean?"

"Senorita, newlyweds would hug or kiss, or something. You make no move, and he make no move. You act like you never met."

"We haven't, until now."

Pio shook his head uncertainly. "I am not sure of anything. Pablo married? You married? Maybe you are sure, but maybe you are not married at all. You see, it will take time to sort these things out. At first I believe you, now I only have questions. Questions you cannot answer. Questions he cannot answer. I must consider." Pausing he added, "I must be about the ranch business. I work for that man until I know the truth in matters which determine the ranch's future. How do they say in English, he gets the benefit of doubt."

He was right of course for she could have just as easily tried to bluff her way into ownership of the estate much like this Pablo was doing. It was hard for her to think about the ramifications of what the imposter's presence meant without tearing up.

"He doesn't speak Spanish," Conchetta said.

"No, but the language he does speak is understood by all men," Pausing Pio continued, "He talks with his guns. Guns are his language and he is very good with them, although the kid may be better. In fact, if the kid ever cuts loose, God help us all."

"What does all this mean? Why would two such men who are good with a gun be here at this place at this time?"

"My dear, you just keep praying as you have been doing, for God helps those who cannot help themselves."

"Didn't you say that wrong? God helps those who help themselves," Conchetta corrected.

"You are mistaken my lady. Watch and see. God helps those who cannot help themselves. You are helpless to hold such a ranch as this one on your own, but God is answering your prayers this very day, is he not?"

Conchetta's jaw dropped a little, "By sending an imposter in place of my husband?"

"Could your husband have handled Dean Reynolds and his men?"

"I don't know. Somehow I don't believe he could."

"So you see, God has begun his work in a mysterious way. You should sleep. I know better what to do in the morning. For now I go round up men. Senorita, say nothing to him, I will be back in the morning with the ranch hands. Before I go let me say this, right now he is all that stands between us and the road. We would be gone already if he had not arrived when he did. You get some rest and I will come back in the morning with the men. You cook big breakfast, no?"

Sliding his chair back from under the table he turned his back on Conchetta and went out the front door without waiting for a response. Once in the corral Pio saddled his bay and walked it through the courtyard entrance. When he was well clear of the buildings he mounted up and rode off. It had always been Don Pablo Mendoza's habit to walk the horses out of the courtyard gate before mounting up to ride so as not to stir up dust. It was a good way, an old way, and the Slash M foreman saw no need for changing habits. He did not like the English language he thought, but for now he would have to practice on his words and endure the new boss's lack of a Spanish upbringing for it was clear senor no habla Espanola and although the man might know a few words of Spanish, he didn't act as if he knew any.

The roundup of ranch hands would take Pio all night, but he had it to do for he'd posted men where they would be able to keep track of the Slash M holdings and herds. It was a ride he didn't relish, but at the same time he wanted things back to the way they'd been before. This new boss, he would make it so and quickly unless Pio was mistaken. From what he'd seen in just a few short hours he was willing to give the hombre a fair chance. No one was going to beat his speed with a gun, and his decision making process was on par with the best ranch owners. He would get his shot. And the girl? She would have to wait.

Chapter 6

Conchetta lay awake in her bed troubling over what become of her husband. The man who'd shown up could not possibly be her beloved mate, even if he did look the spitting image. The vaquero's mannerisms were much the same yet they were all wrong; they were much too different from what she'd known of her Pablo. The new arrival betrayed no desire to so much as try and speak Spanish though he was obviously surrounded by people who did. Spanish had been the only language she'd ever heard her husband speak. Had he received a blow to the head causing him to change so much in so little time? No, this man could not be her husband. There was a surefire way to find out, but she was nowhere near ready to consider such a tactic. Such an outright sin would be the last resort.

Who then was this new man? Who could be so like Pablo that no one could tell them apart except someone who was very, very close? He had no brothers or sisters, at least he'd said as much. He was adopted, but from where? When had the adoption taken place, and would not the fact he was adopted explain his gringo looks? Had Pablo really been an American born baby before he was adopted by the Mendoza family? The man who was now wearing his clothes could qualify as a twin brother, but was he? There were questions she needed answers to and she had no idea how to go about getting them. One thing was certain; Conchetta would not bed the man in order to verify what she believed. Sin such as sleeping with a complete stranger or any type of infidelity was not something she could consider.

They'd only been married two weeks when Pablo received the letter chronicling the death of his Uncle Don Pablo Mendoza. She'd only known him a total of two months before he put her on the train. He'd insisted on riding west on his own, but why? What did she not know? After all he'd been less than forthcoming when talking about his past. If Pablo was fast with those pistols she never knew. He spoke English, yet she'd never heard him use the language in any real quantity. He did, however, have a way of wearing his weapons with ease around his waist. Wearing them and using them were two very different things. The new Pablo carried himself in much the same way as the man she'd married only something was different.

What did it all mean? He possessed all of Pablo's personal belongings, as nothing of her husband's appeared to be missing, and he'd known where the ranch was located. He even rode in on Pepper, the horse his father had presented to him as a much celebrated wedding gift. The matching vest that he wore was something her mother had helped her to make. And those pistols! They'd been presented by none other than Don Pedro DeAguiera the most excellent gunsmith and pistol craftsman in all of Mexico, a man everyone knew and respected as an artist in his trade, yet a man who had no children.

The rumor was that Pablo had saved Don Pedro's life in a skirmish with some Kiowa Indians south of the border, although she'd never pressured her husband about what had actually taken place.

Pablo was a product of the border. He knew well the language of English, but having been raised by the Mendoza family spoke the preferred Spanish. The new man was just the opposite, if he knew any Spanish at all. Pablo had lived among her people, and they knew him. He was considered smart, quick-witted and responsible beyond his years. Everyone knew he was destined for leadership; that is everyone who knew him.

Had Pablo been killed, or was he being held hostage somewhere? What about the patch in the back of the vest? What did it mean? Was Pablo wounded and laid up somewhere recovering? She'd seen the patch when she was pouring Pio another cup of coffee, and while the patch was well placed it was still a patch. The impostor even claimed to be Pablo, but he didn't seem to know anything about him, like the fact he'd taken a wife! Of course no one knew of the wedding except for a few friends and family back along the border in Laredo, then what about the wedding ring? Where was Pablo's wedding band?

Pio had insisted she keep the matter a secret until her husband arrived. As the ranch foremen, he feared for her life if her marriage to Pablo was made public in his absence. Now the foreman was not even sure if she was telling the truth. It took the new man less than two hours to ride in, claim the ranch for his own and leave her in a very uncomfortable position. If her husband were in fact dead she had nothing. She would be completely at the mercy and whim of the new owner. With everything the man had in his possession no one could prove him an impostor. Not even her wedding picture would be sufficient to dislodge the man from his claim, because he looked just like her husband. The picture would only cement his hold on the ranch and bring her sanity into question.

What about the man's uncanny resemblance to her husband? It was a fact which would not leave her mind. He must have deliberately grown the same mustache and goatee to imitate Pablo which would indicate the man had some recent knowledge of her spouse. Could the man speak Spanish like Pablo yet preferred not to? It was a question for which she must have the answer.

For Conchetta sleep was impossible. Her mind drifted back to just a few short months ago when she'd first met Pablo in Laredo. He'd spotted her first, and when she did notice him, he'd been staring at her for a good while. Realizing the attention she was being given by such a man, she blushed and averted her eyes. Several times she'd looked back at him and each time he'd failed to allow his attention to be diverted elsewhere. Eventually she could only glance over her shoulder using her glistening black locks for cover. His attention to her was such as if he were spell-bound. No other maiden was able to distract him, and they'd tried.

When her embarrassment wore off, she slowly turned to measure the man whose attention she'd so completely commanded. It was then he lowered his leg from its perch atop the bench he'd been leaning on and walked over to her and asked her to marry him. At first she'd dismissed his behavior as a lark, only the next day the same thing happened again, and the next and the next. On the seventh day she said yes; for seven in Conchetta's way of thinking was luck. If he'd given up at six there never would have been a wedding. The courtship and engagement lasted but two weeks, and in two weeks she was so in love she never really got to know the man she was marrying. Her ineptitude in the matter was fairly evident now that he was quite literally missing. She knew nothing at all about her husband's past.

Conchetta was upset with herself for not having asked more questions. She knew what he liked to eat, what his favorite things were and how he liked to kiss, but little else. She didn't even know who his friends were or if he'd had any friends at all. His entire allotment of time had been devoted to her since the day they'd met. She'd invested in living so much for the moment she was now in danger of losing her entire future to her naïve and thoughtless courtship. How many women had done the same, only to discover in the end the two parties involved were not compatible? She'd vested so much interest into making everything perfect she'd never questioned anything they'd done together or alone. Only now, with the disappearance of her husband at hand she was aware of her inadequate engagement.

They wed too quickly, she understood that now. They'd been married only a few weeks when Pablo had received word of his Uncle Don Pablo Mendoza's death. The Grand Lord of Sonora had raised no children of his own and on his death he left everything to Pablo, his older brother having preceded him in death. Pablo insisted she go by train and stage, and that he ride Pepper across country; one last big adventure before settling into the respectable life of a married man and ranch owner.

She'd argued against such a separation not wanting to be alone for even one minute in an unknown land, but to no avail. Now all evidence seemed to point to the fact Pablo had taken his last ride indeed, for instead of Pablo showing up, an imposter had arrived in his place to claim the considerable inheritance. Pablo spoke with a Spanish accent born of his years riding along the border in Texas and Mexico. The new man had no such accent and indeed spoke as if he'd no Spanish heritage at all.

What Pio had said was true. He'd faced Dean Reynolds and for now had run him off, but what if the new man also killed Pablo? If so, then he was just as bad, maybe worse than Dean Reynolds. What if the man was a killer for hire? What if he was working for someone else?

Who would be paying him and why? The why was simple, someone wanted the largest ranch in Arizona territory.

When Conchetta learned of the ranch that was to be theirs she'd begun to have dreams of the family they would raise, a family as big as the country they lived in. Now everything she'd dreamed was coming apart at the seams, as if so much scrap from her sewing was all she had left. In the book of one's life the turn of the page was to be expected, but suddenly the most important page in Conchetta's book had been ripped out and all of her life's work misplaced. If her work had not been destroyed, that particular page was now in a place no longer known to her.

If Pablo were really dead she would likely get nothing at all. Yet, if Dean Reynolds had been permitted to take over, she would have already been escorted off of her own ranch. And what of Pio and the few hands which had remained? Would they not also be gone? Most certainly, if not for the ability of one man to take charge of the situation. The man who was now asleep in the master bedroom.

What were the imposter's intentions? Might not he do the exact same thing once he firmly established his control and brought in some more men? The men he wanted? There was nothing and no one to stop him if he chose to fire every man on the ranch and replace them with a bunch of thieves. He was in charge as no one else could be. The imposter now appeared invincible considering the current state of affairs, and he'd been here less than one day.

There was no denying the fact this new Pablo was a wild card and the deck had been reshuffled and stacked in his favor. Consequently the vaquero could lean toward any heading he wanted. He could start the ball rolling in any direction and once it was rolling who could stop him? Short of bringing Pablo's entire family from Laredo who could prove the new man wasn't Pablo? Even she could prove no such thing, and she was married to...

She was now married to a gunfighter! The man was blazing fast with Pablo's guns. He was, for the time being, the man in charge and her hands were effectively tied. She could do nothing. No one could dispute what the gunman pulled off today, and as such no one would be inclined to stop him. Only a fool would step in front of those guns. In just a few short hours things had already gone too far. It was too late to turn back the clock. This new man could pose more of a threat than anyone and had in fact already done so simply by showing up.

A complete stranger waltzed in and took over the Mendoza estate without encountering so much as the slightest hiccup. The only reason he'd gotten away with his plan was the manner in which he'd disposed of the threat posed by Dean Reynolds. The truth was they could use a man of his caliber around here. The ranch would need him if any serious trouble were to rear its ugly head.

To Conchetta's knowledge, her husband had never been smooth or fast with his pistols but the man who'd shown up to take his place was good, too good. Why would anybody but an outlaw be so good with guns? She'd seen him draw from her spot at the front door, or thought she had. The guns appeared so fast it was as if time skipped over the seconds necessary to get them out of their holsters and into position.

Was the new Pablo possibly her husband, only suffering from amnesia? Had he been laid up because of a blow to his head? His skin was no longer so dark, but that could happen lying in bed. Could such a circumstance explain his desire to rely more on the English dialect for now? Had he forgotten his marriage to her? Why had the trip taken so long? His ride should have taken maybe eight weeks, but the venture took several months. Had Pablo really been an American, and only pretended to be of Spanish heritage? Of course, he was adopted. Yet, what had taken so long, a blow to the head and the time necessary to recover? Was the man in the other room really her husband? Why was he the same yet so different? Was her Pablo some kind of a spy for the American government? What about Mexico? The Mother Country certainly had its share of spies!

No, this new man could not be her Pablo, but you'd have to split hairs over the difference. There was one way to verify her suspicions, but she could not bring herself to consider it.

The wedding ring. Where was Pablo's wedding band? The man who was here now did not wear a wedding band, so where was it? If the man was not an imposter, why didn't he wear the ring, if not, why didn't he have the ring?

Was Pablo only hiding somewhere? Had he sent an unknown brother in his place? What in God's name was going on?

The showdown she'd witnessed was in no way planned. The incident itself was irrefutable evidence in the matter. Yet, couldn't such a man be working for the likes of Dean Reynolds? As soon as the thought occurred to Conchetta she dismissed her suspicion. She'd witnessed the rage present in Dean's reaction and noted the surprise in his eyes when he'd failed to draw fast enough. No, this man and Reynolds had never met until today, yet what was it the imposter had said? "I believe you've already tried to kill me once!"

Throughout the night Conchetta examined every possibility both good and bad, but try as she might she could realize only one explanation for the current state of affairs, one she simply could not accept. Tossing and turning with every conceivable thought racing through her mind she eventually exhausted herself and fell into a deep slumber. She had no way of knowing the man in the other room was indulging in some thoughts of his own.

Bobby Joe lay wide awake in the master bedroom staring at the beamed ceiling. He wondered if Dean Reynolds was aware of the kind of ruthless men he was dealing with. Randy Bean and Jack Fuller had a reputation that preceded them. They would ride his coattail for only so long and then if they held true to form they would turn on him with no warning.

Bean had a preferred habit of eventually killing the very men who'd hired him. He'd done as much before and Dean Reynolds wasn't nearly fast enough with a gun to stand up to Bean, let alone both men at the same time. The only guilt he could place on Jack Fuller was guilt by association. Jack never pulled the trigger to anyone's knowledge, but he rode with Bean.

Even after he'd made the decision to fill in for the dead man, Bobby Joe had been uncertain as to whether or not he could actually go through with such a deceitful plan. He'd encountered and dealt with an incredible amount of guilt during the last few days of the ride north and that was before he'd actually done anything, yet the only man who seemed to be dispossessed was by all means a thoroughly rotten saddle sore.

He made a calculated ride over some rough country in order to arrive on the last possible day, and over the entire distance he'd contemplated the right and the wrong of what he was about to do. His plan to arrive at the last minute was to reduce the amount of time anyone would have to dispute his claim. If everything went well he stood to inherit a lot of wealth. If things went wrong he could end up in jail for years, or a dead man like Pablo.

No one would be predisposed to believe his story about flushing out a killer if it became necessary for him to explain his actions. While some folks would give him the benefit of the doubt, most would be suspicious because of the amount of money and land involved with such an inheritance.

He hadn't known the vaquero personally, but suspected the nephew of Don Pablo Mendoza had been of the good and trusted variety. Bobby Joe learned on the streets of St. Louis about the evil that's held within the hearts of men. He was not around when God put things in motion, but he could tell you one thing for certain, the have not's would always be at work trying to beg, borrow or steal from the folks who actually had something. Since the beginning of time it had been so and there was nothing he'd witnessed in his life that gave him any hope the human condition would ever change. What was going on here was pure evil practiced by evil men and if he didn't put a stop to their plans no one would stop them.

He convinced himself he could do no harm to the dead man. Conchetta and Pio both seemed pleased with his arrival now that he was here and even if his plans failed at sunup in the morning, the look on Dean Reynolds face would have made the long ride worth the trip.

Remembering Randy Bean's reaction brought a smile to his face. The executioner acted as if he'd seen a ghost. As soon as the thought crossed his mind he began to chuckle. In fact he'd been seeing a ghost for some time. Bobby Joe realized what he'd been doing to the man and laughed quietly to himself.

"Well, you can't kill a ghost." A fact he was not overlooking and one he hoped Bean wouldn't be able to overlook. Turning the idea over in his mind he supposed the outlaw was finished, at least as far as trying to kill him. He might try to kill others, but Bean's reaction to his presence could mean only one thing, he truly believed Pablo Mendoza to be a ghost!

"Especially one who rides on a horse named Spooky," he chuckled to himself.

On the outskirts of Sonora lay an old boxcar, a car that long ago left the tracks and somehow or other landed upright. Other cars left the tracks at the same time but were destroyed and the wood from those cars utilized to reinforce the one good remaining upright example, now a rectangular wooden shelter that had been converted into a saloon where it landed. Sometimes the saloon was a little too close to the tracks at train time, but not many seemed to notice or care about the noise and the vibration. The sign old Bart hung above the door read, "Train Wreck Saloon."

Tonight was an especially grim one in the back corner where three men sat at the very far end of the boxcar, each nursing a glass of Bart's homemade brand of whiskey, cursing the fact they were not resting in their own beds on the Slash M this night. Instead they were drinking heavily and talking quietly back and forth amongst themselves. Not only was Dean Reynolds infuriated by the fact Mendoza beat him to the draw, he was now suffering considerable embarrassment before his men for not having had the guts to complete the gun battle.

"I swear to God he drew so fast I never even got a grip on the butt of my revolver," Dean said. "If I'd continued I'd be dead right now and you with me Jack. He had his other gun on you and had you covered as well."

Dean's unexpected reaction to freeze his draw was the only thing that saved them. If Jack had made a move and divided the gunslinger's attention he would have never stopped. He would have fired them and both Dean and Jack would be dead men this very minute.

"By rights we should be dead," Jack said.

"What I can't figure is why he didn't go ahead and pull the trigger," Randy added.

"Why Randy, you sound as if you wanted us to get shot," Jack said.

Randy looked at his friend with a puzzled looked on his face. "No, not at all, I just don't know when I've ever seen a man who could not only act, but react as fast as him. I just wonder if he's really human.

"What?" Dean asked. "What else would he be?"

"I'm not sure, but did you see his eyes? I've seen rattlesnake's with more hospitality in them. He had you both dead to rights, and was able to stop what he was doing as soon as he determined the threat was neutralized. Any normal man I know would have never been able to stop the process once he'd drawn his weapons. Such a draw would have been followed by plenty of gunfire."

"You're saying if Dean'd been faster we'd be dead?"

"Pretty much, no hard feelings Dean, but I'm pulling out. I've got a bad hunch about this here hombre. I know you paid me to do a job, and I did my job mind you, but Pablo Mendoza showed up anyway. I swear I shot him dead, and he arrived like he'd never even been winged."

"If you're so certain you shot him, how did he get here?"

"I don't know how, I don't know why, and my better judgment tells me I ain't sticking around to find out neither." Randy Bean waited for the anticipated refusal to let him leave. He'd killed bosses before and if necessary he could do so again. After a few moments of silence, Dean broke the tension that had been building between them, and unbeknownst to him saved his own life.

"Didn't you tell me you shot him in the back, dead center with that Sharps .50? And didn't you also say you watched him with your field glasses to make certain he was dead."

"Boss, that's exactly what I said and it's true. What I didn't tell you was I caught him following me after I killed him. You'll remember where the killing took place," Randy said in defense.

"The Desert del Diablo," Dean said.

"It was a haunting thing, something I never want to experience again."

"Why didn't you try to kill him again?" Dean asked, realizing how foolish his question sounded the moment he asked. A creeping silence followed by total recognition became the pervading influence surrounding their table.

"I did try again, and he along with his horse just disappeared from sight. I never saw him after that because I was still in the Desert del Diablo and I wasn't sticking around to become one of the stories you hear tell of from time to time."

Dean studied the gunman with care. "What you're saying is you got spooked."

Randy sat back, "You can call it whatever you want, but I know I killed him. Right now he's scaring the life right out of me and if I was you I'd take a look at my hole card. Something ain't right about that hombre."

"What do you mean something ain't right?" Jack asked.

"Jack, you've known me a lot of years. Have you ever known me to run from a fight, from anybody for that matter?"

"No I haven't, but then again I never thought I'd see the day either."

"Well you're seeing it, because I'm pulling out. I'm fast with a gun Jack, I'm good with any kind of weapon and so are you, but I saw that man or whatever he is draw when he faced you and Dean earlier today. I'd turned my horse and was watching from outside the courtyard entrance. I'm telling you both there's no way we could beat him even if we put all our speed together in one draw. I've never seen anything strike so fast, except for maybe a rattlesnake. I don't believe anything human can be that fast. You know me Jack, I prefer a long gun rather than up close and personal and you know it. I'm spooked! I'm afraid to try that now." Looking across the table at Dean he added, "Mr. Reynolds, here's what's left of your money, I ain't a thief, but that's the chance you take. Are you coming, Jack?"

"Not this time, Randy. We've ridden a lot of trails together over the years, but this time I'm letting you go. I'm staying on."

"Your funeral." Reaching out his hand Randy stood up from the table. Jack took his hand and the two men shook. "See you around partner."

Picking up his saddlebag from the nearest table and grabbing his Sharps .50 he headed out back where the horses were tethered. Once he had his riding gear in place he grabbed his blanket roll and secured it. Checking his horse over thoroughly, he mounted up and made himself comfortable for the long ride. California was a long distance over some rough country, but even that was preferred over what awaited him if he stayed around Sonora.

The sun receded over the distant purple mountains but a remaining vestige of light illuminated his way as he started across the northern end of the Slash M holdings headed west. Suddenly the air of freedom was swirling about him, the feeling of impending doom left far behind as he rode. The outlaw had no way of knowing he would have lived longer had he stayed. No way of knowing he would be dead before the evening stars filled the sky. No man knows the time of his appointment with the angel of death, not even Randy Bean, and on this night by riding away, the outlaw checked into Hotel Death.

When the bullet struck him he felt its impact and slid from the saddle to lay face up, gazing heavenward with ruptured destiny. His horse trotted off a few yards and turned around to stare at his owner. There was no mistaking the report of the rifle as its function sent Randy traveling over that gulf where the sands of time stand still. The report of the rifle had been simultaneous with the impact of the bullet, unmistakably recognized by Randy only because of its justifiable impartiality. The dying outlaw struggled to focus his thoughts.

Someone shot him in the back from only a short distance away. He tried to look down and see where he was hit but he could feel nothing. His head would not respond. Dizziness was now the order of things, followed by a tingling in his arms and legs as if they were going to sleep. Randy Bean knew he was done for. He tried to fight the overpowering sensation invading every nook and cranny to stay conscious, but the tingling took over his face as well. Then his fingers and toes involuntarily contracted into a hideous shape of their own will, his muscles tearing and clawing mercilessly for oxygen which would not come. He realized he was unable to breathe. He had seen many of his own victims in the same exact situation as he watched them twitch and spasm contorting into a hideous form of human debris. Why? Why had someone done this to him? Then, just before he gave up the ghost he recognized the irony of it all. "Fitting, it was fitting..." he whispered to no one. For one horrible second, and with stunning clarity he knew his heart no longer beat.

Chapter 7

Death in the life of Hughe Rainwater was always nearby. How he managed to stay alive this long was a mystery even he couldn't explain. He rode away from home at the age of nineteen and never looked back. That home was located in the mountains of West Virginia. All he had to his name at the time was his horse and saddle, an old flintlock rifle and a pistol to match. He hadn't stopped riding until he reached the Rocky Mountains. For thirty-five years he trapped fur, fought Indians, and guided various parties across those mountains. He missed the Civil War, but he knew all about the suffering caused by it. He was now an old man, but he was no quitter and had no intention of dying just yet.

He first crossed the plains with James Ohio Pattie in '31, spent the winter trapping and learned the western lands first hand. He took an Indian wife of the Arapaho tribe in '35. His wife died in child birth and he again wandered the plains. He served as a scout for the U. S. Army for ten years during certain Indian uprisings down in Texas and now he was punching cattle for the Slash M out of Sonora, Arizona. Soon as he hired on two years ago he was gored by a half-crazed bull. Then last year he'd been injured in a stampede started by a dry lightning strike. Once again he was fighting for his life, only this time it was no accident. Someone wanted him dead. For him it was hard enough to stay alive without some busybody trying to throw dirt over him. Whenever others made killing him their business, he had the capacity to become a very dangerous man. But time had chiseled him into a more humorous person of late, defining him in ways he would have never expected.

He was given a simple task. Ride to Prescott and return with an Arizona Ranger. He made his ride to Prescott without incident and left a message for the Rangers because they were all out of town. He did his job. The thought of giving up never occurred to a man such as him. The veteran only knew one way when assaulted—to fight back and fight hard, strike on the move whenever possible, but always be ready to move.

He was now an experienced man, an older man who knew a thing or two about how to survive in a desert environment. In fact he could survive out here where others would die not knowing where or how to find water.

He'd been riding home after making the trip to Prescott when he was ambushed. At the time he'd known he was being followed, hence an ambush was the last thing he expected, but exactly what he'd ridden into.

With caution born of days, as the Slash M hand rode into the only pass he would have to ride through, several rifles opened fire from above. Fortunately for him they were shooting downhill and missed their intended target. His horse took the impact of the bullets, and folded to the ground beneath him in a heap of flesh and bone. As the animal collapsed, he kicked himself free and landed on his back next to his dying horse. He lay perfectly still. Bullets peppered the ground near him, but his enemies were obviously not accustomed to shooting at a downward angle so he played possum. He knew if he moved they would be alerted to the fact he was not yet dead. His trick worked and the shooting stopped.

Unmoving, he waited in self-appointed agony, fully expecting a bullet to dispatch him at any given moment. After nearly two hours of torment he heard three men cautiously make their way toward him on the canyon floor. Lying otherwise perfectly still he released the grip on his new rifle and ever so slowly drew his pistol. If ever his shots must count, it was now.

There were three men walking toward him and he had six bullets to work with before he switched back to his rifle. There could be others covering from above as there were more than three men following him, but he would have to take his chances. If these three had gotten ahead of him where were the others? He could only pray they were not watching from up above.

Without turning his head he let his eyes scan the rim of the canyon walls for any movement, the reflection off of a gun barrel, anything that would mean he was being covered. He saw nothing.

Thinking back to the ambush he could only account for three rifles shooting at him. If, as he believed, there were only three shooting at the time, there was a good chance these were the only men he would have to face for the moment. Mentally he recounted the shots and sounds of the ambush in his mind. There were three and three only.

Recalling the terrain he was surrounded by gave him hope for escape. As the men came closer they would be at least fifty yards from the nearest cover and he smiled to himself. They were going to get a dose of their own medicine.

Hastily as the idea of another ambush came to him, and he realized in order to pull off such a thing he would have to get his dead horse between himself and the approaching killers. Shoving his pistol back into his holster, he grabbed his rifle and leaped over his fallen animal in one swift motion.

The approaching men stopped dead in their tracks, immediately realizing the position they'd placed themselves in. A quick glance confirmed what they already suspected. They were sitting ducks in a shooting gallery.

Raising their rifles the men began to shoot their way to cover. They were firing rapidly at a target they could no longer see. No sooner had panic set in, Hughe was taking aim. Squeezing the trigger he dropped the lead runner. The other two men fired wildly as they hunted for cover, but their bullets came nowhere near the Slash M rider.

Taking aim he dropped a second man, and before he could reset his sights on the third, the fellow dropped from view, disappearing into a ravine, which from Hughe's position, didn't appear to exist. No shots sounded from above so evidently there were only the three of them. Had the others been close enough to hear? Was their presence in the canyon imminent? Glancing at the south wall he could see a rope dangling, a rope used by the three men to assist them in traversing the canyon wall. Where were the other four men?

The remaining gunman wasn't in a good position unless he had freedom of movement. Glancing around Hughe realized his own position was no better, but his odds were greatly improved. His dead horse was the only cover he was going to find. The escaped man could move up and down the ravine with ease, if in fact, his shelter was a ravine or wash. Hughe could not allow him to get away.

The Slash M rider was under no illusions; the last man was also a man who would now be more cautious. Where was he? What kind of position did he have? Being pinned down behind his horse for the remainder of this battle did not appeal to Hughe in the least. He knew how to fight on the move and didn't like being tied down to one location. A man who fought from a fixed position was a man who eventually lost. He had to move and soon but where to and how?

Looking around he studied the terrain for anything that might provide him an alternative. The only thing he saw was a rock some fifteen yards away and it wasn't much. If he did manage to reach the rock he would have to remain prone and in a straight line away from the man on the other side of the canyon floor, providing he was still there. At the moment he hadn't any idea where the man was, and therefore no idea how to position himself behind the rock if he was able to reach it.

From deep in his past, he remembered what his father told him as a youngster, "Son, you go as far as you can see and when you get there you'll always be able to see a little farther." If he reached the rock where would he go from there? From where he lay he could see no other cover, but from behind the rock he knew things would look different. Would the difference provide enough of a change to allow him to see something he couldn't from where he was? There was little else to go on.

His first step would be to locate the remaining man. Getting him to reveal his position might not be easy, then again coaxing the man out might take little or nothing. He yelled across the canyon while peeking from around his horse.

"Why are you ruffians so bent on killing me?" he asked.

It made no difference if the man heard him, he already knew where Hughe was located. But if he could get the man to talk, then they would be on even footing and only then would he decide whether to move.

"Why do you think?" the man replied. "You were going after the Rangers in Prescott and the boss is paying five hundred dollars to the man who brings you in draped over the saddle."

"If I was on my way to Prescott I might expect as much, seeing as how I've already been. Killing me now doesn't make much sense."

Hughe was taking notes. The man hadn't moved which meant he could be trapped in a small hole that offered no way out, not a winding ravine or a wash that would allow him ease of movement.

"If your boss wants me dead, the least you could do is tell me who he is."

"Who do you think?"

"Judging by the company you keep, I'd say Dean Reynolds."

"You're pretty smart for a dead man."

He thought to himself for a moment then replied, "You're forgetting one thing." The fellow sounded like a fairly young man, maybe he could use some of his old man savvy and talk some sense into him. Maybe.

"What's that?"

"I've already been to Prescott, and," pausing for effect he added, "I ain't dead yet."

"You will be when the others get here," the young man yelled back.

"How's that going to do you any good?"

"What?"

"By the time help arrives you'll have joined your partners."

A rifle shot rang out and he ducked. Despite his situation, and lack of a good position, Hughe Rainwater was having fun. He was going to taunt this one and if he was lucky make an example out of him. He noted the fact the four remaining men who were trailing him were not present. As he lay behind his horse he began to chuckle, then laughed aloud. It became louder with time and could not have been more inappropriate under the circumstances, but he learned a long time ago to laugh his way out of doom and gloom. The remedy was one he'd learned from his great uncle Orville, although he'd long ago forgotten when he'd come by the habit, but the behavior was now his own just the same. Heck, laughing made him feel better.

Men died here today and not the ones who expected to. More might die before the sun went down, yet finding humor in a stressful situation had for many years been his way. He was also giving his last opponent a good deal of worry. Dealing with a normal old man was difficult enough, but a crazy old man opened up a whole new can of worms.

Taking out his tobacco pouch, he stoked his pipe. If he had to wait he figured he might as well enjoy a good smoke.

For hours the two men waited each other out baking in the heat of the day. Hughe had a canteen full of water that he removed from his dead horse and if he was correct, the other fellow had nothing but his guns.

A six foot long rattlesnake was making its way across the hot desert sand pausing from time to time in order to sniff the air with its tongue. The serpent continued making its way closer to him, slowly, just a little at a time, no doubt a form of curiosity. By chance his resourceful mind stumbled on a dilly of an idea. Using his rifle he lunged at the snake and pinned the viper's head with the barrel of his weapon. Grabbing the snake behind its massive head, he picked up one mad rattler, gathering the reptile into a coil and with both hands he flung the snake across the canyon floor where his foe dozed in the hot afternoon sun.

The viper must have landed close to the unwitting cowboy and having just been manhandled he was mad. He didn't hesitate to coil on sighting another man. A short quick squeal followed by three rapid burst from a pistol filled the air and Hughe once again began to laugh.

"Ain't a soul here yet. I reckon they clean forgot about you," he taunted.

"Those shots ought to bring them running."

Slowly a plan began to develop in Hughe's mind, the product of an overactive sense of humor. "Son, you don't have any friends. If you did they'd be here by now. No one is coming to save you."

He was remembering the six o'clock drums. Only a few miles west of this canyon lay the Zuni Indian village. The Zuni's were a friendly people and did their best to stay away from guns which was why they hadn't come, for surely they were close enough to hear the gunfire. The fact his enemy was young played right into his hands. Chances are he would know of the village, but did he know Indian customs? It was time to press matters.

"You don't want to be in the bottom of this pass when the sun goes down, young man." The silence continued. "This place is called "Walpi" by the Indians. That's Rattlesnake Canyon in plain English. The worst part is this is where those Indians come after dark to perform the remainder of their ceremony." He knew this wasn't Rattlesnake Canyon, but did the young man across from him know it?

"What ceremony?"

Just then the six o'clock drums sounded. From a far off distance they banged, but the echo resounding in the canyon carried an unmistakable message.

"You hear that boy? They started already. They've spent the last week gathering snakes of all kinds, but mostly rattlesnakes so they can perform their sacred dance. They start by carrying them in their mouths, hands, and wearing them around their necks. The whole time they're making their way toward this here canyon. As soon as everyone has handled the snakes and they reach the canyon rim, the last part of the ritual proceeds. It involves throwing all the snakes into the bottom of this here canyon from the cliffs above." Pausing he let his words sink in.

"Now I don't know about you young man, but I'd rather be somewhere else when they get here." The drums continued. He lied about the name of the canyon, the real Rattlesnake Canyon was many miles from here, but likely the kid didn't know that.

"Mister, I reckon I've been a fool. I'm only nineteen. You don't mind if I give myself up, do you? I'd rather not be here when they get here either."

He thought about it then hollered back. "Son, I wouldn't shoot any man what gives himself up willingly. If you'll disarm yourself and come over here where I can get a good look at you face to face, I'll let you go."

The west being what it was a man's word was strong evidence one way or the other whether or not he could be trusted. He watched as the young man stood and removed his guns, placing them on the ground in front of him. Then he chastised himself for having to tell a lie even if it was only a small one.

"Now walk on over here son so I can get a good look at you."

As the young man approached, Hughe stepped forward and punched him with a straight left jab to the jaw using the full force of his weight to make his statement. Quickly he stepped back to avoid any retaliation, covering the youngster with his Winchester.

"What's that for?"

"For trying to kill me, and you're getting off easy. What's your name son?"

"Vince Cole."

"Well Vince, how'd you ever get roped into riding with that bunch?" he asked giving the young man a hand back to his feet.

"Don't rightly remember, but I'd better do some thinking on it. Otherwise, I'll likely end up like Clancy and Sullivan over there."

"I don't suppose you'd help me dig my gear out from under my horse?"

"Under the circumstances I ought to just dig it out for you."

"Here, have a drink before you tackle such a thing." He extended his canteen.

As soon as the young man took a good long drink he capped the canteen and handed it back. Without hesitation Vince bent his back and started doing the heavy work. If you've never dug a good saddle out from under a dead horse you don't know what you're missing. Such a project takes awhile, but eventually the two men got the saddle free and stopped for a breather.

They shared Hughe's water again and then picked up the gear. The trek wasn't easy, but the men ascended the steep canyon wall. It wasn't straight up, yet made for a steep climb to the top of the canyon rim. Both men were huffing and puffing by the time they got there, and the fact the young man stopped to help Hughe several times on the way up was not lost on the old man. Once atop the rim the two men pulled up the saddle which Hughe had tied to the end of the rope.

"What do you figure on doing, young fellow?"

"Call me Vince. I sort of thought I might find those other fellows and mention to them the job is done and let them know Clancy and Sullivan won't be coming home. Then if you don't mind, I'd like to come back and tag along with you for a spell. Maybe learn something from a man who knows what being a man is."

"They won't like it none; you blowing them off and showing up on the other side."

"No, I don't figure they will. In fact, they'll probably get downright mad at me."

Hughe took note of the horses and chose the one he wanted. He began removing the saddle so he could use his own. "I'll take my time riding home so you can catch me once you've told those other fellows what for. I'll be watching my backside just in case."

Darkness was setting in as the two men parted ways. Vince went looking for his companions and Hughe headed for home. He didn't ride far. First he rode over to the Zuni Indian camp to have a few words with his old pal Drop of the Hat. Of course his real name was nothing of the kind, but when they'd been younger and Hughe dropped his hat the fight was on. Old Drop of the Hat would fight no matter the circumstances if a hat was dropped by anyone.

The men discussed old times, buffalo hunts and various fights. Drop of the Hat never laughed so hard as when Hughe told him of the story he told Vince Cole to end the standoff. It wasn't long before the whole camp was laughing at the boy. He had the entire Zuni village in an uproar knowing they would soon have a rich and rewarding sleep. He spent the next two days visiting his old friend, but before leaving he topped off his water supply and let his mount drink its fill.

Hughe found a good spot and waited for two days after visiting the Indians. He only waited so long hoping the boy would come this way leading the extra horse. Not knowing what became of him, Hughe hadn't wanted to risk running into the remaining hired killers if they were still hunting him, so he waited. He wanted dearly to see Vince on the horizon, but he'd been eagerly waiting in vain. If Vince hadn't found the others, they would by now have staked out the only two water holes in the area, making it more difficult for Hughe to get home. If they were still after him, the men would not ride all over tarnation looking for him; they would just go to the water holes and wait.

It was at least twenty miles back to the Zuni camp, and only five miles or so to water, but in the other direction. His decision was made for him. If Vince hadn't disarmed them yet by declaring him dead, those men would be watching the water holes closely. If he reached the water, he would then have to find a way to sneak down to the oasis, fill his canteen, then be off into the night. His enemies would find his tracks now he was moving. No matter how much he thought about his circumstances as he walked his horse, it changed not a thing. No matter what he did, his success or failure would be tied to whether or not Vince had been successful in convincing the other men the job was finished. Suspecting the kind of men they were, he knew if they searched for him at all the search would be limited to a small area in and around the two water holes.

Adjusting the horses stride, he headed toward the northern most water which was the smaller of the two and if not covered by the recent sandstorm he just might get in, get his water and get out without anyone noticing his whereabouts.

Most men would consider the water supply dried up if water was not visible, but he knew better. He understood how to extract the water from beneath the surface even when appearances might look as if there was none.

As the old timer approached the top of the ridge overlooking the smaller water hole he dismounted, got down on his hands and knees to keep from skylining himself in the bright moonlight, then eased forward where he could see. He could not believe his eyes. A lone horse was wading in the pool of water, drinking what it wanted and splashing water on its rump with its tail. No one else was in sight. With the moon high and bright he could see well and the tracks of the horse were well highlighted, yet there was no other sign. He was only two hundred feet from water, but he waited. If there was anyone around he wanted to know before he committed himself. Patience born from the desire and will to live is sometimes the best ally a man can have. He waited, taking his time.

He used half of the night but he retrieved the horse, slacked his own throat and bathed in the fresh water pool. From there, he hightailed for the Slash M. He couldn't believe his luck but he wasn't going to argue with it either.

When he rode into the canyon near Cats Head Creek the following morning he gave a sigh of relief. It was good to be home once again, to set foot on ranch property. Guiding his mount down to the creek he let the horses drink their fill and topped off his canteen after having a drink of his own. Just as he was stepping back into the saddle he heard the shot, and the location told him it wasn't likely to be someone hunting. Putting spurs to his horse he settled into a smooth gallop not knowing what to expect when he crested the hill on the other side of Cats Head Creek.

Chapter 8

A rooster crowed in the courtyard and Conchetta awakened. The old bird was the best clock on the ranch; better than Pio's old pocket watch most of the time. Her restlessness and worry from the previous evening had left her exhausted. Sleep and rest for her became two different things. Groggy and disoriented she dragged herself from the bed and made herself ready for the upcoming day.

She quickly wrapped her long black hair around her head pinning it here and there until it circled the back of her head. Then she dressed and moved over to her dresser, where she poured a little water from the pitcher into a washbowl and dabbed some of it on her face. Picking up a towel she delicately soaked the wetness from her skin. After checking herself carefully in the mirror she turned to leave.

Per habit, Pio was perched on the front porch swing waiting for the sun to rise. He became a watcher of the sunrise since early in childhood. A few minutes later Conchetta watched him smoke his pipe as the smoke curled into the calm morning air, then opened the door and stepped out onto the porch looking for the comfort and support from the ranch foreman. Something she had grown accustom to in only a few short months.

"Good morning, senorita," Pio spoke through around his pipe smoke.

"Good morning to you," she replied as she walked over to the edge and leaned out over the porch rail breathing in the air. There was always something about the fresh morning breeze that gave her the feeling the world had been cleansed during the night ready for a new day. It was especially true out where the desert pinnacles reached for the sky, where the purple mountains always developed a mystic haze as the sun went down. Where the night air filters away all the bad smells with a cool mountain breeze; the smells created by the stifling heat of the day and the small animals who had no one to bury them, those carcasses left to rot.

"Ah, the morning freshness, I just love it! What do you think of him, Pio?"

She masked her question so well Pio was a long moment recognizing her comment as a question at all. Then what she posed began to sink in. Pio, being the slow and cautious type gave a brief moment of thought to her question and removed his pipe with his left hand.

"Senorita, I think this new man is a good man but I do not know all of the circumstances that brought him to us. You know what he has been doing? He has gone over the ranch finances, such as they are, and you know where he is now? He is out riding the range studying the cattle and the lay of the land. He is a man who knows much about beef. And one more thing; he is sharp. Nothing gets by him. He sees all sides of the situation. With him here we have a good chance of full recovery."

"Can he be trusted?"

"I think so. What about you? Can you be trusted?"

"Oh Pio, I don't know if I can take this. Where is Pablo? What has happened to him? What is going to happen to me? I'm scared Pio, I am afraid something has happened to my husband. This man, he cannot be Pablo."

"You are right, but we must not let on for the moment. We must try to find the truth without letting him find out what we know. Once he realizes we know he isn't Pablo there is no telling what will happen, but I do not know any such thing. Do you understand?" Pio asked.

"Yes, I understand. Just like this English. We have to speak it for him. If we don't we would give too much away," Conchetta said.

"Exactly. Conchetta there is something about him I cannot quite put my finger on. The way he carries himself and the way he rides a horse, the ease of his guns. I have heard of this man but I cannot place him. The clothes I think. The clothes are all wrong, yet they are also right. I will ponder the problem and in due time I will know who he is, but we must not get in his way."

"Pio, I am afraid Pablo has been killed."

"Why you think so?"

"Because he has Pablo's guns, his clothes, even his horse. He rode in on Pepper, but what I can't figure out is the wedding band."

"The wedding band?" Pio took another drag on his pipe.

"Yes, I have one and so does Pablo, but he is not wearing the ring. If this new man intends to replace my husband he is missing a wedding ring." Conchetta lifted her left hand and wiggled her wedding band in front of Pio's nose placing all emphasis on the engagement ring and wedding band.

"There is a matching one of these which my husband wore and it goes missing," she told the ranch foreman.

"This man seems to have everything except my husband's wedding ring."

"He has everything I sent to Pablo including the will. He was looking at it this morning. So you see my dear, why I must work for him. This new man is Pablo Mendoza for the time."

"What shall we do, Pio?"

"Conchetta, I know only the man claims to be Pablo Mendoza. I work for Pablo Mendoza. It is you who will have to prove otherwise. My loyalty is with the Slash M and my new boss. Are you sure this man is not your real husband?"

"But, you said you have heard of the man. You said you as much as knew him. If you do then you have to know he is not Pablo Mendoza. The vest he wears belongs to Pablo and there is a patch in it now."

"I have seen it. I am afraid things do not look so good for your Pablo, senorita. I believe you, but you must understand. He must be Pablo. If he is not Pablo Mendoza then the ranch will go to Dean Reynolds. You see, he must be your husband, like it or not. Until your husband shows or we learn of his demise we have no other choice, my dear, providing of course you are telling the truth."

"Oh Pio, how can I find out what has happened to my husband?"

"We can only wait for now."

"But, what if he killed Pablo? What if he is responsible for Pablo's death?"

"Even if he did kill your husband, what could we do? If you had all the evidence you needed to convict him we would only be cutting our own throats. Don't you see what I am telling you? He must-needs be Pablo. You must drop the whole argument for now. If anybody thinks he is not Pablo Mendoza, Dean would have his way and we will be gone." Hesitating he added, "This man, whoever he is, has seen much trouble before, mucho trouble. Can he kill? Yes, but I think only if he is driven to such a point. If this new man were ruthless and unforgiving, Dean Reynolds would have met his maker yesterday when he tried to draw his guns. By rights he should be dead, but your man spared him and you must consider him your man even if what you say is true," Pio said. "This man has known trouble, but he is not a troublemaker. There is a big difference between the two."

"You don't think he could have killed Pablo?"

"I think he has met your husband maybe, but no, I do not think he had anything to do with the fact he is not here. This man has a reason for what he is doing and I am not sure yet what his reason is, but I do not believe he has killed your husband." Pausing he continued, "My dear, out here in the far reaches of the west a man has to learn to measure another quickly. His life depends on his ability to do so. If he doesn't learn to measure men accurately he may die for the wrong reason, for being in the wrong place at the wrong time, or simply being caught in the wrong company. More than one innocent man has been hung with a bad outfit when all he wanted was to share a hot meal over a campfire. You learn to look at the man, how he walks how he treats his horse, his habit, his actions and reactions. You add them all up and make your best call. I think our man has good intentions even if we do not fully understand them at the moment. If Pablo has been killed, as you believe, I would bet my eye teeth our man had nothing to do with it, not him. If your man has been killed I believe someone else is to blame."

What Pio said made sense. He was probably correct as usual. For now they had to go along with the imposter and pretend he was really Pablo. It wouldn't take long to find out if Pio was correct, the man would likely show his true tendencies right away. They would soon know if he was an asset or a life-size bundle of trouble.

Coming through the front gate on the far hill a lone rider ambled his way toward the ranch house compound. Conchetta broke off any further conversation with the ranch foreman and headed back inside for she had recognized the approaching rider from a distance. She did not like the man, but she needed to prepare breakfast anyway. This morning was going to be pot luck and who had the luck remained to be seen.

Pio re-lighted his pipe, puffed on the remainder of his tobacco and waited. About the time his pipe expired, the man wearing a black broadcloth suit eased his horse through the courtyard entrance and over to where Pio was roosting.

"Morning Pio, I thought I would take a ride out this way and sort things out being as the time set forth in the will has not been met. We better do some figuring on what's to happen next." The man spoke all too confidently.

"You have not heard Jeb, Pablo rode in yesterday and so did Senor Reynolds. Pablo saw to it Dean left peacefully. The will stated he must assert his claim by arriving at the ranch within six months. He has done so, but you may as well step down and join us for a good breakfast. The men will be in soon and so will Pablo. He is out looking over the northwest corner of the ranch this morning and will be back within the hour."

Jeb Blackwell was used to getting his way. He orchestrated things in such a manner as to be certain of their outcome. Moreover, he came to expect more of his ability since he opened the bank in Sonora seven years before. He'd known Don Pablo Mendoza quite well, and the ranch owner had been too smart for his own good. Jeb Blackwell knew the legalities of the banking industry and on these legalities he planned to foreclose. Only Don Pablo Mendoza outsmarted him. He stashed money in other banks around the country which Jeb knew nothing about. When he informed Don Pablo Mendoza he must call in the loan made for building, the old rancher hadn't hesitated. "No Problem. I'll wire you the money from my bank in Los Angeles."

"You have money in other banks?" Jeb was caught off guard.

"I was not born yesterday, amigo. I know better than too put all of my eggs in one basket."

Without warning, Jeb's well planned scheme had been thwarted. Who knew the old man was smart enough to place money elsewhere? How much money did the old buzzard have stashed away?

"I was under the impression you were on hard times and I might not be able to get my money. If you have the money, there is no need."

"That's what I thought. You interest me, young Jeb." With that Don Pablo Mendoza turned and left the bank. Well, there were other ways to get what he wanted. He planned to foreclose on the richest plot of land in the Arizona territory. He'd been shrewd enough to get Don

Pablo out of the way, but now, once again, he was coming up a day late and a dollar short. This was not the scenario he had planned.

"I have some other important things to attend to Pio. Hope you don't mind my passing on the breakfast invitation. I'll have to meet Pablo another time," the banker managed politely.

"I understand, senor. You are a plenty busy man. Perhaps you can join us later in the week."

"Have him stop by and see me the first chance he gets. I have some papers he must sign, but I left them at the bank. I didn't know he'd arrived or I would've brought them with me."

"As soon as I see him, I will tell him. You must have camped close by or rode half the night to get here," Pio said.

"I camped nearby, but I need to get back to town. You'll tell him for me?"

"Of course."

Jeb turned his black stallion and slowly walked him out the courtyard gate. It simply wasn't possible, yet he'd been out maneuvered again. Twice now he'd come up short when attempting to gain control of the Slash M range. Even with all his carefully laid plans, Pablo Mendoza showed up anyway. Why hadn't Dean said something? Randy assured Dean the man was dead. What the devil was going on here? How could Pablo be here if Randy killed him in Mexico? Now anything Jeb might try would be hastily planned and closer to home, something Jeb simply did not want to contemplate. He arranged his plans carefully, but the rules of engagement were shifting like sand beneath his feet. Why couldn't the paid gunman just handle his job? Now he was faced with managing the unexpected, yet via Pio he did know the whereabouts of the new ranch owner.

It was good to ride the open range. It gave a man time to think and Bobby Joe Riggins was doing a great deal of thinking. He wasn't counting any chickens either. He had ridden in, made his claim and immediately was accepted. Trouble was something about the entire affair stunk to high heaven, but as with most overpowering smells, he didn't know in what direction to start looking. There was certainly more going on here than he'd so far been able to uncover, but what? The ranch was in financial trouble because all the ranch assets were frozen on Don Pablo Mendoza's death. Not just the local accounts either. Don Pablo Mendoza had upwards of three hundred thousand stashed in four different banks across the country, and the problem was they were all over the country. He would have to loosen up the funds at the local bank first. Once he knew how to proceed, he could do likewise with the others. How long would such action take?

Step two would be the cattle. There were way too much old stock in what he saw thus far indicating quite a spell since the last round up. He would have to get the men to cull the herd. If they needed money, he had Pablo's gold eagles. The twenty dollar gold pieces he took off the unfortunate vaquero weren't anywhere near enough, but they would have to suffice for now.

For the last few minutes he walked the paint, studying the lay of the land trying to get an accurate estimate of what he had to work with. Deliberately he stopped as he topped out on a small rise.

The beauty that lay before him was breathtaking, a beauty of such unusual variety he could have sat for hours just taking in the picturesque scene. He studied the landscape in three hundred and sixty degrees and watched the cattle as they slowly meandered and grazed.

He'd seen Mexican Poppies, Wild Blue Lupine and Owl Clover before but never all together in one place, or in such abundance. The range before him was drenched in green, yellow, purple, and blue with an occasional brittle bush in bloom. Amongst all of this, Chula cacti dotted the landscape as far as he could see, even up the far mountain ridge. The ridge itself was made up of lifeless rock, yet the foreground produced a contrast that made him think those barren rocks were alive.

The ridge ran straight north and south ahead of him. Everything up to a point was on a slight downward slope from where he sat his horse, giving the appearance of a lopsided valley, yet the valley floor succumbed to a breathtaking array of wild flowers in bloom. Even the cacti were blooming, reaching for the sky and showing off their colors. He never dreamed Arizona could offer such beauty. Until now he thought of the desert as barren wasteland covered in sand and more sand.

A fluttering movement caught his eye and he looked to his right to see a hawk nesting in the fork of a saguaro cactus. The nest itself seemed to be suspended by nothing that would actually hold its weight yet the birdhouse was there, and from the looks of things had stood the test of time.

As he watched the goings on in the nest, one of the adult birds pushed a young one from the nest in an awkward attempt to teach the newborn to fly. The baby bird simply fell rapidly making an unbroken straight line descent to the ground below. He winced as he watched the small bird hit, almost able to feel the suffering the tiny creature was being forced to endure. As he sat watching the commotion around the lone cactus he came to a startling conclusion. One of the reasons a bird could fly was it had no fear of falling. He watched as the adult bird flew down, picked up the young, flew back into the waiting nest and pushed the baby bird out all over again. Eventually the baby bird would no longer fear the fall and would begin to try and imitate its mother and father which would eventually lead to flying. Maybe not true with all birds, but it certainly seemed so with this one.

Nudging Spooky forward, the horse and rider descended down the slight grade with grace, weaving in and out between barrel cacti and wild flowers in bloom. At one point he noted the remains of a large snake skin. From time to time a wild rabbit would dart across his path seeking a new hiding place and later as he neared the bottom of the long valley he saw what could have been the snake responsible for the skin he saw earlier.

Continuing to the north along the base of the mountains he noticed a bare canyon on his right. Made curious by the sudden change in landscape he rounded the bend and entered the lone canyon. There he discovered another wonder, cliff dwellings. Dwellings that must have been the main stay of a people from long ago. The houses or homes if they were actually called such were carved out of the solid rock of the cliff they adorned completely encircling the back wall of the canyon.

A full morning was maturing into a beautiful day and an informative one but he recognized it was getting late and he should be getting back to the ranch compound to meet the men. The Slash M hands would be expecting to meet their new boss. Conchetta and Pio would be expecting him as well. He had a meeting planned and as the new owner he'd better not be late.

Turning about he started for home only he never completed the maneuver before being lifted from his saddle by a well-aimed bullet. Just as he was turning he felt a sudden white hot burning sensation invade his side, his first thought being a pulled muscle. Then as he was hitting the ground he heard the report of a rifle, two unmistakable pieces of evidence he'd been shot from his horse.

Without hesitation he scrambled behind a large boulder, the only close shelter he could find. Two more bullets whizzed by searching for flesh to devour as he settled himself behind the large rock. Immediately he pulled back his vest and tore open his shirt to examine his wound. He had been gut shot and the bullet exited his back, but there was no bleeding back there that he could find. Feeling his back once again to be sure, he could tell his intestines were plugging the hole in his back like a stopper. No doubt his stomach was in bad shape and bleeding internally, but at the least he was alive, for now anyway. The bullet entered near his belly button so he might not be in too bad of shape, although if his liver or spleen was hit he knew he would likely bleed to death.

He was neatly boxed in a valley well away from the ranch compound. Tearing off good sized chunks of his shirt he stuffed as much of the material into the open wound as possible, intent on stopping the bleeding. If he could get enough of his shirt to fill the void created by the bullet he knew the pressure would eventually slow the loss of blood if not stop it all together. Slowly and painfully he continued to push the torn fragments of shirt into the small opening in his belly. The wound might become infected in time, but if he bled to death no infection would matter.

Sweating profusely, the pain was almost unbearable. His breath came in short gasps. His eyes seemed to mist over and when he tried to move at all he felt a sudden dizziness. He realized if he passed out he was as good as dead. Eventually the man who executed the ambush would close in and finish the job, especially if the man was Randy Bean. He would not want to make the same mistake twice. Funny, it hadn't sounded like a buffalo gun and the holes didn't appear that big either. Who then?

After what seemed like a long time he heard someone laughing and then a bullet spat dirt near his left foot. On reflex, he drew his feet in as close as he could. The stalker obviously was closing in. A moment later another shot sounded from a good distance off and he heard the man who was now close by do some swearing. The next thing he heard was a horse hightailing it out of there. Seemed someone was coming. At about that time things started to go black for Bobby Joe. He still had his senses as he heard someone approach a few minutes later, yet he could in no way move or respond. His body seemed paralyzed and tingling all over, yet he was breathing, something he could feel and each breath was a reward, a sign he was still alive.

Mentally he strained to open his eyes so he could see the man who came to his rescue, but he was so weak he couldn't seem to open them. Whoever the man was he knelt down beside him and Bobby Joe could feel the man's hand on his neck. Someone was close alongside him, hovering over him, yet he couldn't seem to move. Again he tried to open his eyes, and suddenly they blinked. They were already open and he realized he was blind. He closed his eyes and reopened them, yet there was no change. His heart sank in despair.

"There you are," he heard the man say. "Well mister, I don't rightly know who you are, but I'll try to get you back to the ranch house. If you make the ride there's a chance you'll live. If you don't, you would certainly die if I left you here. We're going to have to take our chances," the strange voice said.

He was picked up. Was it a Slash M rider? The man smelled as if he'd been traveling. It was the last thing Bobby Joe remembered.

Hughe Rainwater brought the new owner of the Slash M home draped over his horse, alive but barely. The man was a fighter, not willing to give up the ghost just yet. The new Pablo withstood the ride and was now resting in his room. As soon as Hughe discovered the man's identity he'd rode back to the sight of the ambush and to try and track the shooter. The tracks went only a short distance the disappeared in the rocks. The killer, for he certainly tried his hand at killing, was a savvy one. Once into the rocks away from sight he slipped burlap over the horse's hooves. This became obvious when Hughe found a piece of the material on a rock. Then he was no longer able to follow a trail. The tracks simply melded into the surrounding terrain and disappeared.

Searching well into the afternoon, he found nothing except what appeared to be another ambush site with all evidence removed. Faring better with the second discovery, he trailed the only tracks he had to go on. By late evening there was no doubt the man who shot the other victim rode straight for Sonora. There was nothing left for him to do but return to the ranch and report to Pio what he found.

Chapter 9

Bobby Joe Riggins opened his eyes gazing up at the large wooden beams crossing the ceiling in his master bedroom, the bedroom having once belonged to Don Pablo Mendoza. This was comfort he didn't know. This was a strange place to him, a place he'd never seen in the daylight. Even if he'd seen it his memory was a short-lived affair and did nothing to help him recall.

"We almost lost you, my dear. You lost quite a lot of blood. If Dr. Bradley hadn't gotten here when he did, you would have died." Conchetta was who he first laid eyes on as he came out of his deep slumber. She sat in the corner of the room in a rocking chair, all curled up reading a Spanish novel. The same spot she occupied ceaselessly for the last few days.

"What happened to me?"

"You were shot three days ago," she said as she came over to the bed.

"Who found me?"

"Hughe Rainwater found you and brought you in. He was returning from Prescott."

"All I remember is a beautiful valley covered with flowers, and...I don't seem to remember anything else. Does he know who shot me?"

"No, the shooter got away. When Hughe found you he had no idea who you were. He believed you were just another drifter riding across the range," she answered in

130

English. "After he discovered your identity he rode back to see if he could trail the gunman. He lost the trail almost immediately in the rocks overlooking the valley where you were shot. He did find another ambush sight where he believes someone was killed, but it is not known who. The place was cleaned of any evidence, and the trail ended in Sonora. It could have been anyone."

"I see," pausing he added, "do you know who I am? I don't seem to remember."

The question caught her completely off guard. She could have told him anything except what she had to and been fine with her answer, but to tell him he was Pablo Mendoza seemed completely and utterly wrong. She did her investigating and determined the man was not her husband. Several times in the last few days she bathed his naked body in private, and by chance she killed two birds with one stone. He had too many old bullet holes in him and none were dead center of his back where the vest had been repaired. Also he was different in other areas. Not quite ready to dive into such uncharted territory she bought herself some time.

"You mean you have no memory of who you are, or what you're doing here?"

"I don't remember anything, just a beautiful valley, and then nothing. Now I find myself here with you, and I don't..." he trailed off.

She turned from the bed and opened his saddlebags on the dresser. "Here, maybe this will help you remember the things you say and do," she said as she handed him the well-read copy of the will. On seeing the document along with her somewhat condescending tone of voice, he sat bolt-upright in bed causing undue and unnecessary pain to his wound. At once he remembered everything. How much did the girl know? It was obvious she knew something, but what? Had he spoken in his delirium?

Just then Pio appeared in the doorway, "Como esta usted, Pablo?"

Wary, he remembered the entire situation he'd placed himself in and the trouble he was about to borrow. He quickly considered who he was and exactly what he'd done. He was glad old Julio had taught him a bit of Spanish before he died but he wasn't about to take the bait the ranch foreman offered. "I've felt better," he answered in English.

Had he said something in a state of delirium that might have tipped them off? Did they know something of his hastily put together plans? Suddenly he was sure of nothing, yet all he could do was proceed as he originally planned. Nothing else made any sense, yet it was clear Conchetta knew something.

"Senor, I am afraid we borrow mucho trouble."

He waited fearing the worst. No doubt the pair had discovered his true identity, maybe his entire scheme. They would never believe he was only trying to force the killer's hand.

"The land here is "muy-bueno," for grazing cattle. Others want it. Many men come because they think the ranch is weak," the foreman continued in English. "We have the best water and best range. Before you came they waited, content to see where the pieces would fit when you arrived. They waited to see how you would handle things, to see what you would do. No longer do they wait, senor. From east, from west they come like wild dogs seeking easy prey. They come from everywhere as when the flies of death are drawn to a carcass. They push back our boundaries, but we have nothing to push them back with." Pio dithered for a moment to choose his words carefully. "We need men, Pablo. We have but six, six very good men, but only six. We have no supplies as we need to hold the other ranches at bay. Also, Senor Blackwell was here again this morning to check on your condition. We have only sixty days to pay off the note he holds on the ranch property. There is nothing I can do."

Bobby Joe's head was spinning. What could he do? He certainly couldn't get on a horse and ride, not now anyway. Things were progressing in a hurry. The news was much more than he bargained for. Pio was correct. Trouble was on them from all sides yet no one seemed to know anything of his ruse, although Conchetta seemed to know something. Had she been going through his things? Certainly she had, for she knew exactly where to find the will. How much did the girl know? Did she know enough to spill the beans?

"Senor, what can we do?" Pio pleaded.

What could they do? The ranch needed men and it needed money fast. Bobby Joe closed his eyes for a moment and just tried to breathe. Abruptly he struggled, laboring for each and every breath.

"I go now, you are weak and in need of much rest," Pio said.

"No! No, wait." Bobby Joe wheezed. "We may have a way out of this yet."

"Senor, I have thought of everything. There is nothing we can do but watch and wait."

133

"Pio, if you are going to ride for the Slash M you need to understand me. I won't be whipped until I'm in my grave. If I can draw a breath there is always something we can do. I want our best man, our most trustworthy. He must be capable of making a long hard ride into Mexico. He'll be riding well south of the border into Kiowa and Pima country and he'll need to be able to communicate with the bandits along the border," he said.

"The bandits," Pio paused. "You don't mean the Comancheros?"

"Pio, I don't know of any other bandits along the border. Do you?"

"No senor."

"I know what I'm doing. My methods are not those of my uncle." He struggled to remember the name of the man who built the ranch into an empire but fell short. Looking back down at the will Conchetta handed him he saw the name Don Pablo Mendoza and suddenly remembered.

"Myself, or Hughe Rainwater are the two most experienced and devoted men on the ranch," Pio said. We are most capable, although Hughe is a bit more gun handy than I. A most wily character, he is the one who found you and brought you home the other day."

"Time is our biggest enemy, Pio. He must be ready to leave by sunup. I hope he isn't afraid of Indians or Comancheros."

"Is very bad land to the south, I shall get him at once."

Alone again in his room with the stunningly beautiful Conchetta, he looked at the damsel with caution. What did she know? When had she become aware, and what was she aware of?

What he was contemplating was a hare-brained scheme, only he no longer had a choice in the matter. The gold had been so elusive all these years, why not let someone else worry about it for a change? His course of action was chosen for him by the circumstances as they were presented. He must recover the Treasure del Diablo, but in order to do so he was going to have to send a surrogate, someone he didn't even know. All he knew of Hughe Rainwater was the man saved his life. There was simply no other way he could preserve the ranch. He was in no condition to go of his own accord. Conchetta helped him to sit up a little higher in bed.

"I had a map in my saddlebag. Could you get my bag for me?"

Walking over to the dresser, Conchetta picked up the heavy bags and handed them to the man who was now in charge whether she liked it or not. Noting her place she returned to her chair in the corner, placed a shawl over her lap and returned to reading her book.

Pio and Hughe walked into the room a moment later and stood at the end of Pablo's bed as he fished for the map that revealed the hiding place of the Cortez gold, the cursed gold of the Inca.

Hughe was wearing a light hearted grin as he observed the boss fumbling for something in his bags. "I'm glad to see you're still with us," the old timer said.

Bobby Joe looked the man up and down measuring him with a glance. He was looking at a man whose trails marked deeply into the lines of his face. The years had worn his skin and chiseled the man's features into a

shrewd character. No one who looked on him would observe anything different. If there was such a thing as the right man for this job, Hughe Rainwater must certainly be the one, and he fit the bill better than Pio could have. Rainwater appeared made to order for such a mission as Bobby Joe had in mind.

"How long have you been working for the Slash M?" Bobby Joe asked.

"I would say two almost three years."

"Pardon me." Bobby Joe picked up a glass of water from the night stand next to his bed and dipped a small wash cloth into it. He put the wet cloth into his mouth and slowly sucked the water out. His mouth was getting very dry making speech difficult, but he didn't know if he could drink anything yet. He made a correct assumption as to why the glass of water and the washcloth was placed on the stand to begin with. It was the only thing he could have for now. Removing the cloth, he continued.

"Are you afraid of Indians?" he asked as he re-dipped the cloth.

"Depends on what kind. If you're referring to the Apache and you know a man who isn't afraid, I don't want any part of his wagon train. If you're referring to the Zuni, well I have friends among them."

"That's good. There are Indian's that scare me, too." Pausing to take another sip from the cloth he added, "Hughe, I need you to do a job for the sake of the ranch. It probably takes two good men, but I can't spare another right now. You'll have to cover some rough country and ride directly through the heart of Pima and Kiowa Indian territory with a pack train of mules. You'll end up south of the border about two hundred miles. Nothing about the trip is easy. It'll require all the skills you've ever learned and maybe a few you haven't, if you're going to make the trip there and back in one piece. I would go myself, but there is no time left for fooling around. I need you to go in my stead."

"I'm willing, but what am I supposed to do? And where am I going?"

Bobby Joe pulled the map from the saddlebags and spread it out before them, motioning for the two men to come around for a closer look. With his index finger he pointed to an X on the map that was placed over the name of a town. A town that no longer held life, a town long abandoned by its people because of war and troubled times. The title at the top of the map said it all; The Treasure del Diablo!

"That mark is your destination. As I said, I would go myself but I am in no condition to make the ride. Besides, I'll have my hands full here while you're riding after the gold."

"You speak of gold, senor?" Pio's surprise was obvious.

"Yes, gold bullion that was stolen from Emperor Maximilian's army twenty years ago. If we can recover the missing gold and pay off the bank, I believe things around here might settle down a great deal, for the better I might add.

"I heard the story one time," Hughe said, "but I don't seem to remember the details."

Pio explained to Hughe, the robbery had taken place not far from the Slash M range. Four soldiers stole the gold from their own command hid the plunder, then when caught they'd been forced to run the gauntlet until they gave up the hiding place, only they never did. The first three men died in their attempts to reach the other end of the column of soldiers. The fourth and last of the thieves ran better than expected. With his hands still tied behind him he ran toward the gauntlet, then at the last second he turned left and ran another ten yards where he launched himself from a water trough onto the back of the captain's free standing and saddled horse.

Immediately the startled horse took out at a dead run. The soldier thief was well under way; making for the open desert with his hands still bound behind his back before the garrison could get mounted and begin an effective pursuit for there had not been another saddled horse present. By the time they got one saddled the thief was well out of sight and riding for all he was worth. The Mexican army never found the captain's horse, the remaining thief, or the gold. He'd simply vanished into thin air.

"Crazy man," Hughe muttered.

"You have a map that tells where the gold is hidden?" Pio asked in disbelief.

"I have more than the map. I used to work with Julio, the only man left who knew where the gold was hidden."

Pio was intrigued. This new ranch owner was full of surprises, and being one who never liked surprises, this was one the ranch foreman did not seem to mind at all.

"How did you come by this map?" Pio asked.

"I once worked for a ranch up Montana way. This particular ranch had an old Mexican cook. His name was Julio and it seems Julio was the one thief who got away. We were good friends for a couple of years, but then Julio took sick. Anyway, once he knew he was dying he called me to his bedside and gave me this map. It was the first I ever knew about the gold and what happened. Since then I've learned that just about everybody knew of it except me, not its whereabouts, but the story. He told me how he and three other soldiers had stolen the payroll from the Emperor Maximilian's army and hidden their gain in an old Spanish water tower. They got caught and the others were killed. Julio alone got away."

"The Treasure del Diablo. No one lives to spend it," Pio warned.

"I spent as much time with him as I could before he died, but he insisted I alone should have the gold. Julio kept telling me, you deserve it above anybody I know. He waited too long to go back for it. I've already tried to recover it once, but I failed. As a matter of fact I almost got myself killed." At his statement he saw Conchetta look up. "That is why Hughe, if you go I'll split the bullion with you fifty-fifty, because you'll have earned it."

Pio had been studying the map. "But senor, even if the gold is there, only one man with so many pack animals, how can he go safely? I know the town you speak of and the distance is over three hundred miles of the worst desert on earth. Not two hundred, not even two fifty. He will ride hard and be careful and still he have no chance. Tis' suicide for any one man to try."

"Maybe Pio, then again maybe not," the new boss said.

"Senor there is no water where you go. Ees why the town is a ghost town, not because of war, because there is no water. The people of Madera moved their town to the north and west of Chihuahua after their well dried up," Pio explained.

"I know the nearest water where the gold is happens to be fifty miles north of where you're going, but there's water beneath the water tower itself if you dig for it. Julio and his friends found it. With proper provisions and this map to guide you, I believe you can make a good ride and return home safely."

"Senor, I beg of you. One lone man is suicide for such a mission as this," Pio protested.

Hughe Rainwater rubbed his jaw contemplating such a hare-brained idea while staring at the map that lay out before him.

"Pio, it's been my experience where gold is concerned one man alone is the perfect number. Anymore and the situation usually becomes volatile, unpredictable, Bobby Joe said."

"Si, you are right again, senor. I was not thinking."

"Hughe," Bobby Joe began. "What you're about to do will affect the lives of many people. Not just everyone here at the ranch, but, others as well. It's a considerable responsibility I'm saddling you with. As I've said, we'll split the sum right down the middle. You'll get half, and the ranch will get the other. When you return, I'll also give you a choice of any quarter of Slash M range so you can start your own ranch if you so choose. In that way we can remain neighbors for a long time, fair enough?"

Hughe was in shock, trying not to open his mouth and present the perfect fool. "Boss, if you need the gold and you need it here on time, I reckon I can deliver the goods, but I don't know what I'd ever do with so much money. I never had enough to worry about, cept'n just what I need to get by."

140

"If you get down there and get back on time, you won't ever have to live a hard life again. You hear me?"

"Yes sir, but I won't need all that much money."

"Pio, how soon can you round up about twenty good healthy mules and get them ready to go? Burros won't work. They can't keep pace with a steady moving horse, especially if the horse has a good gait. The pace'll kill them. I know from experience, it has to be mules. Missouri Mules if you can lay your hands on some."

"I can have just such animals late this evening, or by first light at the latest."

"And Hughe, you'll have to start the mules out easy until you get them used to the distance they'll be traveling each day. Otherwise you might ruin them, and you're going to need every single one of them."

"Yes sir," pausing he added, "Boss, isn't that the gold of Cortez?"

"Yes Hughe, and I know the story. No one has ever lived to spend it, but that's about to change. I don't believe in superstition."

"I don't want to either, but there seems to be something to it."

"I want you to get plenty of rest as soon as you have your gear packed. Pio, I want you to double-check his gear before he leaves. Make sure he has full provisions, water on every mule and his horse, and the necessary gear to haul about four thousand pounds of gold without laboring the mules too hard."

"Si, I make ready, Pablo," and then like wind Pio was gone.

Bobby Joe took the time in between sucking on his washcloth to instruct Hughe on every aspect of the mission, and why the money was so important. "I don't trust many folks Hughe, especially where money is concerned, but Pio says you're the man for the job. You'll be riding into some rough country filled with Indians and Comancheros alike. Avoid the Indians if you can, but if you can't, do whatever is necessary to keep the gold a secret."

"So the only way the ranch can clear its debt with the bank in Sonora is to recover this gold?"

"At present yes. We have much money, more than enough to pay the debt in full, but it'll take time to jump through the legal hoops and get the funds released from the banks where Don Pablo Mendoza did business than it will take for you to ride into Mexico and back. We need money we can spend now."

Conchetta was refilling Bobby Joe's glass of fresh water from the decanter she prepared for just such a purpose. When finished she proceeded to tuck him in a little better, and then returned to her corner rocking chair while the men were still talking.

"We have no more than about fifty-five days. If we don't pay the ranch off by October thirtieth the bank will foreclose, and we'll all be looking for a new home. So you see why your mission is so important, why you must make the trip into Mexico."

"I understand completely, but you said I must avoid Indian's. What about the Comanchero who raid along the border?" Hughe asked.

"I have a brother just south of Nogales."

Conchetta sat bolt upright.

"His name is Miguel. He and his men frequent the border town around Miller's Peak. He is a half-breed and my blood brother. He is," Bobby Joe paused for effect, "a Comanchero. I wouldn't cross him though, as he gets mighty upset over ill behavior that he isn't the cause of."

"Boss, those men are outlaws, ruffians of the worst kind. You're telling me so I can avoid them, right?" Hughe asked.

"Not exactly. We need men as well as gold and he has as many as thirty or forty of the roughest, toughest bunch I ever laid eyes on. With them to help ride herd, I suspect the other ranchers will leave us be."

"You want me to contact this brother of yours named Miguel?"

"Yes, I do."

"Boss, they'll likely cut my throat before I can even tell them why I'm there."

"Not likely. I know them well enough to know they're curious like Indians. Several of them are half-breeds like Miguel. They'll wonder why you're traveling in their neck of the woods. They'll wonder about the mules. I'll prepare a letter for you to give to my brother. I would advise you not to open it as he would consider such a thing to be traitorous. I wouldn't try to read the letter unless he hands the thing to you when he's finished with it, and even then I'd be very cautious."

"Boss, I can't read."

"That's even better. If he suspected for any reason that you read the contents before he received it, he might kill you just to make an example of you in front of his men. I saved his life down in Mexico recently. As a matter of fact, I was on my way here, and he hates owing me for having saved him. He'll want to even the account, so he'll come running unless I'm mistaken."

"Well, if they don't kill me when they first see me, I'll get through all right. I may have to rely on their knowledge of food and water though. I don't know the country very well down that way."

"What I need is someone who'll get down there and recover the missing gold shipment, then ride like the dickens to get back here on time, or die trying. I would prefer you don't die."

"I would prefer it as well. I hope I can do what you ask because I don't have plans for meeting my maker just yet, least ways not for a few years."

"Once you deliver my letter to Miguel, I want you to ride south using this map. Make sure you're not followed. If you are, you may have to kill. It'll be the only way you can remain safe. Also, I wouldn't flash that map around too much. Not in front of Miguel's men or anyone else."

"I understand your concern, but you needn't be worried. I can appreciate exactly what I'm riding into. Your secret is safe with me. Besides, depending on how tough this is I may want my quarter of range when I get back. I won't need all that much money, but the range would be nice."

"And you shall have it. I fully expect Miguel and his men to ride straight north as soon as he reads my letter, and we need those men, Hughe. Whatever you do, don't tell him what you're really riding south for. Some of his men would slit your throat in the blink of an eye if they had any idea you were going after the Emperor Maximilian's missing gold shipment. Not to mention what the Mexican Army would do if they found out."

"How do I explain the mule train? He and his men surely ain't about to miss that many mules heading south. A set up like that will peg me as some kind of miner sure."

Bobby Joe was looking at an old art sculpture hanging on the bedroom wall. It was made from tin and copper. "Tell them you're riding after copper, iron, and tin. Metals we need to do more art sculptures for the ranch." He lifted his finger pointing toward the wall sculpture. "More stuff like what adorns the wall in my room."

Bobby Joe watched a smile come over Hughe's face. He wasn't sure what the man was thinking, but it was a good sign he'd picked the right man for the job.

Chapter 10

An hour after sunup the following morning Hughe Rainwater was two miles south of the Slash M holdings, riding hard for the border. The mules were being stubborn, but they finally moved. He was moving as fast as possible without wearing down his horse. He was aware of the terrain and in many places the country was broken and rough. There were deep gullies to traverse created by flashfloods from long ago. These slowed him down, but not for long. There were occasional stands of rock protruding from the great desert before him, like monuments to the dead, painting the expanse of sky to his south.

He knew the desert and its subtle changes of light. He knew the ways of animals and he knew the habits of men both good and bad. Mostly he navigated them all with common sense. Men who traveled needed water, nourishment for their animals and food for themselves, all of which were restricting or limiting factors controlling ones' field of travel, yet the country before him he read like a book. He could not read the written word, yet he could read the terrain as well as you might read a Charles Dickens novel. He rode a lonely pathway, knowing the importance of this mission, the reasons why he must not fail.

For most men a chance at such money would turn them into thieves, but not him. He was too old and calloused by life's tragedies to give a flying leap. The only thing that mattered to him, at this stage in his life, was his reputation, his name, and his honor. Money, not even massive amounts of the stuff, seemed to fit the picture he had chiseled and forged for himself over the years. He would complete the assignment, but he wouldn't need anywhere near half of the man's gold to make him happy. To him the friendship of Pablo Mendoza was more important.

Where he could, he rode around towns and ranch houses, not wanting to alert anyone to his presence. Nor did he wish to bring any more trouble on himself or the Slash M, something which surely would happen if he were discovered by some crude hombre as he lead a pack train of mules south into Mexico. The only contact he wanted to make was with Miguel Manuel, the boss's blood brother, a half-breed Comanchero who was half Comanche Indian. Mules were worth money and with the border so close he considered it wise to ride shy of any civilization.

The desperados and pistoleros who made their nest in the border towns along the San Pedro River could sense trouble coming like setting hens with a fox sniffing just outside their coup. Like well-trained coon dogs they knew who was where and could smell a rat long before they ever saw it. The last thing he wanted to do was alert them to what was happening to the north, providing they didn't already know.

Most of the men along the border were outlaws of one sort or another, hanging close to the line to escape one side or the other. The border made escape easy for them, yet complicated matters for any posse in hot pursuit. The law could not and would not cross such a boundary. There was nothing to stop the outlaw's from crossing because they were without law or scruples already. His own experience indicated they never had to look far for trouble because they had a tendency to pack the stuff right along with them wherever they went. Generally they created more than they could ever find. If the wrong men down here got wind of what was happening with the Slash M, no good outcome would result.

He rode all night, dozing in the saddle whenever he felt safe, although dozing like that was never really a safe way to travel. As the sun rose in the east on the third day, he picked up his pace and made for his final watering hole before crossing the border into Mexico. A small subsidiary in the San Pedro River that he knew of would offer the cover he needed before moving on. Here he would rest for a day before making his brutish ride into the Desert del Diablo. There would be plenty of grass for the animals, and plenty to drink as the river would offer their last chance to rest up and eat well.

As he waded into the river, several Comanchero unexpectedly surprised him. Rounding the cliff's edge he pushed right into the middle of the San Pedro before he realized anyone else was present. They were standing a hundred yards or so downstream letting their horses drink at the water's edge. He could only hope he'd ridden into the right bunch of men. As he pulled his mules into the water showing no fear for having seen them they streamed around him single file, surrounding him. His only option was to remain calm and pretend he had every right to be there with twenty mules. He said nothing and paid them no mind, as if they were not present at all. He made no eye contact whatsoever until he was spoken to.

"Senor, your mules are drinking in our water. You have good reason, no?" The speaker was a tough looking hombre with large shoulders and narrow hips. He wore two guns tied down with two ammo belts draped over his shoulders much the same as Pablo wore when he found him on Slash M range. Those ammo belts were full as if he were rationing the ammo for his men. None of the others were so well-fitted. Looking around at the other men Hughe concluded he was right. Every man-jack of them was unarmed, barren of useful weaponry except for the one who addressed him. They may have guns, but they had no bullets. He smiled to himself. That was the trouble with riding outside of the law. You couldn't trust anyone, not even your own men. The big man's guns still had the thongs on the hammers, so if trouble started Hughe would shoot him first. Likely the other men would scatter and run unable to defend themselves.

"You ride hard," the man said. A challenge was being laid down and no one was more aware of the challenge than Hughe Rainwater. If he answered them incorrectly or failed to satisfy their curiosity they would try to kill him.

"I have come for Miguel Manuel. I have an urgent message for him. Do you know where I can find him?" Hughe asked.

"What message do you bring?"

"That I do not know. It is sealed. I don't know what it says, I can't even read. I'm just a messenger. I'm to deliver a message to Miguel Manuel and him only."

"What if I kill you and take it anyway?"

"I wouldn't try it. Not unless you want your men to see you gunned down."

"The big man let out a roaring laugh. "Senor, surely you jest! We have you outnumbered ten to one."

Hughe didn't smile, he didn't flinch, he looked the big man right in the eye with a menacing look of his own. "As men go you have me outnumbered ten to one. As loaded guns go, I have us even at two apiece. And amigo, your thongs are still on."

Startled, the big man looked around for evidence that might betray what he knew to be the truth. The stranger was correct in every detail and had him dead to rights. He did not trust his men and therefore collected their ammunition whenever they were traveling, never giving out ammo unless it was absolutely necessary for his men to go armed.

"With your guns anchored, you would be dead before you could pull them, amigo." For good measure he laid his rifle across his left arm, pointing directly at the outlaw.

Laughing again the big man waved off the implication. "You have me, senor." Pausing he added, "I must rethink our travel arrangements."

"You do that. In the meantime, I need to find Miguel Manuel."

"We will be glad to take you to him, but senor, I would not ride to Miguel's hideout with those mules. You will surely lose them."

"How far is his hideout?"

"Maybe two hours ride."

"Why don't we do this my way? You ride in and tell him I'm out here waiting for him. Tell him I have an urgent message for him from Pablo Mendoza. I believe they're blood brothers. You get him here quick and I'll await your return."

"As you say senor, but I warn you. If you are lying or playing a trick in any way, if you try anything at all we will hunt you down and kill you!" The big man laughed again, "If Miguel Manuel doesn't kill you first."

Sinking spurs the man went out of the water and around the cliff the way Hughe came in, his men following in unison like the tail end of a large alligator. Up out of the water and around the cliff they rode hell bent for leather. The Comanchero would return, and he had best be ready.

To his way of thinking the Kiowa, Pima, Apache, and Comanche's were still at war with the white man. The Mexicans and the notorious Comanchero were trading back and forth with them, and from what he knew, the Comanchero could hold their own in any fight. The only way you were really safe was if you were one of them, and even that wasn't foolproof. He'd been lucky so far. The fact he'd noticed their guns and ammo arrangement was no doubt the reason for his success in the recent event, but he would have to remain on his toes. The next time he saw those gents, he was certain things would be different.

Stripping the mules of their gear one at a time he tethered them near the water so they could drink and forage at will. Then he started a good hot fire just under the cliff's edge out of the wind. While coffee brewed he refried bacon strips. Slapping them on a tortilla he folded them together for a quick but satisfying meal. He ate his fill then relaxed. From time to time he would wake for more coffee then nap lightly in the afternoon shade. This was an old trick he'd taught himself, to sip coffee on a full stomach allowed him to rest, but not sleep deeply.

The land by the river was a broken and jagged mass of rock formations. The shallow San Pedro snaked its way through the canyons at this spot, while the water carved its way downstream. The San Pedro's water was responsible for the only vegetation in the area.

In the distance, mountains rose to the sky. From where he sat he could see Miller's Peak to the west, easily seven thousand feet to the top. The land of Mexico lay before him like a wide open sea of sand. From here he would have to push on to the southeast. There was still more than three hundred miles of baron wasteland to cross before he reached his destination, providing Pio knew of what he was speaking, and in Hughe's experience the slash M foreman would be correct.

The sun was sinking in the west he heard the riders coming from a good distance away. He hoped the Comanchero were returning with Miguel. As the bevy of horses slithered around the cliff he got to his feet to greet them. His Winchester 1873 was in his left hand and his pistol hung loosely in the wedged holster on his right just below his hand. He was ready. A well-dressed man by Comanchero standards wearing a yellow-stained white shirt and a tan leather vest spoke first.

"Are you the gringo who looks for Miguel Manuel?"

"I am, provided you're Miguel?"

"I am. What is this message you bring from my brother?"

"Before I go giving out anything to a complete stranger, I need to know for sure. I don't intend to get myself killed for any reason."

"This man who sends message, he saved my life. We are blood brothers, no."

"That's what he said." Hughe waited. He was going to need more proof than common knowledge.

"This man rides a black and white paint, wears a black and white vest to match. He is big man about six feet four, maybe two hundred fifty pounds. All muscle, with dark hair. He has two of the most beautiful Russian .44's I ever laid eyes on." The Comanchero paused, "he is also the fastest pistolero in all of Mexico."

"Well, you've pegged him. Pablo would be real upset if I gave this letter to the wrong person."

"Pablo?" The Comancheros memory was jogged.

"Yes, my boss Pablo Mendoza, he is your blood brother?"

Miguel was acting peculiar. "Pablo has sent me a letter, no?"

"I reckon you are who you say you are." Reaching into his saddlebag he pulled out the sealed letter and handed the envelope to Miguel. Hastily opening the letter the Comanchero unfolded the piece of paper and began to read. He was working at it slowly, but he was reading. Hughe made a mental note to learn to read if it was the last thing he ever did. Slowly the man began to smile. Then his smile turned into a chuckle, then a riotous belly laugh. Something was very funny, but the robust Comanchero was the only one laughing. By the time he'd finished reading the news, he was doubled over and laughing so loud he could have awakened the dead. He tried to speak several times, but was too overcome with hysteria to proceed. "My brother is crazy I think." The man spouted between laughs. "Does he really have this ranch he speaks of?"

"Yes he does," Hughe said, his curiosity growing. "He never spoke of it to you?"

"No senor, and for good reason. I would have killed him for such a place. But now, now he is firmly in place. The estate is his and everyone will know he is boss. To kill him would be murder; therefore I can only help him. This brother of mine, he is smarter than I was prepared to believe," Miguel added for clarification. He was laughing so hard because Bobby Joe tricked him. He told him all about the murder of Pablo Mendoza and how he intended to flush out the killer, but he'd said nothing of the ranch at stake.

"We camp here for tonight. In the morning we ride. My brother needs my help." Miguel turned and yelled to his men after which he continued to laugh.

"I am just beginning to understand the breadth of Pablo's intelligence myself," Hughe said, realizing what would become of any interlopers who happened onto Slash M range once Miguel and his men took over the riding duties. God help them.

"You are safe with us senor, we will bring you no harm. You ride for Madera?"

"Yes, although I've never been that way before."

Miguel Manuel dropped from his horse and handed the reins to a subservient rider. Tossing the letter into the fire he ordered his men to make camp. "No worry, you have an easy ride, if you can avoid the Pima tribe. I show you easy route, water all the way but for the last forty miles." With a serious look on his face the man's tone changed immediately. "Why do you ride to a ghost town with so many mules?"

There it was. The last question Hughe wanted to answer was the first one they wanted an answer to. These men were not going to play with him. He knew if they found out about the gold he was as good as dead.

"Didn't Pablo say anything in his letter? Surely he must have told you."

"He said nothing of you only that you ride for him to Madera."

"Yes, I ride for him. He is sending me to the abandoned mines around Madera to gather iron, tin if I can find any, and copper for making things the ranch needs. We have an old smith on the ranch named Moses, who makes whatever we need, horseshoes, bridles, and bits, or he can fabricate art work to be hung on the wall for decoration. He's that good."

"What could Madera have for you? It is a ghost town cleaned out long ago."

"Pablo believes the abandoned mines have enough copper and iron to provide what we need at the ranch without buying in town. Our relationship in town has been strained of late, and you boys sure ain't going to help smooth things over when you arrive, if you know what I mean."

"Ah, I see. He must have been riding north from Madera when he found me," Miguel said.

Hughe was uneasy. He wasn't used to making things up as he went along. He was uncomfortable with the thought of deliberate deception, but he would be even more uncomfortable if these men found out about the gold he was going after.

"Are you sure it is copper and tin you are after my friend?"

"What else would I be after?" Immediately Hughe wished he'd said anything else.

With mischievous eyes Miguel retorted, "Gold! You ride after gold," he accused.

"Miguel, if I may say so; for something as valuable as gold Pablo would have sent more than one man. He would have sent an armada. He would want to defend such riches as gold. No, you miss guess. Would you trust just one man with such a cargo?" He was appealing to the outlaw nature of the man now, and he had him. "If you were to send your men after something like gold wouldn't you want enough men to guard the stuff and keep an eye on one another and make sure the shipment got to its destination? No, not gold senor Miguel, just copper, iron and some tin if I can find some."

Miguel picked up a stick and churned the letter into the fire so Bobby Joe's letter to him would burn all the way. No one else needed to know what he knew. He was satisfied for now and poured himself a hot cup of coffee. If all went well he would be at his brother's ranch in two days ride. If they rode hard the trip could be made in one day, but he'd tried such a maneuver before and it had been costly as far as horses go. No, they would take their time and leave out in the morning.

Eventually all seventeen of Miguel's men drifted up to the campfire and had coffee, and those with food ate as they drank. Miguel seemed satisfied with the answers he'd received. While Hughe was responsible for taking care of his own food stores and as such, there were several frying pans on the fire well into the night hour. As they passed around their frying pans filled with beef, antelope and deer meat, the Comanchero informed the men where they were headed and why they would do so without complaint. Unexpectedly a small wiry man of about thirty continued the chatter about the fire.

"You mean we're going to have a real roof over our heads, regular like?"

"It looks that way," Miguel answered.

"It'd be worth the ride just to have a place to sleep where we won't be sharing our blankets with wild critters."

"I figure we're going to have to do some work boys, and I wouldn't do such a thing for anyone else, but Bo... Pablo saved my life and I owe him. I figure once his troubles are behind him we'll be even." Miguel was going to have to mind his tongue.

"What trouble?" It was the wiry fellow again.

"It seems many of his neighbors are getting land hungry and they are trying to push back his boundaries by pushing their herds onto Slash M range. We're going to let them know they're trespassing and push them back. We'll probably cull the herds while we gather the stock."

"Did you say the Slash M?"

"I did. And my brother Pablo is the sole heir to the biggest ranch in Arizona territory. I plan to see that he keeps his place. Do I hear any objections?"

"What are we riding into, a range war?"

"That would be my guess," Miguel said.

After the short discussion no one said much. It was one thing to whoop and holler and take what you want. It was quite another to have to abide by the laws of the land and work for your keep, and still another to defend a range with weapons if necessary. Every single man among them knew the fun and games of the last three and a half years was over. It was time for them to ride into an uncertain future, and to a man they were ready.

By the time the campfire was dying down in the wee morning hours everyone knew who they would be riding for. Pablo had resided among them for nearly two months when he brought Miguel in with three arrow wounds. They also knew him to be the fastest thing they'd ever seen with a gun. Miguel Manuel was the kind of leader they could all enjoy, and if they'd learned anything of the man who had stayed with them only a short time ago, they knew he would not put up with indiscriminate behavior. He would allow a man his fun, but he would never allow him to go too far.

Miguel provided well for them considering the circumstances they'd all been dealt, but now they would be able to do for themselves even better at the Slash M. Miguel was aware of the implications before the men were. He knew if they got comfortable at the ranch, they would never leave. Oh well, they couldn't expect to continue to drink, fight, and create a ruckus everywhere they went without someone paying the ultimate price for his behavior. It was better for them to settle down, while they still had a chance.

As the sun grayed the sky around Miller's Peak in the east, Hughe was two miles south of last night's camp heading for the ghost town of Madera. Miguel offered his knowledge of water in the area, marked additional water holes on the map that Hughe could use and given him advice for avoiding confrontation with the local Indians if he happened to come upon them. He also explained the easiest way to avoid the local Indians all together, a tip Hughe greatly appreciated.

There was no doubt he had left a hard bunch of men back there on the river, and if they were going to be on the Slash M, folks around Sonora were going to be a little gun shy about pushing their herds onto Slash M holdings. As he thought of the menacing Comanchero band a smile lit his face. A smile. It'd been a long time since he'd been able to really smile about his life and his role in it, in truth, only since Don Pablo Mendoza's death. Maybe, things were shaping up again.

This nephew Pablo Mendoza was no pilgrim according to Pio and his English was better than expected. He seemed to understand Spanish but preferred not to speak the language. Well, it wouldn't be the first time. Other than the fact he'd been shot, he was very capable of handling a gun. Pio had also stated the man was more than capable of handling the day to day operations of such an estate. That the Comanchero along the border respected him was a testament unto itself. If Pablo Mendoza could control such men as the ones he'd just spent the night with, there would be no denying the Slash M. Pablo Mendoza would be able to handle anything that came his way.

As he meditated on such things he developed a respect for his new boss that demanded unwavering loyalty. His loyalty had been to the ranch for he was a hand who understood what it was to ride for the brand, only he was veering toward a loyalty for the ranch owner, a loyalty he'd never quite been able to give. It was with a new knowledge and respect he headed into the Desert del Diablo leading his mule train.

He never thought of himself as a leader, and was much better at receiving orders than giving them. In his element now, he knew what he was capable of. The Comancheros would be an unknown element at first, but no ranch in the region would test them, not if they wanted to live. Outlaws were outlaws and the Comancheros were of the worst kind, but if Pablo could control them he would possess a very intimidating army, and might even be able to tame the Indians if such a thing were possible. Don Pablo Mendoza had fought Indians every year just to keep his ranch in one piece, although such incidents became fewer with time. If Pablo was able to maintain order with the Comanchero, the men who traded with the Indians, there was a good chance he could develop a working relationship with them himself. The more he pondered the possibilities he began to find himself steeped in respect for this new boss.

Chapter 11

Conchetta spent the last several days taking care of a man who might be the killer of her husband, a man she did not know, an obvious imposter who was getting away with an entire inheritance that belonged to her and her husband, and if Pablo was dead the ranch belonged to her. Yet since the man's arrival she'd learned a few things. He was a basic common sense sort of man, yet when forced to play a tough situation he was more than capable. When pushed into a corner he struck out like a rattler. She also believed if he thought he was in the right he would back up for no man. In short, Conchetta Mendoza found herself torn; admiring the qualities the man possessed, yet afraid he might be responsible for the death of her husband.

So many men who lived in the west were heedless of anything but the present moment, she assumed the reason was because so few of them planned to stay in any one place for any length of time, or were too busy fighting drought and disaster to think of a thing like beauty. Something about this new man was different. He seemed to notice everything around him. She realized in many ways, he was more than her Pablo. She now doubted her husband could have held the Slash M for this long, but the new man? He was someone to be reckoned with, but who was he? She was certain he was quite capable of handling anything that might come his way, that he was a man to ride the range with. A man to stand with, she was certain, but the question remained who was this new Pablo? These were the things Conchetta noticed, leading her to doubt the man was responsible of killing her husband.

There seemed no doubt someone wanted Pablo Mendoza dead. Had they succeeded in killing him, only to be thwarted by...?

Suddenly Conchetta understood. The new man must have known of her husband's death, and knowing how much they looked alike he assumed her husband's identity and rode in to claim the inheritance, knowing the killer, or killers would try again. She could think of nothing else that would explain the man's arrival and the happenings since. Was it possible others knew of the man's intentions concerning the ranch?

It was quite possible others would want Pablo Mendoza dead and out of the picture, thank God they were as of yet unaware of their success in the matter. Otherwise she would have had to make her presence known, and consequently she would make herself the next target.

The new man rode in with everything that belonged to her husband, including the letter from Jeb and a copy of the will. Therefore he would have firsthand knowledge of her husband. Where had they met, and when? Were the two men actually brothers engaged in some exotic conspiracy? Did the new Pablo know who she really was? Was the new man protecting her, or maybe her real husband? Was her husband still alive, but hiding out somewhere? Then she remembered the bullet hole patched in the back of the vest, and the fact the new man did not have a corresponding wound. No, her husband was either dead or laid up somewhere fighting for his life.

Conchetta had thoroughly gone through the man's possessions while he lay in his room unconscious. Nothing in his possession would indicate any knowledge of her, or that he might know of her presence here at the ranch, unless he'd found Pablo's wedding ring. He had everything else, why not the ring?

She was mentioned nowhere, yet she wouldn't be. She and Pablo had only just married when the letter came from Jeb informing them of Don Pablo Mendoza's death and the subsequent will. These were the thoughts she experienced as she prepared dinner for the ranch hands, eight men in all including Pio and her husband's impostor.

Footsteps sounded on the hard wooden floor. Conchetta turned to see her ward of the last week spin a chair around and straddle it as though he were sitting a saddle, although he eased down into the chair a might slower because of his recent wound.

"Hope I can keep food down. I really need to eat something tonight. My stomach thinks my throat has been cut," he commented.

"You must be feeling better." God he was handsome she thought to herself. How could two men look so much alike and be so fundamentally different. She could feel her womanhood stirring, conflict and desire welling up all at once. It scared the daylights out of her, the feelings she was having for this new man. She found herself fighting her own primeval urge of desire for this new Pablo. It made her angry with herself, although she wasn't certain why. She didn't even know if her husband was dead or alive, and here this man was stirring her up inside. Had she married the wrong man?

When the man didn't reply she turned from her work once again and took a good look at him. As she did several of the hands trooped through the front door and seated themselves at the table awaiting their dinner. Only a moment later the rest of the ranch hands came into the room with Pio in tow, and again she busied herself with setting the food on the table. She placed plates in front of them all, serving the host first. She noted, though starving he must be, he was gracious enough to wait until everyone had been served before he dug in himself.

The men ate with very few words amongst them, stealing glances of curiosity toward their new boss as they ate, for they were meeting him for the first time. They all knew what happened, and were respectful of what he'd went through, yet their curiosity was piqued by the fact no one saw him for the entire first week he was present at the ranch, save for those who stayed in the big house. Not one of them knew the kind of man who inherited the Slash M. They waited in anticipation to learn. Only Pio knew anything of the man, and he'd chosen to say nothing. A couple of the men tried to get him to talk about the new owner, but Pio would only discuss the rancher's physical condition, addressing only how Pablo was recovering from his gunshot wound. Normally Pio would have prepared them for such a meeting as they were about to have with their boss, yet for some reason he'd given them little or nothing to go on this day. They knew nothing of Pablo's concerns, his worries or his fears.

The big man before them nibbled at his food, afraid of what eating too much would do to his insides. They were not getting an accurate picture of him as he picked at his food and ate slowly.

Bobby Joe waited for the men to finish their pulled steak and beans before opening up the conversation. While picking at his own plate he'd noticed there were still six hands present at the table. As he'd sent Hughe south, it appeared there was one too many men seated around him.

"Pio, didn't you tell me we only had six hands left?"

"Si, we only have six."

"Well, I sent Hughe into Mexico and I am still counting six men. Have we picked up a stray somewhere?"

"Si, there is a new man if you will have him, Senor Pablo."

Pio nodded his head and a young man in his late teens or early twenties leaned forward and introduced himself. "My name is Vince Cole, sir."

There was one at the table who looked even younger. This one wore a long colt dragoon pistol hitched about his hips. Both were no more than kids. What was going on here?

"What brings you to the Slash M?"

"Well sir, Hughe Rainwater told me I could find a good riding job here and to look him up when I was ready. He's gone right now so he can't speak for me, but I can ride herd, rope and shoot."

"Well it may come down to shooting. You're welcome if Pio hasn't any objections."

Everyone waited for the rest of the story, for the other men already heard it from the mouth of Vince, but not yet the boss. Pio nodded at the young man again as if to say go ahead.

"Sir, I reckon I know what I'm letting myself in for. I was riding for Dean Reynolds up until about ten days ago. Mr. Rainwater had every right to kill me like he did the others, but he let me go. We ambushed him between here and Prescott while he was on his way back from seeing the Rangers. Anyway we didn't have anywhere near enough men. The others are dead, and I want to ride with Hughe, provided you'll let me."

Bobby Joe's surprise was obvious. He lowered his fork to study the young man. Even Conchetta was hypnotized by his words and ceased working, turning to see who the young man was, having paid no mind up to that point.

"You were riding for Dean Reynolds, and now you want to ride for Mendoza?"

"If you will permit sir, I can explain."

"Go ahead, I'm all ears," Bobby Joe motioned with his hands and sat up a little straighter in his chair.

The young man took a quick glance around the table and then began. "It's like this. Dean suspected you would try and sneak someone through to the Rangers in Prescott, so he sent seven of us out to scour the countryside looking for the rider. That's when we ran into Hughe Rainwater, sir."

"Are you telling me that seven of you took on the likes of Hughe Rainwater, and you're the sole survivor?"

"Well sir, I don't rightly know just yet. We set out to stop him and we surely paid the price. Two men are dead and four others unaccounted for." Glancing about the table he continued, "It didn't take long for me to realize I was in over my head, and I said as much to Hughe. At the time he had me pinned down in a wash in Rattlesnake Canyon. I told him how I figured I made a big mistake and asked him would he let me go. He said he would, and he stuck to his word. He showed me right then what it means to be a real man. He could have shot me dead like the other men I was riding with, but he didn't. He let me go like he said he would." Making a point to look Pablo straight in the eye he added, "I've come to the conclusion if I was to hang around with a man like Hughe, maybe some of what he knows and his good sense would rub off on me. He didn't get to be his age without knowing a thing or two.

"You see, I grew up on the streets of St. Louis with no real upbringing to speak of because my parents were killed during the war. My hope is Hughe could get me set in the proper direction."

Bobby Joe looked around the table and noticed more than one of the men had faces that were turning red. Were they holding back laughter? Looking around, he could see he had a good humored bunch, and nothing was more important when the chips were down. Even Pio had developed a slight grin.

"Son, I..." He almost slipped up and told the young man he had grown up on the streets of St. Louis too. He was going to have to watch it. "If you want the job it's yours, but let me warn you. If I find out you are feeding information to anyone, especially Reynolds, you won't be able to ride far enough or fast enough. Another thing, you are to ride with a partner at all times until I say otherwise. You have no decision making power."

"I still want the job sir, and the conditions are just fine, because when Dean Reynolds finds out I'm riding for you he's going to blow his top. I'll feel much safer if there's someone else riding with me when that happens."

After a short silence, Bobby Joe changed direction and got down to ranch business. "Gentlemen, I know you've been anxious to meet me. I am Pablo Mendoza.

"If you ride for the Mendoza ranch you're riding for me. I know the pay's been slow in coming, but that's about to change for the better. Also we've been low on men, and that too is about to change for the better." Suddenly he had their attention.

"As you all know by now I was shot last week. However, it's given me plenty of time to study the situation and range conditions on the ranch. Moreover, I was able to see most of the range beforehand. We've got our work cut out for us, and I do mean work. If anyone here is afraid of hard work you'd best speak up now."

Looking around the table at each man in turn, making eye contact as he went he asked, "Does anyone here know how to use dynamite?"

The room was so quiet you could have heard a feather land on the floor. Not that the dining room hadn't grown quiet beforehand. His question raised the silence to a new level creating an uncertain stillness in the tense atmosphere. Positively disturbing, the calm silence in the room gave way to nervousness.

At the opposite end of the table a hand slowly appeared. After a few seconds the hand was barely holding itself steady above the table top, but nevertheless a hand it was. It belonged to a fellow in his mid to late forties a beard hanging well below his shirt pocket. His hair was dark but beginning to turn a shade of gray and his pupils, one dilated larger than the other was not exactly pointing straight ahead, giving anyone who didn't know the man the idea he was not all present. In reality he was anything but. The crow's feet that garnished the deep brown eyes promised a hint of insanity.

"What's your name?" Bobby Joe asked.

"Harley Simms."

"Do you know what you're doing with the stuff, or do you just know a little bit?"

"I figure I can open you a hole all the way to China if you get me enough powder."

"Good. Do you know where the small channel branches off from the Little Apache and runs down through the narrow canyon?"

"I know the spot."

"I want you to take Vince and teach him how to use the stuff. I want you to blow those canyon walls down into the creek thirty to forty feet deep, create a natural dam that will allow us to hold more water on our range when the rains come. A good lake should help us get through the dry spells easier."

"But senor," Pio protested. "That will shut off the water supply to our neighbors to the south."

"You mean the ones who are trying at this very moment to push back our boundaries? Pio, there's an awful lot of cattle being taken out through that narrow tract of canyon, right through the creek. I want it sealed because from what I was able to see, those cattle are not coming back."

"Si, I had not thought in such terms, but your point is taken."

"There is more. I want you to ride into Sonora with the men and get the supplies we're going to need. I want you to buy all the ammunition you can lay your hands on, even if it doesn't fit anyone's gun. Clean the town out as much as you can. If anyone else is going to purchase bullets I want them to have to ride for them, or wait for them, do I make myself clear?"

"Senor, we will need money. All of our credit is dried up."

"Bobby Joe stood up and dug into his pants pockets and produced the seventeen twenty dollar gold pieces he found in Pablo's saddlebags, along with two hundred dollars in paper money he'd managed to save. The men stared. He knew what they were thinking. They hadn't been paid in months and here he was passing over all kinds of money he'd been sitting on.

"I want you to take the men to town with you. Get Harley the dynamite he's going to need, and any extra you can lay your hands on. You can buy the men a couple of drinks beforehand, but once you have the supplies, I want you out of there. I want you back on the ranch and back to work. If all goes well in a few weeks you'll be given your back pay, and I'll include a one hundred dollar bonus for each of you, including Vince. By then you'll have earned it. You may well earn it again before you get it and with any luck the financial trouble the ranch has been experiencing will be behind us."

The only black man in the bunch spoke up. "Moses Carter, sir. You said something about more men?" Moses was one of the many known black cowboys in the west at that time.

"I did. They should be here any time providing Hughe got my message through to them. If he didn't, it might be a little longer."

"Are they good men?"

"That depends on what you mean by good. Let me put it to you like this. They are good for us. I don't think anyone will bother us too much once they arrive."

"Why would no one bother us?" Harley asked.

"You may as well know it now. They are Comancheros."

A man Bobby Joe hadn't yet been introduced to whistled. "Comancheros. They're an unruly bunch of outlaws on either side of the Mexican border. They're very unpredictable men, Senor Pablo."

"And your name?" Bobby Joe asked.

"Rex Collier."

"Of course they are, Rex. That's why I sent for them. I don't want a bunch of sissy's trying to hold off range hungry ranchers. I want hard cases, and I, in no way, mean to imply you men are a bunch of sissy's. You have done a fine job up till now. However, your notoriety as gunmen has done nothing to keep our neighbors from pushing their cattle onto Slash M holdings. Once Miguel and his men arrive, I believe that situation will change."

"They'll take over, you can't control them," Rex warned.

"Normally you'd be correct. However, these men, their leader in particular, owe me his life. I saved him from certain death recently. He'll want to clear the debt. He does not like owing it I think."

"How many men does he have riding with him?" Pio chimed in.

"I'm not sure exactly, maybe twenty or thirty, but any help he can provide will be greatly appreciated. Another thing. These are the worst of men but they are on our side. Let the other ranchers and anyone else who wants a piece of our range worry about them. We needn't concern ourselves with such worry at all."

Harley Simms was beginning to smile as was Moses Carter. It'd been several months since the Mendoza brand held the upper hand. One week of leadership under Pablo Mendoza, though wounded badly, was turning the ranch fortunes around.

"Senor Pablo," Moses said, "for one, I believe things are going to get fun around here for the next few weeks. I wouldn't miss it for the world."

For the last several months the ranch hands had been little more than observers, yet they were all players. For months they'd been holding pat, not showing their hand, doing no more than required. Never mind every rancher in the territory knew the plight of the Slash M ranch, knew the trouble they were in and knew they couldn't fight. Now new cards had been dealt, along with a new boss, and their attitudes altered with the knowledge. The ranch would survive, as none of the men would contemplate otherwise. It'd been a while since they felt any confidence in the matter. Before the men left the table on this evening, Bobby Joe took the time to meet and greet every one of them. He wanted to know them, their quirks, their strong points, and their weak ones. Sending Hughe after the gold had been a good idea, but he couldn't count on the gold alone. He instructed the men to start culling the herds so they could make a drive to the railhead. The ranch was going to need more immediate money.

Chapter 12

L ater the same evening, Bobby Joe stood alone on the edge of the verandah leaning against a pillar, sucking on his toothpick. He let himself forget about the superb dinner Conchetta prepared and the meeting that took place. He stood favoring one side soaking up the night air, feeling the breeze that played softly against his clothing. Without question he'd been a lonely man, a drifting man with no ties, no sense of belonging to anyone or anything, not since Sue and Manny Riggins, his adopted parents died. He wanted desperately to stop, to ride over his own land, to watch his own cattle grazing on the pasture. He longed to sleep in his own bed at night. For this more than anything he came to Arizona.

For the first time in his life the person he wanted to settle down with had a face and a figure, and boy did she have a figure. Until now there had been the thought of a good woman, no definite features, nothing he could recognize, only the thought. Now after meeting and being waited on by the pretty young Conchetta he believed there could be no one else. He grinned as he thought of such a beauty sharing his life. How could he even think of such a girl marrying a drifting cowhand? Especially a cowhand who assumed other people's identities.

Standing on what was to be his own front porch, he knew he no longer wanted to drift. He wanted to stay right here, to remain Pablo Mendoza. He wanted more than anything to stay on, to be the boss, but his plan had been designed to flush out a killer, to trip him up, to get the man to make a mistake. Now he was firmly in place as Pablo Mendoza with no one the wiser. Every reasonable thought spoke to him, telling him his plan was going too smoothly, that it was too good to be true, but he had another thought, he also wanted to settle down. What would the young maiden's reaction be once she discovered he was not really Pablo Mendoza?

Not to imply the name Bobby Joe Riggins meant much, for it didn't, except where tough men gathered. Stories about him drifted from one territory to the next in the way such stories have a habit of doing. He was not a reputed gunman, but he was known as a tough and capable man. Back down the trail there were men who would tell you he was a man to leave alone.

This was a wild new country, a lonely land, but a good one. If he was lucky he might yet have sons to grow up strong and tall beside him. This is what he wished for. No longer did he look to the far horizons, he wanted to enjoy his own hearth fire, to draw water from his own well, and to see the heads of his own horses looking over his own corral fence. He wanted peace and serenity, and in seeking it he'd ridden smack dab into the middle of a land on the verge of range war.

Through the courtyard entrance a man rode a strangely marked horse; a true leopard appaloosa, white with black spots with a small patch of gray covering the right shoulder. The man did not ride alone. His dog walked beside him and a strange pair they made. The dog was graced with the same spots without the shoulder patch of gray. It was a dog such as Bobby Joe had never seen. The old lizard that called the Slash M home hardly stirred from its slumber.

The pair drew up. The horseman sat his saddle, while the dog squatted as if waiting for some specific command. The horse spread its nostrils to catch whatever scent was in the air, pricked its ears and looked eagerly ahead. The rider was a tall, slim middle-aged man narrow at the hip and wider of chest, his shoulders broader than any Bobby Joe had ever seen. He was a fairly big man, but this young man carried more meat on the bone. His features were stern and rugged, although not an unhandsome sort. There was a tough confident look about him, the kind that commanded attention wherever he might go. As he sat his horse he studied Bobby Joe with discriminating eyes.

Familiar footsteps sounded behind Bobby Joe and Conchetta came swishing through the doorway in a fresh evening gown. Light reflected off of the big man's badge as the front door opened and then closed itself to the night. Conchetta moved up beside him and stood motionless staring at the strangely marked horse and matching dog.

Bob Haslam was in his second month of being an Arizona Ranger. He'd ridden for the Pony Express nearly fifteen months before and earned the nickname Pony Bob. He'd been one of the first riders all those years ago who helped deliver Lincoln's inaugural address to San Francisco via fast flying horses. He'd been shot on that trip in 1861 by disgruntled Paiute Indian's but managed to escape their grasp. When the telegraph signaled the end of Russell, Majors, and Waddell's Pony Express in

October of 1861 he saddled up with his friend, Nat Love and headed for Denver where the two were hired to ride for the United States government. They were scheduled to deliver counterfeit plates that were recovered by the federals to Camp Floyd in Northern Utah. Halfway to their destination they were ambushed. Nat Love went down in the first volley of gunfire, but managed to survive, Haslam evaded the pursuit altogether and delivered the plates on schedule. All by the time he was seventeen.

To sidestep his responsibility or dodge his duty never occurred to the man. Life demanded the finest he could give it, and nothing short of his best effort would do. To Pony Bob, all who didn't perform their dead level best sooner or later ended up in a mess of their own making. There was no room for delinquent behavior in Bob Haslam's world.

As a newly appointed Arizona Ranger, it was his job to enforce the law, catch the bad guys and keep the peace. Laws were the rules that allowed society to prosper, which made civilization work. Without the law of the land, life would be chaos.

In such a vast land as the one he lived in it was customary to settle a dispute with guns. Sometimes the right party won, sometimes they lost, but a gunfight was cut-and-dry most times. Consequently, men were more guarded around one another, and more cautious as a result. They were more respectful of one another and more polite in general. Murder was rare, but it did happen on occasion, and now Bob Haslam had a murder on his hands. Worst of all he had no experience at solving such a crime. He was a common sense sort of man who only knew one way to do anything; so he started coping with murder just as he would anything else, one step at a time.

"What can we do for you officer?" Bobby Joe asked in order to break the ice and seek control of the conversation.

"My name's Bob Haslam, folks call me Pony Bob." The ranger said. "I'm looking for a man going by the name of Pablo Mendoza."

The way Bob said it left no doubt as to what he meant, "a man going by the name of Pablo Mendoza." How much did the lawman know? His accusation was cleverly disguised as a question, but it was an accusation nevertheless.

Abruptly Bobby Joe realized just how dangerous it had been for him to assume a dead man's identity and carry on such a silly charade without having informed the law first. All he wanted to do originally was to flush out Pablo's killer, and if he inherited a one hundred and fifty thousand acre ranch during the process, so what? Now, looking at the stern jaw on the ranger he wanted out. However he knew with every bone in his body it was too late to back out now.

"I am Pablo Mendoza, how can I help you?"

"I'm not inclined to believe you, mister." He waited expecting Bobby Joe to fill in the blank. When he made no such attempt the ranger continued. "I have evidence to the contrary. You don't mind telling me what your real name is, do you?" The lawman was fishing.

Suddenly Bobby Joe felt his skin crawl, he thought for a moment it was going to crawl right off of him and leave him exposed, defenseless. The ranger studied him from the back of his horse with a critical eye and stern set jaw while Bobby Joe languished in the silence that corrupted the evening.

How many times in his life had he faced fear, known fear, yet he'd never known fear such as this. Every nerve in his body was on alert.

"Sir," Conchetta broke in from somewhere beside him, "I am afraid you are mistaken. The man before you is Pablo Mendoza."

"I would like to believe you ma'am, but I can't. You see I have recovered a log which describes in detail the killing of Pablo Mendoza. It's quite convincing considering it came off of the body of a known killer for hire. I've also been advised that this man is an impostor and may be involved in trying to steal this ranch from its rightful heirs."

Conchetta felt as though a knife had been thrust through her heart, but she stood perfectly still. At least now she knew the man who'd shown up in his place was not the killer of her husband, providing the ranger was telling the truth, and why wouldn't he? Instantly she realized she could not let her husband's death be confirmed. She would never be able to hold such an estate by herself. She would lose everything. Whether he deserved it or not she could do nothing but come to the impostor's rescue.

"No doubt sir, the killer made a mistake. He may have killed someone, but it was not Pablo."

"And why not...?" Bob asked, unaccustomed to having a woman challenge his judgment.

"Because sir, I am Conchetta Mendoza. I am his wife. If anyone should know the real Pablo Mendoza it is I."

Stepping closer she reached out her left hand and encircled Bobby Joe's arm with both hands, just as two lovers might do at a ball, and then she looked directly into his eyes having made the announcement. Only now did Bobby Joe realize the girl wore a wedding ring.

He unexpectedly felt weak. His head was spinning and he was getting dizzy.

"I need to sit down," he said desperately to the young lass, the girl's touch unexpectedly sapped his strength.

"I don't doubt it." Conchetta almost whispered in his ear, she did not hesitate however to add, "Someone did shoot my husband. As you can see he is still weak," she said as she helped Bobby Joe to the front porch swing where he could get off his feet before he fainted, whether from weakness or shock neither was sure.

Straightening Conchetta added, "My husband was shot, but he is not dead as you can see. He is however still very weak, far from a full recovery."

"I hate to be troublesome ma'am, but I don't suppose you could provide me with some proof to back up what you are saying?"

Bobby Joe closed his eyes and took slow, deep breaths. He was in shock and somewhat stunned. He seemed on the verge of giving up the ghost, but the act of sitting provided him a second wind. He was also out of the loop as far as he could tell, doing his level best not to hyperventilate and pass out completely.

"You just sit right here my love, while I get the proof the ranger needs. Don't try to get up. I'll be right back." Swiftly Conchetta whisked herself away leaving the two men in silence. Bobby Joe was afraid to open his eyes, afraid he'd give his scheme away to the lawman if they made eye contact. Mysteriously this cat and mouse game had twisted into a living nightmare. Conchetta had known the entire time. Wishfully, he now wanted more than anything for this frightful chain of events to end. A visit from the Arizona Ranger was more than he bargained for.

Before his thoughts could betray him further, Conchetta returned with a small picture frame. It was their wedding picture and with it the license. She didn't hesitate to hand the items to Bob who took them and examined them in the light of the front porch lanterns.

"As you can see we are legally married and have been since February first of this year. And like I said, I should know my own husband."

Bob Haslam turned the items into the light to get a better view. It was simple and straight forward, the license from Laredo, Texas was as official as they come. There was no mistaking the man in the picture; it was the same man who now sat on the front porch swing, although now a mite thinner and more gaunt.

"Ma'am, I am truly sorry to have bothered you, but I had information describing the killing of Pablo Mendoza. I got it off a dead man I found right here on your ranch. Seems he kept a log of all his killings, thirteen in all—, your husband being the last," he said handing the items back to her. "Apparently he was mistaken about his last victim's identity, leading me to make a mistake of my own. When was your husband wounded?"

"A little less than a week ago, why?"

"Just wondering who was really killed down in Mexico. It's no less than a three week ride south of here at best. Seems he laid for someone he thought to be your husband, but I'd say he made an error. Poor fellow probably never knew what hit him, whoever he was."

"Maybe he shot my husband. Someone did."

"I doubt it. Randy Bean logged all his murders," the ranger said tapping the killer's notebook propped on the pommel of the saddle then dropped the evidence back into his pocket. "My guess is someone killed Randy from ambush, maybe the same someone who shot your husband. Randy Bean did his killing with a Sharps .50 buffalo rifle. Randy was shot with a Winchester model .73."

"We believe my husband was shot with the same caliber weapon."

"It seems I still have a killer on the loose, and I don't know where to begin to look for him. Finding the likes of Randy Bean would have been easy, but now what?"

"It is well known locally that Dean Reynolds would like to get his hands on this ranch. Maybe you should start there," Conchetta said.

"Fact is, he's the one who tipped me off that your husband was an impostor. I believe I'll have a talk with Mr. Reynolds when I get back to town. Mr. and Mrs. Mendoza I have no doubt you are who you say you are, but I still have a problem. I have a murder on my hands, and though he may have been the worst of outlaws he was still murdered, and he was murdered on your land. Also his log describes the killing of someone named Pablo Mendoza taking place months ago south of the border."

"Sir, my husband was ambushed south of the border a few months ago, and he was wounded, but he recovered and made his way here only to be shot again by someone else," she lied. "He was unconscious when Hughe Rainwater

182

brought him in and he has been fighting for his very life, but as you can clearly see, he has survived both attempts. The doctor was out here for two days, and had he not been able to stay, my husband would likely be dead."

Bob tipped his hat and started to leave.

"Hold on a minute, officer. I am getting mad," Conchetta said. "There is someone trying to kill my husband at every turn, and all you want to do is solve the murder of a killer. You may want to find out who is trying so hard to kill my man if you value your position. He only has one life, and you can do no more to help the dead. Meanwhile my husband still lives."

"I reckon you're right ma'am. I hadn't thought of the situation quite in those terms. I might be slow to get my mind around an idea and for that I apologize, but once I do, I don't let go so easy. Please accept my apology. What I can't figure is why Dean Reynolds would tell me such a cockamamie story in the first place?"

"Officer," Bobby Joe broke in as he was beginning to get his wind back. "Just where did you find Randy Bean if you don't mind my asking?"

"Considering I found him on your ranch I guess you have a right to know. It may be an area you want to avoid until I solve this thing. I found him over on the northwest portion of your range. He was not too far from some old Indian cave dwellings."

"That's where Pablo was shot from his horse, but why would the killer stick around after shooting either of them? And I can't figure why Hughe Rainwater didn't find something when he went looking."

"Hughe Rainwater is a good man," the ranger added.

"Sir," Bobby Joe interrupted.

"Call me Bob. I've a feeling we're going to know one another quite well before this trouble's over."

"Okay, Bob. I don't think Dean Reynolds is behind this. In fact, I'm almost certain of it."

"Who do you think is?"

"I haven't got the slightest clue, but if you sort of made it known you'll be watching our ranch and our range a little closer, I'd sure feel a lot safer on my own land."

"Not a problem. I was going to do so anyway after what the little lady said. Your land seems to be where all the action is." Pausing he added, "Well folks, it was a pleasure to meet both of you. I have a lot more questions than I have answers, but I figure it's the nature of my job. Ma'am, I will do my best to protect your husband, if I have to ride with him everywhere he goes. I'll be back out soon. In the meantime get some rest Mr. Mendoza," he said. "I want to see you in the saddle acting like a real rancher."

Chapter 13

Pablo Mendoza as he'd presented himself sat on the front porch swing dumbfounded as the Arizona Ranger and his dog left through the courtyard gate. Bobby Joe was in more trouble than he'd ever encountered in his entire life, and understood the implications. If Conchetta was really Pablo's wife, and he was certain she was, why defend him knowing full well the ranger was correct in his assessment that he was an impostor? Turning to look at the young woman as if seeing her for the first time, he gazed on the woman he could have spent the rest of his life with and cursed himself for seven kinds of a fool. Now look what he'd done. He had a snowballs chance in the Desert del Diablo of ever knowing her.

He would have to ride away. Only a fool would attempt what he'd done, and right now he was the biggest fool of them all. He'd fooled no one but himself.

"Ma'am," he said, "I reckon I've played the fool. When I found your husband's body down in Mexico, I got mad clean through. Randy Bean shot him in the back and left him for dead. Realizing we looked so much alike I got the idea I could show up, take his place and maybe flush the killer out or get him to make a mistake. On the way I had grand illusions, the kind that can get a man in trouble, apparently. I thought, what if no one challenged me? What if the ranch became mine in the process? Who would know? Who knows, if things worked out, well maybe I'd end up with a ranch like I'd always dreamed about and nobody the wiser. I'd no idea Pablo was married. What's more, I knew to do such a thing was wrong when I thought of it, but the only man I seemed to be depriving was Dean Reynolds, so I gave it a try anyway. I'll gather my things and ride come morning."

Conchetta stood near the swing so when he got up she would have to move to let him by, only she didn't. He stopped when he realized the girl was not inclined to move. She stood so close he could feel her breath on his exposed arm. With no warning, the lovely Conchetta threw her arms around his neck and hugged him tight. They were the only two people on the ranch at the moment, and he found himself wanting to pull her closer, to hug her in return, but his recent exposure held him in check.

Letting go her stranglehold on his neck, she stepped back and quickly composed her emotions.

"Where is the wedding ring?"

"Ma'am?"

"My husband's wedding ring, where is it?"

"I don't know, I never saw a ring," he said.

"I cannot let you go," she said while looking downward. "I do not know your real name, but you have proven to be a good man. Even though your motives were questionable, and I'm no longer certain to what extent that is true. You came and were shot. Why? Because, you were trying to flush out the killer of my husband. Is that right?"

"Yes ma'am, but..."

"You almost died for your decision, but now we both know who killed Pablo, and it wasn't you."

"Ma'am, I can't stay on the Slash M after what I've done. It wouldn't be right."

"You are mistaken, because not everything you did was wrong. Senor, if you leave now I will lose everything."

Both looked up as Pio and the men returned from town. In a rush she said, "I cannot fight the other ranchers even if need be. Strength and the showing of it is a man's undertaking. If it was known I'm Conchetta Mendoza the widow, I would lose everything tomorrow. My life would be in danger just as yours is. Pio is a good man, but he cannot do the things you can. He cannot free up the bank held money. He does not possess the decision making savvy you have demonstrated. Would Pio have thought to blow up those canyon walls to create more water for ranch needs?" Hesitating, she added, "I need you now more than ever. I know my husband is gone and I can do nothing to bring him back, yet you are here and everyone already believes you are him. I am very pleased you were not responsible for killing my husband, for I thought in the beginning you could be. I'm not ready to be so young a widow," she pleaded.

She took a step back and straightened her dress, but not too soon. She wanted the men riding into the courtyard to see them posing as lovers up close, together and personal when they arrived. She was not to be disappointed.

"If you must go, I cannot stop you." She leaned forward and whispered into his ear, which to the men riding up, she knew would appear to be a kiss. Then she turned and entered the house, leaving Bobby Joe standing on the front porch in a vacuum.

He stood there cold and alone watching the men filing into the corral one by one. The feeling of Conchetta's closeness left with her, but he was unable to recover from her touch. If everything failed right now, this very moment, all would have been worth the price he paid, to feel her touch, her arms around his neck, the whisper in his ear. He knew with every bone in his body he should cut and run for the hills, but the scent of her was still swirling around him, overpowering any thought he had of taking leave.

Only a few moments ago he'd known his ruse was over, his intentions uncovered and exposed. Now for reasons completely unexpected and unknown, the girl was giving him another opportunity. She was the one he wanted, and she was giving him another chance. To do what? If he left now he would never know.

Pio walked up the front steps with boxes full of supplies. Bobby Joe, realizing he had his arms full, grabbed the front door and opened it for him. Once Pio entered, Bobby Joe followed him into the big open foyer. Pio placed his boxes by the hearth in the living room and turned to look at the man he only knew as Pablo.

"Is everything all right, senor?"

"I do hope you will stay on," Conchetta said as she walked to him and took him by the arm. "I need you. We need you," she said as she led him over to a large comfortable chair in the corner. She almost pushed him into it, and Bobby Joe was helpless to stop her.

"I take it the two of you have met formally," Pio said.

"I know Pio feels the same way I do. We need you. If you leave, the ranch will fall apart in no time."

"Si, it would be good of you to stay, senor."

So, they both knew? Good Lord, how stupid could one man get?

"Who else knows I am not Pablo Mendoza?"

"No one at all. The ranger thought he knew, but he is now convinced you are Pablo. Does anyone else know this man is not Pablo?" Conchetta asked Pio point blank.

"No, I don't know of anyone but you and me who know the truth."

"I do," Bobby Joe said. "His name is Miguel Manuel. He's on his way here. If I'm going to stay, you should know my real name, or at least the one I go by. It's Bobby Joe Riggins."

Pio was surprised, yet he should have known. The name explained everything except what the man was doing in Arizona. He heard the name and the story just as every other man in the west. Bobby Joe was working a line camp up in Montana. One morning he got up and saddled his horse, rode out to check the cattle. The entire herd had disappeared without a trace. Fifteen hundred head of prime beef stolen right out from under the young man's nose. The thieves had made one mistake; they hadn't killed the man responsible for those cattle. At the time Bobby Joe had been a boy of seventeen, a cowboy just like the name implies.

Bobby Joe had heard of the outlaw trail that ran all the way from the north into Mexico. Supposedly the only men who rode the trail were outlaws or someone with a death wish. If you were not one of them, you were taking your own life in your hands because they could spot an intruder a mile away. Usually it was a man's appearance, or his attitude that tipped them off. Then it was only a matter of time before they killed you.

At seventeen he'd not only ridden the outlaw trail and lived to tell about it, he also buried every man-jack that was responsible for rustling his boss's herd. Then on returning to Montana he offered up the money the outlaws had gotten from the sale of the herd and presented the cash to his boss. There had been other stories, other gunfights, yet Pio remembered there had been thirteen hard-bitten outlaws, men who would never see the light of another day. Bobby Joe had returned without a scratch. It was the kind of story men out west did not forget. If Bobby Joe Riggins was the new Pablo Mendoza, the other ranchers surrounding the Slash M were in trouble, not the Mendoza clan. Pio grinned at the thought.

Bobby Joe interrupted Pio's musing. "I'll gather my things and take them out to the bunkhouse, and sleep with the men. I'll stay out of your hair and work hard ma'am. I owe your husband that much for saving my life."

"He saved your life?" Conchetta asked.

"Not exactly, but if his horse hadn't found me when he did, I'd be pushing up daisy's right now. I'd be just as dead as your husband."

"I see," Pio said scratching his jaw. "Senor you must stay in the house. If you do anything to let the men suspect you are anyone but Pablo the ranch will be in trouble."

"I'm not quite sure I follow you. The two of you want me to carry on this charade?"

"No one else can fill Pablo's shoes. We have no choice, you have no choice," Pio added.

Conchetta seated herself beside Bobby Joe in the other chair. "It is very simple. Other than your man Miguel as you call him, Pio and I are the only two people on earth who know the truth of who you are. To everyone else you are Pablo Mendoza the new owner of the Slash M holdings. Your arrival was just in time and your presence here on the ranch is the only reason it still exists. For months our neighbors waited, but as of right now the other ranchers are testing your resolve to see what Pablo Mendoza will do. Without you here there is only me, and senor no woman could hold onto a one hundred and fifty thousand acre ranch, even if she did know what to do." Hesitating she continued, "If anyone believes for one minute that you are not Pablo Mendoza we would lose everything in a matter of hours."

"You're suggesting I continue to pretend I'm Pablo, and your husband? I gather you two have had some time to think things through and talk this over. I understand now why you were so quick to act when Bob Haslam accused me of being an impostor."

"If what he said was allowed to stand, the ranch would be in Dean Reynolds' hands by morning. I could not allow such a thing to happen. I had to step forward. There was no other way to save the ranch."

"You almost gave me a heart attack, you know that?"

"I am sorry, but there was nothing else I could do under the circumstances."

"I know, but I sure could have used some warning."

"Listen well cowboy, if you plan on being my husband you'd better get used to such things happening. I'll warn you now if you stay you will be letting yourself in for more trouble than you bargained for. I don't believe my husband had enough experience to hold onto such a ranch as this. I was afraid I might become a widow, only I never expected it so soon. He never had a chance. However, now we know what we're dealing with. If you stay you will no doubt be shot at again. Who knows what else might happen?"

"You are the only thing holding the wolves at bay. Are you game?" Pio added.

Bobby Joe smiled to himself at Pio's question. Since childhood he'd weathered the storm of death, always in close proximity, always taking others but not him. Although he was never foolish or reckless he'd been skirting death since he could remember. If need be he could do so again.

He was an interloper here, yet the man's place he'd taken was dead. Perhaps he could do a good job of carrying on in the dead man's place, making the ranch safe for those who remained, but he would be subservient to such a woman as Conchetta? Was that really a bad thing? Not from where he sat.

He stood up. "I'm exhausted, but I'll do as you wish. I'll stay on and pose as your husband." A moment later he was headed down the hallway to his bedroom.

The new ranch owner was sleeping soundly when Conchetta entered the living room from the kitchen and placed a hot cup of coffee in front of Pio where he sat in the boss's big chair and smoked his old pipe. Pio looked up at the young, beautiful girl, noting the worry of the last several days seemed to have departed from her.

"For better or worse it has begun, senorita. What do you think now?"

"Pio I feel I should be mourning the death of my husband, but for some reason I do not. This man has come for a reason, only God knows."

"It is this new man. His presence here is meant to ease your pain. God is answering your prayers."

"For some reason I don't feel bad. I feel relieved."

"Maybe it is because he looks so much like your husband you don't miss him so much."

"He looks so much like Pablo I can scarcely tell the difference. I miss my husband, but he is still here, at least I keep telling myself so."

"Who can judge how a woman in your position should feel? I have never heard of such a thing as what we are involved in, nor could I have dreamed up such a tangled web of circumstances," the ranch foreman admitted.

"You are correct. I never dreamed such a thing could happen as this, but things have worked out thus far."

"Let me add, I ride for the Slash M and as long as I can draw a breath I pledge myself. That means to you and Pablo," Pio studied his swirling pipe smoke. "You are not afraid?"

"No, not anymore. He faced Dean Reynolds without hesitation, and he has faced the Arizona Ranger on this night. He has sent for more men and he sent Hughe after the gold we are going to need to get things going around here. He is making very good decisions, and besides, I like him more now that I know he didn't have anything to do with my husband's death."

"Si, this man can use a gun, but more importantly he knows when not to use one. I do not worry so much about our neighbors now he has sent for these Comancheros. They will be a new piece in a big puzzle. I hope he is doing the right thing in bringing them here."

"He will make it work. If his actions so far are any indication things will be just fine."

"You are right of course, senorita."

Chapter 14

Help was on the way in the form of certain border outlaws known as Comancheros. A Comanchero was cautious, sometimes careless and veterans of many campaigns or raids into American territory. So there was no surprise among them as they began to understand the lay of the land into which they were riding. The land was baron of grass but over infested with jagged rock formations that hindered quick travel by any group of men. Cacti dotted the landscape at every turn and required much accuracy in the steering of their mounts in order to prevent them being stabbed with the protruding thorns that protected the plant's showy flowers.

As the men rode north the landscape changed and opened up. Grass appeared here and there along with small shrubs that were harmless to the exposed legs of the horses. The much anticipated Comanchero gang had been riding Slash M land for almost an hour when Antonio, the point guard returned with half expected news of the tracks that revealed much.

"Senor Miguel, someone is rustling your brother's stock."

"Are you sure?"

"There is no mistake. They are moving slowly trying not to stir up dust and the riders are all wearing a different brand. We can stop them I think."

"We will stop them. Lead the way Ant. No one is going to steal my brother's stock as long as I am breathing. Not if I can help it."

As one, the cavalcade of seasoned Comanchero fell in behind Miguel and Antonio. In a matter of minutes they were about to ride into a sea of cattle. As they neared the head of the long column they pulled up to await the first rider. When the point man saw his way blocked he knew he had been caught flat-footed. When he drew close enough to talk, he halted his horse.

"Senor, you are going the wrong way no," Miguel said.

The lone rustler held his ground and studied the men before him. There was nothing in what he saw that gave him comfort. He'd heard of these men and from what he'd heard they were capable of killing without warning. They didn't even need a reason. If reports were accurate, and one thing you could always bank on in the west, reports and descriptions of men were accurate. But, why were these Comancheros so far north of their usual haunts? They were border men. Reynolds insisted rustling cattle from the Slash M would be a piece of cake. Mendoza only had six riders left there was no way they could watch all of the cattle.

"You are not speaking, senor. Is something wrong? I know you are dumb because you are trying to steal my brother's cattle. Are you deaf also?"

The rustler was going to die right here and right now. Abruptly the man understood his fate. All he could do would be to warn the others who were breathing in the dust of impending trouble. If these men were allowed to ride in without warning they would surely all die. Hoping to take one or more with him the castigated rustler drew his pistol and was dead before he could pull the trigger, but he had done his job, he had warned the others something was amiss.

As if shot from the same canon the other nine rustlers fled while cattle swarmed in all directions. The rustlers scattered to the four winds but they were outnumbered by a bunch of bloodthirsty wolves that were practiced at overtaking their prey. With art and precision of long practice the Comanchero divided into two's without an order being given and rode down their victims in a matter of a few desperate minutes. Their pursuit was a work of art. How they overtook the rustlers and reined them in befit a well-trained army. Six men were still alive although two of them were slightly wounded. In all, four died and the Comancheros wasted no time in securing the dead men to their mounts then riding back to the scene as they had done many times before, but for different reasons.

The cattle scattered when startled by the gunfire, but ran only a short way before settling down when they realized the mêlée of bullets was not intended for them. Slowly the Comancheros pushed the herd back together then started them toward the home ranch while guarding their captured prey. Each outlaw was securely fastened to his horse and there were no glad tidings among them. They knew their lot and knew their destiny, but they each prayed for a better ending as criminals often do when caught, yet knowing of certain what fate awaited men who rustled cattle.

At noon the following day the men arrived at the home ranch with prisoners and four dead men in tow. Only the night before had Conchetta, Pio and the new Pablo sorted the ranch's future out, and Ranger Bob

Haslam had been out for his visit. Everyone stopped what they were doing and watched as the herd pushed ever closer to the home range. Bobby Joe and Conchetta were sitting on the front porch swing discussing the arrival of so many when the Comanchero departed the herd and started toward the main house. Over the low rolling hills near the ranch and the adobe wall that surrounded the main compound the two were able to see the dust of many cattle along with everything else that was taking place to the south.

"Conchetta, that would be the men I sent for. It looks like my brother has already run into some trouble," Bobby Joe stated.

"That is many men. I cannot cook for so many. I will need much help."

"It is a lot of men, but we need them. The ranch has been short on manpower for too long."

"We must send for Anna. She knows how to cook for so many."

"Who is Anna?"

"Anna was the ranch cook before I arrived. With no pay she went to work in town."

The young couple watched from the front porch swing as the horsemen pulled free of the herd and stopped pushing them letting the cattle scatter at will. They watched as rider after rider emerged from the dust. As the cattle settled down the dust also dissipated and riders appeared as if from a cloud. The new Pablo Mendoza arose from his seat looking on in wonder.

When the riders entered the courtyard with Miguel leading the captured and deceased, Conchetta rose taking her place beside her fill-in husband. Bobby Joe spoke first as he had given much thought as to how he would greet his brother in front of his men who were lined up behind the prisoners sitting their mounts.

"Welcome gentlemen. My name is Pablo Mendoza. My wife, Conchetta and I will be your host for as long as you stay. I hope you had a safe journey, my brother." This he spoke directly to Miguel. He paused as he recognized Dean Reynolds and Jack Fuller in the bunch with their hands tied to the pommel of their saddles. Dean had a dumbfounded look on his face, as if he were trying to understand what just happened. Bobby Joe now recognized the fact Reynolds had not known Conchetta was the wife of Pablo Mendoza.

"You are Conchetta Mendoza?" His question was directed at the young lady of the house.

"Yes, I am Pablo's wife. Mr. Reynolds, I am sorry to find you in such a compromising position."

Jack Fuller dropped his head as if he was finally defeated. He knew of the young maiden living on the ranch, and he'd fantasized about what she would be like if he could ever get her alone. Now he was certain of only one thing—how big a fool he was.

"It seems you have already found trouble." Pablo once again took control of the conversation. "Why are all these men tied up?"

"We have captured some rustler's, brother. Shall we hang them for you?"

Several of the tied men panicked at the thought. They struggled and kicked in an effort to free themselves from their bonds. Jack Fuller had tears streaming down his cheeks, otherwise he showed no emotion. They were stripped of their guns and the Comanchero had commandeered those. The bottom line was the rustlers were helpless and at the mercy of their captors.

"Miguel, this is not Mexico. I understand justice, but I will have to give the fate of these men some thought. I did not expect to have such a problem on my hands so soon."

"It's no problem. We'll ride back down to the border and hang them in Mexico."

Several of the Comancheros prodded and poked their captives with pistols and rifles alike, smiling at the prospect of torturing them on a long ride back to the San Pedro.

"It's going to be a very hot day today. Tie them to the corral fence and leave them in the sun without water for a while. I'll make a decision on what to do with them shortly. There must be a dignified way to arrange for their disposal. A legal way." Pointing to Dean Reynolds and Jack Fuller, he added, "I want those two staked out on the ground in front of the rest of these men."

Snapping his fingers and circling his index finger in the air Miguel gave the signal for his men to follow through as Pablo ordered.

"Si, as you wish my brother." Stepping from his horse as the commotion began behind him the fearless Comanchero bounded up the front porch steps and gave his brother a big hug in front of everyone for old times sake. "We have much to talk about, no?" The border outlaw suggested.

"That would be an understatement," Bobby Joe said. "Let's go inside where we can talk in private." Conchetta was already holding the door open for the two men.

"My men, they might get carried away if I am too long gone. We must make this quick for the prisoner's sake. Otherwise you may lose some rustlers."

Miguel took in the ranch house as he entered and thought to himself he had just entered the Pearly Gates of Heaven. The home was magnificent in construction and architecture. Here he could live a noble life, here he could put down roots, here he could stop being the wandering vagabond he'd become. As soon as the two men were seated in the two big chairs facing the hearth, Conchetta poured them each a cup of coffee.

"How many men did you bring with you," Bobby Joe asked.

"I have seventeen altogether. Seventeen and if we need more I can raise the ante."

"Are your men any good with cows?"

"We have never had cows, but we know how to rustle a herd, I think for my men have been good at stealing American beef and taking them south across the border, and we have brought your cattle home, but in your letter you said you needed guns."

"I need both."

"Then they are both," Miguel smiled displaying his spaced front teeth.

"We're going to have a supply problem right away, I can see that much," Bobby Joe said.

Just then the front door opened and Pio stepped in. The foreman had something on his mind yet he was unsure how to proceed with Miguel in the room. How much did the man know and better yet could he be trusted? To spout off without knowing anything about the man was no good. He stood in the doorway holding the front door open.

"Senor Pablo I will ride to town and get our old cook. We will need her with this many men about the house."

"Miguel, this is Pio. Pio is my ranch foreman."

"I am pleased to meet you, senor." Pausing Miguel added. "Are you sure you are telling me everything my brother? What is this thing you have gotten us into?"

Pio closed the door behind him as he entered the room, sensing immediately what was going on. He needed to be satisfied himself that Miguel was a true ally. He looked at his boss and at Conchetta for both understood the dangerous foundation upon which they were building their uncertain future.

"What is going on here?" Miguel shifted in his chair as all eyes settled on him. It seemed to Miguel all three of them had something to say, yet no one was talking.

Bobby Joe studied his new friend for a long moment. "Only Conchetta, Pio and now you know what my real name is. Can I count on you to keep such a secret?" Bobby Joe asked.

"Brother, brother you do not trust me? I owe you my life. I think you can trust me. I will not say anything. You have always been, and from now on you are Pablo Mendoza. My men know you only by that name, you know this yourself. I burned the letter you sent me. It would not do any good for someone to read such a thing. I would have to kill anyone who read it, so I burned it. And brother, my lips are sealed."

"That's good because if anyone were to get the idea the real Pablo was dead the lid would blow off this country like a powder-keg."

Conchetta interrupted. "Senor Miguel, I trust Pablo to do the right thing as he has managed so far. In fact, I must trust him with my very life. You see, I am his wife Conchetta. This man before you is Pablo Mendoza from now until all eternity. He is my husband, I am his wife."

"You never told me you were married, my brother."

"I wasn't, but Pablo was."

"Gentlemen, may I interrupt?" Pio cut in. "You must forever remain Pablo Mendoza. This can no way be a temporary situation. What we are doing must be permanent," he said speaking directly to both men and Conchetta. "This is no game. You must assume Pablo's identity forever as Conchetta suggested. You can never go back."

"He is right," Conchetta stepped forward. "You must forever be my husband whether you want to or not. Nothing else will work."

"Aye yah yah!" Miguel exclaimed. "You get the ranch, the girl and the money! Are you sure you can handle being such a man, my brother?"

"I can handle things on my end, but you must never tell our secret."

"No one would believe me. To everyone already you are Pablo Mendoza. I would look like a fool if I said anything different." Miguel smiled.

"I have given much thought to what must happen and temporary will never work. Someone will slip up or make a mistake. If it is not forever," Conchetta said as she measured Bobby Joe's reaction, "then we might as well throw in the towel now." She studied Bobby Joe's eyes to see what was in them and then looked at Miguel.

"Do you know what you are saying?" Bobby Joe wondered as their words began to penetrate.

"I know well what I am saying, for there can be no other way," Conchetta replied.

"She is right, my brother. We are the only four people who know this and the life of Bobby Joe Riggins must be put to rest here and now. If you leave next week, or ten years from now she would lose the ranch. A woman can do many things, but holding a ranch such as this is not one of them. I am afraid you must forever be tied to her. I myself will slip up unless we put the name Bobby Joe Riggins to rest right here and now."

"Pio and I agree. The issue must be buried once and for all, Bobby Joe must now disappear forever, never to be resurrected," Conchetta said.

"You are saying the ranch is forever to be mine and I am forever to be your husband?" Bobby Joe puzzled at their resolute stance in the matter.

"That is exactly what must happen. Your wife has presented the only possible solution," Miguel said.

Bobby Joe let Miguel's words sink in and turned to look at the beautiful Conchetta. "Are you certain this is what you want?"

"I must forever be your wife. Take me or leave me now, but we can exist no other way. There is no other solution that will allow us to survive, not now not ever! We have become stuck in our little game of deceit, but we're okay, no?" Conchetta emphasized while she leaned on the arm of his chair and ran her fingers through his hair.

Bobby Joe thought things through to a point, but he never figured on not being Bobby Joe Riggins. Living the remainder of his life as that of a dead man was an aspect he'd not thought of and was much more demanding than any prospect he'd been prepared to accept. Yet this new plan meant Conchetta would be his. Could they really be happy as husband and wife? The whole idea was crazy, yet what everyone said made sense. Such a scheme was risky when he alone knew what he was doing, but now three other people were involved, and any one of them could finger him as an impostor at any moment. Yet, were not their fortunes tied to the success of the ranch as well? To finger him as an imposter would derail their own fortune.

"This all made a bit of sense when I alone knew what was happening, but now there are too many people who know the truth," Bobby protested.

Conchetta grabbed Bobby Joe's whiskered face with her right hand and turned the familiar face only inches away from her own and looked directly into his eyes. "There is no one in this room you cannot trust Pablo, especially me," she said as she planted a kiss full on his lips while holding his face in her hand. Letting go she added, "Need I remind you some more?"

Both Pio and Miguel chuckled. This was a spectacle neither expected to witness. The girl was driving home her point with the precision of a hammer striking a nail on the head.

"Okay, you've made your case, but I'm going to need all of you to assist me if we're going to conspire to live our futures together and handle this ranch. You must call me nothing but Pablo Mendoza. You must see me as no one but Pablo the owner of Slash M range otherwise we are doomed to fail in our efforts."

"We make a pact here and now," Pio said. "A pact between the four of us. We must forever consider our future as if we were one person. Miguel, you and I must for the remainder of our lives pledge that we will never speak of this again. We must always base our decisions on the best interest of the ranch for Pablo and Conchetta's sake and we must swear on our soul that we will each uphold the others no matter what."

Pablo stepped forward and held out his hand. Each got up, placed their hands one upon the other.

"Repeat after me," Pio instructed. "I pledge my life,"

"I pledge my life," they repeated in unison.

"My breath."

"My breath," they repeated.

"And my sacred honor to the Slash M ranch."

"And my sacred honor to the Slash M ranch."

"So help me God," Pio finished.

"So help me God." They agreed in unison and then Miguel added, "Senor Pio, my men are making trouble, shall we go fix them and leave these two lovebirds alone?"

"I think we shall," Pio replied. "Congratulations you two."

As the two men ducked out the door, Conchetta laid her hand on Pablo's and said. "We'll be fine. Pio and I have been discussing this very thing. At first I didn't want to consider such deviltry at all possible, but as I thought about my situation I realized there could be no other way. I married Pablo Mendoza. You are now Pablo Mendoza, no?"

While Conchetta touched and stroked the back of Bobby Joe's hand it seemed as though his entire past was being sucked out of him, literally erased with each touch of the girl's fingers. The emotion she stirred within him left no room for Bobby Joe. He only thought of her and how Pablo Mendoza would be spending the rest of his days with such a beautiful woman on such a grand estate. He could handle this, he was meant for such a life he told himself.

"It won't be as difficult as you think, Pablo. I will make things very pleasant for you, my husband. I won't be any trouble at all." Slowly, deliberately, she got up and took him by the hands and said. "Follow me."

Hand in hand she led him down the long hallway toward the master bedroom where she stopped and turned to face her new man. "Tonight we must begin to live like a husband and wife." Leaning into her tiptoes she kissed him full on the lips then lowered herself back down. "I will get my things together and put them in our bedroom."

Bobby Joe realized as she stared into his eyes she was either correct or he was the biggest fool to ever set foot on the planet. If she was going to act in such a manner, masquerading as Pablo Mendoza would not be difficult at all. He felt terribly sinful for what he was about to do with another man's wife and full of guilt for what he'd already imagined, but the scent of the woman and her touch on his lips along with her promise was more than he could bear. He knew that he could no more resist her than he could raise his own parents from the dead.

"I don't know if I can control myself. You're very beautiful and I'm getting weaker by the moment," he said.

"Pablo." She blushed. "You still do not understand." Again she raised herself on her toes and planted a kiss full on his lips, only much harder, deeper and longer until he started kissing her in return. Until there was no longer any misunderstanding of the feelings between them, until he knew she wanted him for the man he was and not for the man her husband had been. They clung together for several minutes after the kiss and felt the closeness of flesh each of them had longed for. Neither wanted to let go, their touches driving away the problems of the moment.

"Just one thing before we get too carried away. We must get married immediately," the girl said. I must say my vows with you and you must share your vows with me. I can live no other way."

"If it will make you happy, I'm all for it."

"You do not think it necessary?" Conchetta asked.

"Of course it's necessary. We must say our vows and know we mean them. I could no more let your previous husband speak for me than you could speak for your own mother."

"With you as Pablo and me as Conchetta...?" She quizzed.

"Yes, with no misunderstanding of the family we really are. There is one thing you should know however. For years I never knew my real birth name. Bobby Joe Riggins was the name I was given by my adopted parents when my mother died. The most I was ever able to find out was the name Westmoreland, nothing else. My adopted parents died in an earthquake in southeast Missouri and I was left to fend for myself. There is one thing more. My mother died giving birth to another baby when I was one year old. I was never able to determine if the baby lived or not. When I turned your husband over and saw his face, I thought certain I'd found him. Only for a moment, but the thought was there."

"Are you kidding me?" Conchetta gasped and put her hands to her face.

"I wish I were. The truth is, not knowing my birth name makes becoming Pablo Mendoza a good deal easier. I have experience in such matters because Bobby Joe Riggins isn't my real name either!"

"Good Lord almighty, then you could have been brothers and Pablo was probably not my husband's real name. He was adopted too!" Conchetta said.

"If we were family we'll never know, not now."

"Before I forget, you need to know one more thing. I am your wife, not a slave to those bad men you have imported. I will help cook, but I will not become a slave in my own household." She laid down the law as she looked Pablo in the eye.

Her statement jarred the new ranch owner from his lover's daze. "I'll handle the situation in another manner. You needn't worry about becoming a slave my dear. I could never treat you as anything but my queen. In fact I need to go outside and handle a few things while you're moving your personal belongings," Pablo said.

Bending down he gave her a kiss on the cheek and added. "I'll be back in a couple of hours."

When he stepped out onto the front porch and the door closed behind him several eyes turned his way. He noticed right off the men had followed instructions and staked Jack and his boss out in the yard in front of the others. Descending the steps he walked over to the two rustlers and looked down on them.

"What happened to him?" Pablo asked looking at Jack Fuller.

"He got smart with one of my Indians. He was the wrong man to insult, so Huachuca here took a couple of fingers for souvenirs," Miguel said. "He collects them. I do not know why."

"Cut these men loose Miguel, cut them all loose. I know what I'm going to do with them now."

"Cut them loose!" Miguel shouted to his men.

The Comanchero cut the bindings of their captives and stood back to observe, training their weapons on them. Every man among them was curious as to how their new boss would handle the situation.

"Now gentlemen, take off your boots, all of you. You deserve to be hung. However, I'm not going to order it. I think you know by now the Slash M is a place to avoid at all cost. I want you to tell your friends, if you have any, to stay off Mendoza land."

Pablo saw Miguel watching with curious eyes as he paused for emphasis. He knew the Comanchero wondered what he had in store for such a forlorn bunch of cattle thieves. Inwardly, he smiled. His voice parted the silence in the courtyard like a bolt of lightning depositing a crack of thunder on the deck.

"It's twenty-seven miles to Sonora. Leave your boots where they lay and start walking!"

Reynolds looked at him in horror. "You're joking!"

"Dean you brought these men in here and tried to steal my cattle. You were caught red-handed. Anyone else would have strung you up already. You and your men are getting off easy. Your horses, guns, saddles and now your boots belong to the Slash M ranch. It's a small price to pay in exchange for your life. Now take your boots off and get going!"

Like a played out herd of cattle the men dropped to the hard packed earth and removed their footwear. As a disheveled group, they slithered towards the courtyard entrance dreading what they knew was ahead. Some of them were grumbling, one was limping already, but all were moving in the direction Pablo ordered.

"Don't worry about your dead. We'll take care of them for you. If any one of you dare get caught trespassing on my range again you will receive the hanging you averted here today. My men won't hesitate to carry out the sentence," Pablo yelled after them.

Not one man turned back to listen. They could hear just fine. Every man in the bunch knew he meant what he said and was certain he would do as promised having just witnessed Jack losing two of his fingers.

"My brother, I do not think I want to cross you. Not only are you very good with a side arm, you may be more dangerous than I have previously believed," Miguel said.

"Count on it. We'll have to make do on the food by roasting a beef until we can recover our ranch cook from town."

"Roasting a beef over an open flame is a most excellent cause for celebration. And, we must celebrate our reunion my brother!"

Pablo studied Miguel for a long moment. "A celebration is welcome, but it will not last past this evening. In the morning we have much work to do," Pablo said.

"Antonio! Go cut out that wounded cow. She is to be our dinner tonight!"

Antonio wasted no time following orders. The heifer was slaughtered and brought in for roasting with flawless execution. Several of Miguel's men had experience building fire pits such as the ones they would need to accomplish the feat, yet the Mendoza ranch already had a flame pit for just such an occasion near the well and the fire was handled with the equal precision of habits long practiced. Practiced on what animals from what herd was another matter.

In no time the fire was just the right size with a half steer roasting above the heat in the middle of the courtyard, the other half going up not twenty yards away over another. No doubt Miguel's men had roasted beef over an open flame before this, but out in the wild they hadn't the readymade pits. Pablo Mendoza looked on with appreciation as the men worked in harmony to prepare their supper for the evening.

Miguel walked over to where Pablo stood and looked on as his men handled every aspect of the cook out, except for the sauce Conchetta brought to them, which was a masterful stroke on her part. With one unselfish act the young Conchetta had bought the loyalty of each and every outlaw among them. They always ate their meat plain, with haste, ready to move at a moment's notice, but to have a sauce applied such as the lovely Conchetta prepared made each one of them feel as if they'd suddenly become respectable somehow. Then she topped the meal off with civilized drinks of lemonade and tea.

Knowing the ways of such men, she thought to treat them better than they were treated by themselves if they were going to be staying on for a while. As soon as she finished moving her things into the master bedroom the idea struck her so certainly she went straight to the kitchen and prepared a recipe handed down from many generations in her family. Not even Pablo had tried it yet; either Pablo she noted.

Pablo stepped down from the front porch and pulled the ranch foreman off to the side and gave Pio special instructions. The man was the undisputed ramrod for the Slash M brand. The new Pablo was placing a vital charge into Pio's hands, one which must be carried out with utmost scrutiny. Pablo knew Miguel watched them talking, yet he knew Miguel was aware of his place and wasn't worried about what his brother did. He was to keep his men in line and Pablo watched him go back to celebrating.

Finally they broke up and Pablo went into the house. Pio headed for the stables where he hitched up a horse then placed the animal and carriage in front of the hitch post which were on either side of the front porch steps. A few minutes after he went into the mansion he returned forthwith and stepped into the coach. He waved goodbye to Pablo and Conchetta.

Pio slapped the rump of the animal with the reins and walked the horse out of the courtyard. Once outside the gate he put a quirt to his animal and cantered off.

Later in the evening, as the sun was setting, Pablo looked out over the courtyard from the front porch swing. Four dead rustlers were buried with each one's head facing either north, east, south, and west face down. They'd been spread out, unmarked and placed so the cattle would walk on their graves just as he'd ordered. The new men had their possessions placed in the bunkhouse though the ranch was one bunk short. They made do as always. Huachuca, the wild Indian, chose to sleep under the stars where he seemed more comfortable anyway. It was well after midnight when the men finally went to sleep on full and gorged stomachs. It had been a red-letter day for the Slash M ranch and everyone was exhausted.

Chapter 15

Pio did not partake in the festivities. Instead he was headed for town. Not trusting the rustlers had been adequately searched by Miguel's men, he rode warily around giving them a wide berth and an impossible target to hit in case one of them still held a hide-out weapon. Late in the evening Pio rode into the town of Sonora and pulled up in front of the livery. Stepping down he handed his reins to the old timer who tended horses.

"Feed him some oats tonight will you? We must return first thing in the morning."

"Yes, senor. I would have done so anyway."

"I know, Zeek. I was just making pleasant conversation."

"You've been making a lot of conversation around town, and you haven't even been here," the old hostler said.

"You mean people are starting to talk?"

"That's what I mean."

"What are they saying?" Pio asked.

"Your new boss might not be who he says he is."

"Zeek, my new boss is none other than Pablo Mendoza, and you should know he means business. He sent me to town the other day to get all the ammunition I could purchase, and all the dynamite I could lay my hands on. Right now this town is completely defenseless until such a time as new supplies arrive. He wanted it done on purpose. We can defend the Slash M with ease."

"With only six riders…?" Zeek asked.

Pio smiled. "With twenty-four riders. His brother rode in this morning with seventeen of the toughest Comancheros I ever did see. That's why I came to town. We need Anna back out at the ranch. She still down at the cantina?"

"Si, we'll be sad to see her leave. She is the finest cook in all of Arizona I think."

"I don't think, I know. One more thing," Pio said, "Pablo has a wife out at the ranch and her name is Conchetta. She arrived several months ago. Now that Pablo is here we believe it no longer necessary to keep her identity a secret."

Anna DeSalto was a robust woman of forty-five years. She'd been the ranch cook for Don Pablo Mendoza for ten of those years and had grown used to the ways of ranch life. She'd not wanted to leave the ranch, but when it could no longer afford to pay for her services she'd been forced to move into town. A woman needs things. She was a self-sufficient woman, having never married. She liked what she did and the satisfaction on her patron's faces was all the reward she'd wanted from life, but she missed her room and quarters at the Mendoza ranch.

When Pio entered the cantina she knew instantly why he had come. His smile betrayed his purpose, for until today he had always told her, "not yet." This time the smile that adorned his countenance revealed to her things were different at the ranch. She'd heard rumors of late, but they were just rumors. She had no facts and no information of real substance to go on until Pio came to town. The ranch foreman would bring news of the new owner, his wife, and the conditions at the ranch. Now though, he was obviously returning for her.

"Hello, Anna."

"You have come to fetch me home then?"

"I have indeed."

"I will be ready to go at first light. How are things on the ranch?"

"They are much better than I expected. We have many new men, and Pablo is a very capable rancher. He is a good man, but not a man to cross. He is proving to be very tough and thoughtful. Even as we speak, he has forced six rustlers to walk back to town in their bare feet. Four others were buried on the ranch this day. Scattered about the range face down, as was his instructions," Pio said.

"Such a story will travel far, very far," she admitted.

"Si, and to make matters worse it is Dean Reynolds and Jack Fuller doing the walking."

Anna smiled. "I miss the old days when Don Pablo Mendoza and Consuelo ran a stable household. I must meet this Pablo Mendoza. I think I may enjoy working for such a bold one."

"You don't know the half of it. His new hands are Comancheros, two of which are full-blooded Comanche Indians and one is half-breed Apache."

"You are kidding, no?"

"I am not. Their leader is Pablo's blood brother. Pablo saved his life somewhere down in Mexico and then rode north to claim his inheritance, only after making sure the man would survive being ambushed by renegades."

"The ranch is safe for a woman such as I?" Anna wanted to know.

"If I didn't think so, I wouldn't have come for you. I'm in love with you Anna, or did you not know?"

"I know you love me, but you have never said so." The cook smiled.

"I am saying it now. Will you marry me?" Pausing to study Pio's eyes the cook looked him up and down.

"I will marry you if we are married before we return to the ranch tomorrow. I see no reason to wait."

"I'm not getting any younger my dear, but we must wed at the ranch and bring the priest with us."

Undoing her apron Anna hollered toward the kitchen, "Jose, I am going to get married, you must finish the evening without me," Anna hollered toward the kitchen.

Grabbing Pio by the arm the two wasted no time in trotting out the front door onto the street. There was only two blocks to navigate before reaching the old Spanish Mission and the priest would be there. He was always there after the sun went down.

At the ranch things were different. Pablo and Conchetta slept together in the same bed for the first time. They were alone and under such conditions the two consummated their agreement from earlier in the day, but not by making love. The ultimate test of trust was now underway and having considerable obligation to one another, they both lay awake with doubts about their future.

"Can you exist as Pablo Mendoza?" Conchetta asked.

"My dear Conchetta, if I have any problem being your husband you'll be the first to know. But I should tell you, I have no experience at believing in a life this good. My life has been fraught with trouble from the very beginning. I want to believe, but I have no practical experience in such matters."

"Do you like my love so far?"

"Well, I do like the way you're treating me. I've never had a woman to be so forward the way you have."

"But you have had another woman?" Conchetta sat straight up and looked at him.

"My dear, you are the first and only woman I've ever kissed. How about you? Have you ever given yourself to another man?" Pablo turned the tables.

"Pablo only, and since you are now Pablo, I must say no, never! But, you understand why we must wait until Pio returns with the priest," Conchetta added.

The two laughed at her statement and in no time were deeply engaged in conversation. What did it all mean? Why had such things happened to them? Could they make their new life work?

The only movement on the ranch late that night was Huachuca surveying the herds. These new beasts were not like the great buffalo herds of old. Nothing was missed by the Indian who'd been an insomniac since seven years old when a mountain lion tore into his family's wickiup and killed his siblings before his father could subdue the animal. It was a terrible fright for the young Indian brave to behold, and he had not slept after the sun went down since. He would catch a few winks during the early morning hours if necessary, but usually it wasn't.

At noon the following day, Pio and Anna returned to the ranch with news of their impending marriage and

brought the priest with them as Pio had been instructed. It was a festive moment, for the two were clearly made for one another. Conchetta helped Anna get her things situated in her quarters and then the two ladies turned to making a meal for the men who still loitered around the main ranch compound. One ceremony was held in public view for all to see, and one held in the house in secret.

The Slash M had a wine cellar, a wine cellar in the middle of nowhere, but a vast array of wines was present to witness the two marriages. Having known of the Stone Hill Winery in Hermann, Missouri from his several excursions to the town and the fact he'd been born there, Pablo only needed to select the right bottles.

It was nearly two o'clock before the ranch hands were able to eat, and as they ate the women worked on supper. Anna did not want Conchetta's help but the younger girl insisted. It would not be allowed to become a standard, but Anna was grateful for the help on this day. The table was only capable of serving twelve guests at a time, making it necessary to have the ranch hands eat in two shifts. Other than eating there was much to do about the ranch, and the new hands were up for the task, as were the old ones.

"Were you able to get all of the dynamite I asked for?" Pablo asked Pio during the first sitting.

"Si, we have enough to blow up the whole territory if it comes down to it, and we purchased all available ammunition as you requested. I didn't leave so much as a shotgun shell. Most everything was allowed on credit now that the merchants know you are here."

"Good. Harley, today would be a fine day for you to teach young Vince how to use the stuff. I want the two of you to ride out to where that channel branches off from the Little Apache and blow those canyon walls in on themselves. If my guess is right, we'll control virtually all the water on the southern range once you do it. I want the canyon approach sealed off as soon as possible. Take a couple of Miguel's men with you to keep an eye out. I don't want to hurt anybody, just solidify our rankings in the ranching community amongst our neighbors."

"Just like you want it boss, I'll have the blasting finished before the sun goes down tonight."

"Good. Pio I want you to take Miguel and six men. Leave three each at the two line camps up on the north end of the range. We'll do the west and south range tomorrow. I figure to switch a man out each day at each camp. No man will be away from the ranch for more than two days at a time if we do things right, and no one will have to starve. They can carry enough grub with them to handle a two day riding job."

"Two day rotation is good, but once Harley does his job, we won't have to watch the south camp so much. No cattle are down there," Pio said.

"Then put some young stuff down there. I don't want any of our neighbors getting the idea we don't need the southern section."

"Si, you are right again, senor."

"Gentlemen, I want complete coverage of our range for the next three weeks. Don't do anything from habit. Mix things up, but I want the entire range covered. If you see anyone trying to push a herd onto Slash M holdings, I want them pushed back. If you catch someone trying to thin our herd I want them brought in to me dead or alive. I want it known Conchetta and Pablo Mendoza, the new owners of the Slash M will not tolerate any monkeyshine from outsiders who hope to gain a little land because of our perceived weakness." Pausing he added, "Miguel, if your men feel like a lark now and again its fine with me. I witnessed their behavior south of the border and I must say their games are interesting to watch. As long as such games do not endanger the ranch or the men themselves they're fine. We're going to be working hard for the next three weeks, but I want the men to have a good time as well. I want you and your men to select horses from the Slash M remuda so no one will mistake who you are. I want our neighbors to know everything is normal around here. This is still the Slash M and will remain so for as long as I'm alive."

"Si, and it shall remain so as long as I live my brother," Miguel added.

"Pio, do you have any questions?"

"No senor, I understand the plan most excellently."

"Gentlemen, let's get this done. You both know what I expect and I'll accept nothing less than your best."

Moses Carter had been with the Slash M since before the Civil War. He'd been given his freedom and passage to wherever he wanted, providing he never returned to the Georgia plantation where he grew up. Master O'Neal swore to tell everyone he'd been a real hero, having won his freedom by saving the life of O'Neal's daughter. The girl had been frolicking in a nearby meadow picking flowers when two strange white men bore down on her and began to tear her clothes to shreds. Throwing the girl to the earth one of the men mounted her, but he never finished his move.

He knew instantly when he witnessed their behavior the young lady was in real trouble. His axe blade took the man in the back, dead center from twenty yards away and the man fell forward on top of the girl, dead. The one left standing turned to run, but times being what they were, Moses knew he would be hung as a murderer if the man got away to tell his lies. With equal precision of throws long practiced his long knife that he carried for work on the plantation, penetrated the back of the second man and sank to the hilt.

He immediately went to the girl and uncovered her as she was struggling to free herself from the weight of her dead attacker, wrapped her in the now torn, ragged dress and carried her home. Young Callie was crying and sobbing on his shoulder the entire time. The sight was horrible as everyone was in from the fields for the day and witnessed the girl being brought in by Moses, but Master O'Neal quickly took control and gave explicit orders to every slave he owned. Soon Moses alone stood at the door. He was given his writ of freedom and traveling money, even told in what direction to run so none of his family would see him. The year had been 1858 and Moses boarded a ship for Galveston Island in the gulf and then drifted west where he signed on with Don Pablo Mendoza to fight Indians and hold the range against savages, rain, flood, drought, and the harsh winters.

Now he had a new boss, his third in succession and Moses Carter was no green-behind-the-ears cowboy. He'd ridden west before anyone ever heard of the term cowboy or Civil War. He traveled the toughest of trails and he'd survived. He'd witnessed the fruit of both good men and bad. To Moses, Pablo Mendoza was a good man, and

Moses was appreciative of the fact. He'd worked hard to become a cowboy and this new boss seemed to show him a respect he'd never had, not since that day long ago in Georgia.

"Moses, do you know the area where I was shot?" Pablo asked.

"Sho'nuff do, boss man."

"I want you to go up there and have a look around. See if you can find anything Hughe might have missed. Randy Bean was killed in the same area about the same time I was shot. There's someone up there who doesn't want anybody nosing around, and the problem is, that range belongs to the Slash M if I'm not mistaken."

"Mister boss dat's been Slash M land long as I been here."

"I'd been expecting Randy Bean to try and cut me down. Bob Haslam tells me Randy was dead a day or two before I was shot. Nothing makes much sense right now, but I need you to find me some clues, evidence of anything that happened up there. And be careful. I don't want to lose any of my men, especially my best ones."

"Yes, mister boss, I's be careful as all git out." Without waiting for any further instructions, Moses Carter excused himself from the dinner table and headed outside. "My, but it sure is nice to have a boss again," he mumbled as he headed for the corral.

"Billy, I have a letter prepared, a letter that must reach its destination if the ranch is going to return to complete and normal operation. I want you to ride into Sonora and get it in the mail for me. It's very important to the well-being of everyone who lives on the Slash M. Do I make myself clear?"

"Yes sir."

Pablo reached into his shirt and withdrew the letter, handing the sealed document to young Billy. The young man got up and took the letter immediately and followed Moses to the corral.

Moses was almost done saddling his horse when Billy threw a rope on his own mount.

"That new boss is no pushover," Billy commented.

"Naw-sir he ain't. Might be he's de best I ever did see."

"Might be you're right Moses, I'm going to try and learn all I can from him."

Stepping into his saddle, he leaned on the pommel and said, "You's be careful, young Billy. Dis thing ain't over by no means. Maybe just be startin'. These next few days gonna to be interesting, dangerous but interesting," he said. Turning his gray toward the courtyard entrance, the savvy Moses headed out of the courtyard and up into the hills.

The distance was a good half a day's ride to Sonora and Billy wanted to be there before nightfall. Nudging his horse with his boot heels, he settled into a distance eating cantor the moment he cleared the courtyard gate.

Chapter 16

Pony Bob Haslam was sitting at his temporary desk at the sheriff's office going through Randy Bean's belongings the following morning, trying to understand the implications of the log book he'd found on the killer.

Two shots echoed through the room at almost the same time, then one more. Jumping from his chair he hastily locked up the evidence and headed out the door. Once in the street he couldn't believe what he saw. A young man that appeared to be all of fourteen or fifteen stood over a dead man lying in the middle of the street, his gun still smoking. A whip lay close by his side and the man's gun appeared to have been dropped where he stood. There were two bullets in the man. One entered the chest dead center and the other pumped huge amounts of blood from the gaping hole in his forehead. The ranger looked on in amazement as the young man pulled the spent bullet shells from his gun and reloaded his revolver, dropping the still warm gun back into his leather holster at his side. Seemingly, the young man was unaffected by the fact he'd just killed a man.

"What's your name young man?"

"William Bonney sir, but most folks call me Billy."

"Well, what happened here? I am Arizona Ranger Bob Haslam and I need to know."

"I came to town to deliver a letter for my boss Pablo Mendoza of the Slash M and this man tried to stop me by using a horsewhip on me. He smacked me once with his whip from out of nowhere and I turned, unloosed my leather thong and told him to draw. I'm not going to allow any man to get after me with a horsewhip, nor stop me from doing my job."

"I see."

"It was a fair fight, officer. This here young man braced the fellow just like he said and made him drop his whip. He even let the fellow draw first but the boy here was quick as greased lightning. Never in all my born days have I ever seen a gun put to action as fast as this here young man. Why, it weren't even close."

"What's your name?" Bob inquired of the stranger.

"My name is Carl Pratt. I'm in town from Sharp's Corner, New Mexico a good ways east from here."

"It all happened so fast nobody even had time to get off the street," another bystander added.

"I've met your boss. I suppose he knew what he was doing when he sent you into town to do a man's job." Pausing he continued, "Don't go anywhere Billy, at least not until I get a chance to talk with you and clear this matter up completely."

"Yes sir. I'll be right here in town," Billy replied as he turned and walked down the street toward the express office. As of yet he'd not sent the letter.

"Does anyone here know who this man is?" Bob asked the shell-shocked crowd.

"I saw him in the bank earlier today," a middle-aged lady replied. "Might be someone from there knows him."

Looking over the lady's shoulder, Pony Bob picked out Jeb Blackwell meandering near the back of the crowd. "Jeb, do you know this man?"

Jeb Blackwell was the owner of Sonora Bank and Trust. He was a fairly young man, his father having set him up in business a few years earlier. He was six feet tall, slender and carried himself with a dignity which stated to all who knew him; I am the strongest, most confident man in these parts so don't cross me. Stepping forward, young Blackwell took a look at the unfortunate man, thinking he had best not lie.

"His name is Eli." For appearance sake he added, "I'll have to check the bank records to remember what his last name is." Jeb Blackwell was thanking his lucky stars he'd made the man open a bank account with the money he'd paid him.

"If I need to know anything further after going through his belongings, I'll get in touch with you," the ranger stated.

"Whatever you may need, Ranger I'm at your disposal."

"A couple of you men grab him for me and carry him down to the sheriff's office. I just want to have a good look see and make sure things are on the up and up before I have him buried."

Three bystanders picked the dead man up and followed Ranger Haslam down to the sheriff's office. Once the body was laid out the men departed, leaving Pony Bob to study things on his own. He stepped back and studied the body for a few minutes. Ultimately he concluded young Billy Bonney was not a youngster to be trifled with. All accounts and evidence indicated he'd given Eli first draw and the man was dead with one bullet through the heart and another right between the eyes. Maybe he'd just made the boy real mad, but Bob didn't think so. He was too calm and cool to have been very mad, and a mad young man would have never placed two bullets so square on target. The man had to be moving or falling when the second shot took him and in either case, whether a head or chest shot, the second bullet had found its mark also. Pony bob whistled and shook his head.

Going through the dead man's pockets Bob found nothing that indicated who the man might be. Only thirty-two dollars and change. Then the ranger had an idea. The man must have a horse and a saddle, maybe even saddlebags stored somewhere. Where had he been staying?

No one was present when Bob reached the stables. He saw nothing that he could identify as belonging to the man. Zeek would know, but where was he? Leaving the stable he went back down the street to the Cactus Diner, a small restaurant on the edge of town. Zeek would be having his lunch about now, and he would be listening to all the talk about what had happened. As the ranger from Prescott entered the diner he saw Zeek sitting at his usual table in the back corner. Crossing the dining room he made himself at home across from the sturdy yet stubborn looking old timer.

"Zeek I need some help. By now you've heard about the shooting. You didn't happen to notice what the dead man was riding did you?"

"He was riding a big sorrel when he rode into town yesterday. I got him down to the stable right this minute."

"Did he leave anything else with you?"

229

"Just his saddle and rigging, like most folks normally do, he took everything else with him over to the hotel."

"Thanks Zeek, I owe you."

Bob Haslam got up from the table and went directly to the stable. As he walked down the street he couldn't put his finger on it but something about this whole investigation stunk to high heaven. Hughe Rainwater had informed him of the pending trouble looming at the Slash M by the note he'd left in Prescott, but everything happening here could not be a result of greedy men longing for the Slash M range. Was there something else going on? He had no idea what was happening, but if he could locate the remainder of the man's gear he might at least come away with a clue. Entering the stable all he found was the man's sorrel and saddle and other horse accouterments. A few minutes later when he entered the hotel he was greeted by the innkeeper.

"Howdy Bob."

"Jake, the man killed out there in the street this morning had a room. What room was he staying in?"

"Why, room four last time I checked."

Flipping the guest register around Bob looked at the list just long enough to find the name. Eli Wilkes. The ranger said out loud, "You got a key?"

"You know I do."

"Get it and come with me."

Together the two men went down the hall to room four and Jake opened the door. There on the footboard of the bed hung the man's saddlebags. His other belongings were neatly arranged on the bed. "I reckon that's all the help I need for now."

"Any time you need me."

As Jake went about his business, Ranger Bob Haslam picked up the man's belongings and took them back to his own room. There he went through the man's personals but found nothing to indicate what he might be doing here, or where he'd come from. His horse wore a B & B Connected brand, yet there was no listing in the stockman's association handbook for such a brand. In the end he found nothing that told him any more than he already knew. Just as he was putting everything back in the man's saddlebags a thought occurred to him. Why was the man picking on Billy?

Pablo Mendoza had been shot twice, by all accounts once by Randy Bean and then shot again by someone unknown. There were the ranch holdings, and Dean Reynolds had insisted the man known as Pablo Mendoza was an imposter, yet he'd known nothing of Conchetta, indicating his knowledge of the situation was suspect. Randy Bean was dead, shot from ambush much the way he'd conducted his own killings. Was there something in the list that would tie any of those killings to the current situation?

Grabbing up Eli's personal belongings, he walked down to his temporary office, dug out Randy's things and took another look at the killer's log. There had to be a connection yet as he looked over the names nothing was obvious. Had Eli Wilkes been known to Randy? Nothing indicated that was the case, yet it seemed an obvious conclusion. Locking up the sheriff's office he headed back down to the hotel. On entering he spotted Jake.

"Jake. Where is that young man Billy staying, in what room?"

"Upstairs beside you, in room thirteen."

"Thanks again," Bob said and headed up the stairs toward Billy's room. Without hesitation he rapped loudly on the door and a moment later it opened.

"Come on in, officer. Like I said, I'm not going anywhere."

Bob stepped into the room and closed the door behind him. The wallpaper was laced with flowers carved straight from someone's imagination and lacking of sufficient color. A wash basin sat beneath the flue and between the two windows in the room. One bed nestled itself against the north wall and a nondescript rug graced the dark wooden plank floor.

"Billy, why would Eli Wilkes be trying to pick a fight with you?"

"You got me there, . I don't have a clue, only some men have a mean streak built into their manners which leads to no good," Billy said as he spun his pistol and dropped it into the holster.

"I suppose that's true enough, but I believe there was something else. What did you come to town for?"

"I had a letter to put in the mail for my boss. The express, mail and telegraph office was closed when I got here last night so I got me a room and figured I'd wait until this morning."

"Does anybody here in town know you have the letter?"

"Anyone who was in the Cactus Diner when I rode into town. I asked no one in particular when I walked in where I could find the person responsible for the operation of the mail. The place was pretty full , but a tall thin wiry man in a black broadcloth suit told me I might as well get a room for the night. The gentleman lived out of town and wouldn't be back in until this morning. He was the banker."

"That would have been Jeb Blackwell. He owns the bank here in town with his father Horace. They own the B & B Con..." Pony Bob paused realizing the implication of the brand he'd failed to connect earlier, and wondered why it was not in the stockman association handbook. "He told you right, son."

"Ranger, you think that man was trying to stop me from mailing my letter?"

"I don't know for sure Billy, but it's a good possibility."

"Who was he?"

"His name was Eli Wilkes."

"I never heard of him before."

"Don't look like anybody ever will again either," the ranger said.

"I'm sorry about that, Ranger, but he came a-hunting trouble, he surely did. I won't draw on a man lessen he gives me good reason to. He just didn't leave me any choice."

"I believe you Billy, from now on be more careful while you're in town. Someone else may try to stop you, and knowing how fast you are on the draw, they won't walk right up to you and pick a fight next time, they'll just shoot you from ambush and hope they get away with it."

"I hadn't thought of someone trying to shoot me from cover. Thanks. I'll be real careful."

"One more thing before I go Billy. Your boss, Pablo Mendoza, do you believe him to be the real thing?"

"I'll tell you true. Even though I'm quite young, I've had a few riding jobs and no one's treated me better. He doesn't make a decision what doesn't benefit or improve the ranch in some way. He handles men better than most twice his age, and as for his guns, I wouldn't want to brace him. I thought I was fast until he showed me how he does his draw. Is he the real thing? You bet he is."

"Thanks Billy. If you need anything, or if you think of anything what might help me put a stop to these killings, don't hesitate to come and see me."

"Yes sir, the last thing I want to do is be a problem."

Pony Bob left Billy's room and returned to the stable to look at the horse Eli had been riding. Looking around once again he found the man's rifle sitting in the rifle rack at the door. Why hadn't he thought of it before? Taking the weapon down, he looked the gun over then headed for his office.

Sitting at his desk, he made a list of his findings. What was the man doing riding one of the Blackwell mounts? Had he stolen it? Not likely. It would have been reported stolen by now. And why wasn't the brand listed? Who was the Blackwell family anyway? What was their stake in what was happening and why didn't Jeb know more about the man if he was riding a B & B horse?

There was no question Pablo Mendoza had arrived on time to claim his inheritance. He was this very minute out at the ranch with his wife and they were swiftly gaining the respect of the locals, even if they'd never been seen, their stories and exploits were preceding them. Apparently the couple was here to stay, so who wanted them dead and why? Dean Reynolds was too obvious a choice. He was a ruffian, but Bob didn't think him capable of the planning necessary to accomplish what had been done, nor to do the things that must be done. There was no denying Dean Reynolds and Jack Fuller were a factor in what was going on. Even Pablo suspected someone other than Reynolds to be behind the killings.

Eli Wilkes's rifle was of the wrong type to be considered the gun that killed Randy Bean and wounded Pablo. Now this, another killing right here on the streets of Sonora. Only this time things had gone awry. Picking on a youngster is usually a safe bet for any bully, only Eli picked on the wrong one and the move had cost him his life.

Something bigger than the obvious range war was brewing here, and he wasn't going anywhere until he had answers.

There was simply too much taking place in and around Sonora for him to consider going anywhere else at the moment. There were more killings in the offing unless he was mistaken.

He'd not been present when Hughe Rainwater had summoned him, but arrived within a few days of the man's departure from Prescott. As soon as he read the message Hughe left, he mounted up and rode out. Trouble was brewing and his presence was needed in Sonora. There were two other rangers working in the Arizona territory but they'd also been out doing their own investigations just as he'd been doing. Having been the first one back and the first to read the note, the duty fell to him. Suddenly, the ranger had one more question. Where was Hughe Rainwater? He should be right here in the thick of things.

What he knew was little enough. Pablo Mendoza and his lovely wife inherited a ranch the likes of which he'd never seen. Someone thought to be Dean Reynolds was willing to kill for it. He'd asked around enough to know Dean had been running with Jack Fuller and Randy Bean, two no accounts by any man's standards. Now Randy was dead, shot in the back much the same way he was reputed to have killed his victims and if his log was any indication, it was no rumor. He fell asleep at his desk thinking over what he knew, trying to assemble the pieces to this strange puzzle.

The following morning, Bob's office door opened and Billy stepped in. "I need to be getting back to the ranch unless you need me to stay on."

"I do have a question for you before you head back. Silver City, New Mexico. You want to tell me what happened?"

"Now, how in...?"

"You're not under arrest, Billy. I just want to hear your side of what happened. If what you say is right, I'll send a letter to the sheriff and clear the matter up for you. The sheriff is a friend of mine. I don't like seeing a bad thing hanging over a young man's head when he's trying to live right. Now I don't know one way or the other, but if you'll tell me what happened and be truthful, I'll see what I can do."

"The man attacked my mother and it looked like he was trying to kill Ed, who was a good friend of my mother's. I had to stop him. If Ed had been killed, then my mother would have been next."

"But with a knife in the back? That's like shooting a man in the back, Billy."

"I was twelve years old. I didn't know any better, . I was simply trying to save my mother who died shortly thereafter anyway."

"I'm sorry to hear that Billy." Bob paused. "Are you telling me you know better now?"

"I've been studying the law some and it's my wish to be on the right side of the law whenever possible. I ain't the criminal a lot of people are making me out to be. I just don't want to be taken advantage of. The man I killed yesterday wasn't going to be satisfied until he'd pinned my ears back. Well sir, I don't believe I did anything wrong in defending myself. If I'd only wounded him and embarrassed him, he would have waited until he was well and then he would have hunted me down out of revenge. I saw he was that kind of man right off. I don't figure on being dry-gulched."

"I see. How many men have you killed, Billy?"

"Just the two and I didn't start the trouble either time."

"That's good enough for me, but I do have one more question. How old are you?"

"I'm seventeen."

"God help us all. You look to be all of fourteen." Pausing he added, "I reckon you can head on home but be careful, and tell your boss to do the same. He's not out of the woods yet."

"Yes sir. I surely will."

Closing the door behind him, Billy left the sheriff's office and headed to the stables to saddle his horse. Zeek was leaning back in an old rocking chair he'd scrounged from somewhere, tipping it back and forth with his toes and chewing some of his Carolina tobacco.

"You riding on?" Zeek asked.

Stopping at the entrance Billy sized the man up for the first time. "I'm riding back to the Slash M if that's what you mean. I feel sorry for anyone who tries to stop me."

"Me too. I saw you draw that Colt dragoon on Eli. He always figured himself fancy with a gun in any kind of a fight, but I tell you what son, he wasn't even close."

"I've got a tip for you. My boss is a might faster. Maybe even a bit more accurate than me. You might save someone's life if you'll sort of spread the word around. And one more thing, we're fully staffed now. The Slash M is no longer shorthanded. Dean Reynolds and his bunch should come wondering into town either late this evening or first thing in the morning, barefoot. They may need some medical attention. You might want to give the doc a little head's up."

Without waiting to see Zeek's reaction, Billy went back to the stall where his mustang waited. Before he could lay hands on his saddle, Zeek was up the street starting the gossip and looking for Doc. Of course real gossip has at least a hint of falsehood in it. As far as Billy knew, he had stated nothing but truth and facts as he understood them to be.

As the young gunslinger rode out of town he shifted from his usual route and took another one. It would be best if he didn't become a creature of habit. Crossing the Little Apache, he made his way out of the well-trodden paths and into the wide open, untouched countryside. Anyone who wanted to follow him could, but on this chosen route no one would be lying in wait for him.

Chapter 17

The perplexed ranger sat in the Cactus Diner eating his breakfast while his dog Toby lay in wait on the boardwalk outside watching the coming and goings of men. He was about to take another bite when he noticed a commotion at the end of the street near the edge of town. Getting up from his window seat, he went to the door and stepped out onto the boardwalk. Six men were limping into town barefooted. From the looks of things the cowhands lost their mounts, their boots and their guns. They were struggling for each step they took.

Chuckling to himself, he went back inside to his breakfast and finished his meal. He was just about to get up when the horseless six entered the diner. Lowering back into a restful position he waited, certain the men would fill him in on what happened. They didn't. He expected them to ask him to recover their belongings, but they didn't do that either. The exhausted men never said a word, surprising, considering they were missing so much. They ordered and paid for their meals, ate in silence and then literally stumbled from the diner to the hotel a few doors down.

For the next two days no one saw hide nor hair of the desperate men, only Jake running to and fro all over town to get and gather the things they needed. When they did emerge from their rooms, it was apparent to all they were recovered from their ordeal, except for one who now walked with a permanent limp, and Jack Fuller, who folks instantly began calling, "Three Finger Jack." The outlaw was missing two fingers and everyone in town knew the story about what happened. The good folks of Sonora were snickering and laughing behind the backs of all six men. They got themselves into quite a pickle and came out on the short end of the stick, but what didn't help their plight was the fact Pablo Mendoza and his hands had been responsible, Bob later learned.

Pony Bob observed the comings and goings in town trying to put together the pieces to a larger puzzle. He didn't miss the show when all six men entered the bank at the same time a few days later. A bank robbery? But the men had no horses, not yet anyway. Almost immediately four of them stepped back outside and waited by the hitching post, leaving Dean Reynolds and Three Finger Jack inside.

He loaded his greener and two extra pistols then waited. If it was a robbery they'd never get clear of the street. What were the men doing at the bank at the same time? What sort of business were they conducting? Jack Fuller, now being called Three Finger Jack was a known outlaw, but he wasn't wanted in Arizona territory. Dean Reynolds was a bad sort, but he wasn't wanted either. What business could they possibly have at the bank? He made a mental note deciding he would have to talk to Jeb Blackwell to see if he knew these men and why? Later at lunch, he sat across from David May, the bank teller. He bought David's meal and started his inquiry. As the two men ate he asked the questions.

"David, the six men who walked into town barefooted the other day were all at the bank this morning. Do they all have money in Blackwell's bank?"

"Yes sir, all six of them have an account."

"Did they get money out today?"

"No sir. They only came to settle up with Jake at the hotel. Jake got all their furnishings for them as you know, and he needed to be reimbursed."

"Why would Jeb do business with known outlaws?"

"Everyone has a right to a bank account, . If they are such evil men, why are they not in jail?"

"You have me there. I can only do what the law allows me to do. I can't arrest them for something they haven't done yet."

"Jeb figures if a man is capable of walking in and opening an account, he's eligible to have one."

"Yes, I see what you mean. No banker I know of would turn his nose up at anyone opening an account, not even unsuspecting children."

"Dean and Jack did spend some time in the boss's office this morning, but I have no idea what they discussed. I was tending business out front."

"Is this the first time they've talked?"

"All together it is, but most of them have been in on their own, one time or another."

"Do you know what they are talking to him about?"

"No sir, but I can tell you what I do know. I said they all have an account, but they didn't open it. Jeb Blackwell opened each account for them and Jeb puts money in them regular like, some more than others. Something else you should know, he's closed up five accounts in the last week or two including the four closed today, all deceased.

I can't say what he does with the money, but I think he puts their cash back in the general bank funds, only never mind me, I'm not snooping to find out. I need my job."

"Thanks David, you've been a great help."

"There is one more thing, . Sometimes Jeb leaves for days at a time. No less than three and no more than a week. He's not going to the ranch, he just rides off somewhere. I've noticed it's every third week on Monday when he rides out, so he'll be riding out again on Monday unless I miss my guess."

Bob thought about the information for a moment, "So the last time he rode out was a little over two weeks ago?"

"You're right on the money."

"What does he say what he's doing?"

"He says he is going hunting but he never brings back any game."

"Thanks David. Thanks a lot."

David May took one last drink from his cup of coffee and got up, took his hat from the peg by the door and walked out, leaving the ranger to think and ponder over the information he provided.

A moment later, Horace Blackwell entered the diner and took the seat across from Bob, his empty dishes still gracing the table.

"Ranger Haslam," the rancher seemed ruffled. "We have a problem."

"What kind of problem, Horace?"

"Pablo Mendoza!"

"What about him?" Bob asked, waiting for the complaint he knew was coming.

"He's gone and hired a bunch of Comanchero cut-throats, three of which are outright Indians!"

"So? How are the men he hired your problem? Is it because you and your riders can no longer push your beef onto his range? Listen Horace, and listen to me good. I'm a lawman. No law has been broken by the Mendoza ranch. He can hire whoever he thinks can do the job. He can hire blood thirsty vampires and he won't have done anything illegal. If the men get the job done that's all that matters. You are quite welcome to do the same."

Horace was bewildered. He'd been certain the would react to the Comancheros in a negative fashion, but apparently Mendoza bought the man's respect with such a move instead. The ranger was obviously content to sit back and watch things play out.

"Listen, you know I would never hire such unpredictable and undependable men, but there's one more thing you should know. His men have dammed up the Little Apache with dynamite. There's no more water coming through the gorge. Also, there's not one round of ammunition left in this town. He's bought every last round and moved the ammo out to the Slash M Ranch."

Pony Bob choked back a laugh, yet he was able to withhold his shameful outburst for the time being. "Horace, does Jeb ever bring fresh killed meat out to the ranch?"

"What?"

"Does your son ever bring you fresh killed meat?"

"Now what kind of question is that? Of course he doesn't. The only time I see him anymore is when I come to town."

"He never rides out to the ranch for a visit?"

"Not for the longest time, that I'm aware of," the old man answered. "Look ranger, what are you going to do about the Mendoza problem?" he asked.

"Did he block the water on his section of the range?"

"Yes, he did," Horace grumbled.

"As long as he confines his improvements to his section of range and makes changes on his land there's not a thing I can do. When he blows up something on your land, then you come and see me."

"But Bob, my men are afraid to go anywhere near the Slash M. Those Comancheros the man has hired are a pack of bloodthirsty wolves. There must be twenty of them and they're riding the range like a bunch of half-crazed bulls just looking for trouble. They already killed four of Dean Reynolds's men and sent the rest of them back to town barefooted."

"Doesn't Dean Reynolds and his men work for you?"

"What?"

"Dean Reynolds, Three Finger Jack as they now call him, Randy Bean, Eli Wilkes? Don't they all work for the B & B Connected? That's your brand isn't it?"

"I don't know what you're talking about."

"Eli's horse is still in the stable. It wears a B & B brand. He was killed right out there on the street the other day. Tried to horsewhip one of Pablo's men."

"I don't know what you're referring to, but I'd sure like to see for myself. The horse I mean. None of the men you mentioned work for me."

"Why isn't your brand registered in the stockman's association handbook this year?"

"What?" The rancher narrowed his brow, incredulous.

"You heard me. The B & B Connected is not in the Stockman's Association handbook, yet you're one of the largest brands in Arizona."

"What do you mean it's not in the handbook? My brand has been in there from the get go."

Bob tossed the handbook onto the table in front of Horace, "Has been. Show me where it's listed now."

Opening the book to the correct page, the page where his brand had always been listed, there was nothing. Horace then fumbled through the book from front to back. It was only seven pages of listings so his search didn't take long.

"What in God's name is going on here?"

"I was rather hoping you could tell me."

Horace was dumbfounded. "Jeb's took over the financial end of the ranch along with the bank when we opened it three years ago," Horace said. "Other than an occasional glance at the books to ensure the ranch's still making money, I turned everything over to my boy. He's going to inherit anyway. I don't understand why he didn't reregister the brand."

Horace knew brands came went with the wind, but the B & B brand was still a thriving entity. But then, Jeb may have something more on his mind than just the ranch.

Horace studied the ranger. "I need to water my beef. There's no more water coming down the Little Apache. What do I do?"

"I don't know," Pony Bob stated. "It's not my problem. I've got murders and attempted murders on my hands right now, and Pablo Mendoza has done nothing outside the law. If his men killed four of Dean's riders I'll have to question him on the matter. If my guess is correct however, he'll probably be cleared of any wrong doing. If you need to water your cattle why don't you go and talk to him. I've met him. I think he's likely a peaceable man when he isn't being shot at or put upon by his neighbors."

"He hasn't left his ranch since he arrived, and with those Comancheros on the loose I ain't about to go waltzing in there like its Sunday go to meeting."

Exasperated, the big rancher got up, took his hat off the table and went through the front door with his hat in his hand. It was going to be a long day and things weren't looking too good for his B & B Connected. Horace started down the boardwalk toward the bank. His son was going to have to answer a few questions. Maybe Horace had been wrong to help the boy so much. He'd seen such lack of appreciation before. A man helps his children to the point they think they know more than their parents, only they don't, because they've not been tried by the fire yet, but you'll never convince them of the idea they're wrong. As he walked, he thought of what he would say to the boy. What could he say?

Jeb sat with his feet propped up on the desk, dropping them to the floor and closed his desk drawer.

"Why didn't you re-register the brand on time?"

"What?"

"The B & B is not in the stockman's handbook this year, why not?"

"Pa, you're the one who wants that old ranch, not me. I don't care to have it. I have the bank."

"You're my only son, and you'll inherit that old place someday. Regardless, the brand should never have been allowed to lapse."

"As you wish, but I'll just sell the place. I don't even want to be a rancher."

"What in God's name are you talking about? Why you wouldn't even have this bank if it weren't for that old broken down ranch as you call it."

"Look Pa, things are changing out west. Not everybody has to make a living on a ranch. I might keep the place, but I'll not be the one running the day to day operations, I have no desire."

Flustered, Horace did an about face and stormed out the door, almost knocking Dean Reynolds over backward as he left the office. "Get out of my way!" Horace snapped at the oncoming pest. Suddenly he realized who was in his way and he stopped, grabbed the man by the shirt and pulled the slightly bigger, but surprised man up to his face.

"Why would Ranger Haslam believe you work for me? What are you and Jeb up to? You didn't get the Slash M and sure as there's a fire in hell you're not going to get my spread. Now, get out of my way," he said as he shoved the discombobulated Dean to one side.

Jeb leaned back in his chair as Dean entered his office and closed the door behind him. Dean Reynolds had been useful up to a point, but now his ability to serve was severely damaged. The fact his sister had been married to senor Don Pablo Mendoza years before no longer mattered. Dean would never be able to inherit the estate now that Pablo Mendoza had an iron-clad claim. Randy Bean assured them Pablo would never show up but the sidewinder had been wrong and was now dead himself.

Served him right, he'd been paid to do a job and he'd failed miserably.

Now Jeb's only option was to try and foreclose on the Slash M before the new ranch owners could find or figure out what other accounts Don Pablo had stashed in other banks around the country. He'd been shrewd, able to thwart Jeb's efforts, but the new owner, maybe he didn't know as much. Dean took a chair in front of Jeb and took a cigar from the humidor on the desk, cut the tip, lighted it and leaned back in his chair.

"What do we do now?"

"I think I'll go it alone from now on. I no longer need the services of you or your men. You lost four this week, you have five unaccounted for, the ones you sent after Hughe Rainwater..."

"Four. Young Vince is riding for Mendoza."

"What?"

"Somehow he is riding for the Slash M."

"Let me get this straight. You sent seven men after Hughe Rainwater, two turned up dead, four are missing altogether and one ends up riding for Mendoza. What good are you? Randy Bean is dead, Jack Fuller is missing two fingers, and the rest of the men are crippled from walking. Eli was shot graveyard dead right here in the street the other day. You can't even buy bullets for your new guns because Mendoza had the foresight to buy the town dry."

"You really don't want my help anymore?" Dean stuttered.

"I can't make myself any more plain, Dean."

"Just like that, I'm of no use."

"Just like that Dean. You can keep the money you've been advanced. I won't need your help from here on out. Besides, Pablo Mendoza and his wife seem to have the complete ball of wax sewn up to perfection," the banker lied, or so he believed.

"You're giving up?"

"What else can I do? You and your men accomplished not one of the tasks assigned to you. It's over, unless you want to start killing people wholesale. Face it, a smart man knows when he's been defeated, and he knows when to quit. The whole plan has gone up in smoke unless you have some new revelation you haven't told me about."

Dean Reynolds was stunned. So this was how his dreams ended. He'd tried everything he knew to become the new owner of the Slash M, but to no avail. But, Jeb wasn't telling him everything, of that much he was certain.

Getting up from his chair Dean walked to the door. "I won't give up until the ranch is mine, so stay out of my way!" he said, opening and closing the door behind him.

Jeb stared through the window of his office as Dean left the building. His words meant nothing, nothing at all. What Dean was is what he'd always been, a distraction, a decoy, a pawn in a chess game. If he stirred up enough trouble now, he would only eliminate some of the heat Jeb was beginning to feel from the Arizona Ranger.

Since finding gold on Slash M range Jeb looked to find a way to get the ranch, and so far he'd failed. He found the gold by accident, but he couldn't let on the ore was there, or where he was getting such a thing. His small placer mine was on Mendoza land, and therefore legally belonged to the Mendoza family. His prize had been a strange find, an abandoned find left by the Spaniards in years gone by. He'd found a few old helmets, swords and shields at the location, and the evidence strongly suggested there had been a battle fought with Indians long ago. The Indians were gone now, and so were the Spaniards. But the gold, the gold was still there by the bucket loads.

Then he had seen Conchetta and wanted her, not knowing of course, she was already married to Pablo. Why hadn't the girl said who she was when she arrived? Of course, her life would have been in danger, but not really. He wanted the girl and she could stay, but she had no way of knowing what he was up to. She was a beauty!

Randy Bean was dead because he'd gotten too close to the gold. Pablo had been shot for the same reason. Who else would he have to shoot before he managed to get his way?

Originally his plan involved using Dean Reynolds to acquire the Slash M Ranch. Randy Bean and Jack Fuller were brought in to cement his position in the matter. If Dean balked at turning controlling interest over to him, he would simply have Randy Bean or Jack Fuller kill him and take over anyway. Nothing had worked out. His only satisfaction had been when he was able to shoot Randy for dereliction of duty, then Pablo from ambush. The fact Pablo hadn't succumbed to his wound was unfortunate. Also the fact Hughe Rainwater arrived on the scene unexpectedly had been disadvantageous. His only option at the time had been to skedaddle.

Now he found himself in the position he'd never expected to find himself in, people were starting to become suspicious of his dealings at the bank, and suspicious of him. Anything he might try now would have to be done very carefully.

Several Comancheros occupied the Train Wreck Saloon outside of town for the day and the regular patrons were fighting shy of them. The truth be known, they were becoming soft quickly, too easy going and spoiled by the cooking at the ranch, but a few of the men resented the fact. They wanted things like they used to be and it seemed to these men Miguel was taking advantage of his brother's kindness just a little too much. Still, the men knew better than to brace him. He was too fast and swift when it came to dispensing his own brand of justice. What Pablo did to the Reynolds outfit was nothing compared to what Miguel could conjure up, and to a man the Slash M crew knew this to be fact.

The Comanchero leader's disposition was just so when Horace Blackwell stepped up to the bar in the Train Wreck Saloon and ordered a whiskey from a bartender he'd never encountered. Horace was not used to doing business on this side of the tracks.

"Whiskey," the rancher demanded, and every eye in the place turned on him. Tossing the drink down he turned to look the men over. Pablo was not among them. Horace Blackwell was losing cattle, two hundred in the last week alone and they weren't being rustled. They were dying from lack of water. Never before had Horace been in a room filled with so many unfriendly faces. The silence was screaming to him, "Get out of here now, you fool!" But, his need for help was greater than his fear of dying at the hands of such men as he now faced.

"I'm looking for Pablo Mendoza. I need to speak with him."

"He is not among us, senor. My brother is at home." Pausing Miguel added, "What do you want with Pablo?"

Stumped, Horace didn't know what to say or quite how to respond. "You're Pablo's brother?" The rancher managed.

"Si, I am his brother. What do you want of him?"

"My cattle are dying, and many more will die if I don't get them to water soon. My ranch is all I have left. I want to ask your brother if I might water them on the Slash M until the dam he created on the Little Apache is full enough to let the water start running across my land once again."

"So you own the B & B Connected," Miguel said.

"Yes I own the B & B. I lost two hundred head last week. I can't afford to wait any longer. Normally I would mind my own business, but I need your brother's help." Pausing he added. "I am asking for his help."

Miguel thought what Pablo would do and then he said, "You can water your herds on the closest land to yours to include the lake until the water again flows across your land, but it will cost you two head of beef each week. We must eat, senor." Looking the man over, Miguel continued, "If we find your men anywhere else on our range the water will be cut off and we will kill your men. They will be considered rustlers looking for cattle even if they are alone. Do you understand?"

"I understand perfectly. And sir, you will not have any such trouble from my men. I thank you. What you have done is noteworthy and I won't forget it anytime soon."

Stopping at the door Horace turned back, adding, "If you or your men ever need anything at all, just come and tell us what it is. We'll be there. I'll not turn away you or your men."

Ducking under the shallow doorway of the Train Wreck Saloon, Horace headed for the café where his men were having their lunch. On his way up the street he ran into Ranger Haslam sitting on a bench in front of the Cactus diner feeding his dog Toby.

"Pony Bob, you were right. I didn't get to talk with Pablo, but I did get to speak with his brother and they'll let us water our cattle on the Slash M until the water starts flowing over the dam again. Right there is the toughest bunch of hombre's I ever did see," he gestured toward the saloon, "but, they're not unreasonable."

"That's good, Horace. I knew if you just talked to them something good would come of it. Pablo is a fair man. As long as he's given a chance to do the right thing I've noticed he usually does it."

"Evening, Ranger." Horace tipped his hat and headed on down the street to where his men were eating.

Chapter 18

After no less than five weeks of complete domination of the range by Slash M riders, the folks around Sonora came to one unanimous conclusion, the Slash M was a ranch to leave alone. Everyone who lived within three hundred miles of Sonora knew about the Comanchero, and more of them kept showing up. As long as the pistol-bound men from south of the border were not breaking any laws, Ranger Haslam was content to give Mendoza his head.

No one in town missed the parade of riders Saturday afternoon except for Jeb Blackwell who said he was going hunting on Monday and had yet to return. The Slash M rode into town in full force. No less than twenty riders guarded twenty mules laden with gold, and Conchetta Mendoza was along for the ride. For the first time, the townsfolk were getting to see the wife of Pablo Mendoza and Pablo himself.

They didn't miss the pack train or the armed guards who rode beside them, nor did they miss the fact that Hughe Rainwater led them. Hughe hadn't been seen around town for months, and folks had begun to talk. The cavalcade of riders rode straight to the bank and relieved the mules of their burden, then entered with the whole town watching. As the Mendoza riders filled the bank lobby, Pablo Mendoza and his lovely wife approached the teller, David May who was befuddled to say the least.

"Sir, we have a deposit to make," Pablo stated in no uncertain terms. He lifted a saddlebag and started dumping the refined gold shipment onto the counter. "This place doubles for the land office doesn't it?"

"Yes sir, it does," the teller said.

"Let's figure out how much money we have here and you can give credit to my account. All this gold makes me jittery," Pablo said.

Every Slash M rider brandished a rifle or a shotgun so David May was just a little on the nervous side. Conchetta recognized his uneasiness immediately and began to put the bean counter at ease.

"Miguel, post your men outside please, they are making our friend nervous." Turning back to David she added, "We are here to do business and to make a rather large deposit. You must understand the guns were necessary to protect our interest. Once the gold is safely in your hands our men will stand down."

"Yes ma'am," David replied as he began to weigh and measure. "This gold is already refined. It'll be worth much more than the raw ore we usually see. It is much heavier and more pure."

Conchetta smiled in return

Pony Bob was the one man who could pass by the Comancheros guarding the bank outside, and he did just so. He walked right through the men, parting them, then entered and walked over to where Mr. and Mrs. Mendoza stood. He looked at what David was doing, and then focused on the gold. "What's going on, David?"

"The Mendoza family is making a rather large deposit and it's pure gold."

"Do you know how to account for all of it?"

David nodded. "Yes sir, Jeb's shown me many times. He trusts me more than he does himself when gold is involved."

Shaking his head in disbelief the ranger yielded to the situation. "Mr. Mendoza I need to speak to you before you leave town. Will you stop by the Iron Kettle later this evening? I'm situated at the sheriff's office temporarily, so I'd rather meet you at the Kettle." Turning his attention to Conchetta he added, "Ma'am," tipped his hat and walked out of the building.

By noon every soul in town knew the story. Pablo Mendoza and his men recovered the lost Mexican gold shipment of over twenty years ago, gold that had been stolen from the Mexican government by four Mexican soldiers. It was rumored to be the cursed gold of Cortez. The Mendoza family deposited over nine hundred thousand dollars in refined gold bars into the bank. It was also noted by everyone that with such a large quantity of gold on hand, Jeb Blackwell was nowhere to be found. Pablo was in a little bit of shock himself. He had fleeting thoughts the entire life of Pablo Mendoza might be nothing more than a myth ready to evaporate at any given moment.

Pablo posted his own guards at the bank until the gold could be shipped. He knew it would not take long before every outlaw in the territory would be trying to figure out a way to get their hands on the bullion.

Later the very same evening, Pony Bob sat in the Iron Kettle waiting on Pablo. Most of the regular patrons at the café had already said their goodnights and headed home. Finally around nine o'clock, the couple arrived together, waltzed over to his table and took a seat across from him.

"I hate to burden you at this late hour Pablo, but I have a few matters to clear up with you."

"Bob, if anything needs clarification, I want it cleared up too. I don't want any suspicion hanging over my head, or the heads of my riders."

"I'm glad to hear that. My first question concerns four dead men. Dean Reynolds and his men swear you killed four of his men from ambush."

"My brother was riding up from the border with his men when they spotted ten riders moving Slash M cattle south toward the border. They were already off Slash M range. A gunfight ensued and four of Dean's riders were killed in the process. Miguel wanted to hang the remainder of them, but I suggested they walk to town barefooted to give them time to think over what they'd done. I also confiscated their guns, ammo, boots, and their mounts along with their saddles and rigging. They were caught flat-footed rustling cattle from Slash M range. I averted a hanging, sparing their lives."

"Do you know the names of the four men?"

"No sir, you'll have to bother Dean about that, but I did bury them."

"I see. That makes more sense than anything I've heard so far. Do you want to press charges?"

"No. I figure they learned their lesson about messing with the Slash M cattle. I told them if they ever set foot on my range again they would be hung on sight." Pausing Pablo added, "I was hoping you could help me figure out a thing or two."

Pony Bob put his hand up between them as if to say hold on. "First, let me advise you. If you or your men hang anyone without a fair trial, I'll be obliged to arrest you or them for murder. I won't stand for such behavior. Now what's your question?"

"What possible claim could Dean Reynolds have on the Slash M?"

"You mean you don't know?" Studying the inquisitive faces before him he decided the couple really had no idea. "Dean Reynolds used to have a sister. She was married to none other than Don Pablo, your uncle. If you hadn't arrived when you did, if you'd been one day later, he would have inherited the ranch de facto! Dean Reynolds would have had a claim on the estate every bit as strong as yours, providing you hadn't shown up of course. As it stands he's out in the cold with no more claim than Jessie James."

"I see what you mean, Bob. Someone's been trying to stop me ever since I left Texas. I've been shot at and left for dead more than once," here he included the shooting of the real Pablo. "I don't believe Dean Reynolds is smart enough to be pulling the strings of that outfit. I think he's a front man, someone's using him."

Bob thought about what Pablo said for a moment, and he was under the same impression. He had some ideas, but couldn't elaborate on them or disclose them at this time. "I'm trying to solve a murder that I happened on while coming here from Prescott, that of Randy Bean on your range. He was killed at almost the same place you were shot. I believe whoever shot him, shot you and several others. I can't prove anything yet, and I don't have any evidence as to who it might be; only that each shooting seems to be identical in circumstance. I still have a lot of missing pieces to the puzzle, but I will eventually find out who the man is. If you or any of your men should stumble on any evidence that might shed some light on these killings for me, notify me immediately will you?"

"Certainly, I want his murder solved more than anyone. Right now I have a big target painted on my chest and I don't like the idea. I stand a much better chance of growing old if we can figure out who's pulling the trigger. I sent Moses Carter up range looking for sign. He says he's getting close, but I haven't seen any results yet."

"You tell him to be careful. That man is liable to show up at any time, and he doesn't seem to want any witnesses," Bob warned.

"Ranger," Conchetta intervened, "we only want peace and to raise a family. I do not feel I can raise a family in such upheaval. I am afraid always. When can I rest in my own home without worry?"

"Soon ma'am, real soon, in fact as long as you have those Comanchero and Indians on the place I would rest easy. Real easy! There's not a soul in this territory right now who'd risk getting caught on Slash M range. I'm afraid to ride out there myself and I'm an Arizona Ranger."

"Thank you Ranger Haslam," she said as she patted the back of his hand. "I hadn't thought of my safety in those terms until now. I will rest much easier because of what you have said. Thank you."

He did not fluster easy, but he suddenly found himself flush around the gills. "Ma'am, you take my word for it, you're safer than anybody in this territory, me included. Now I've got things to do. I take it you're staying in town for the night?"

"Yes, it's too late to start back now, and we don't come to town very often," Conchetta said.

Excusing himself he left the Iron Kettle and headed to his room. He hadn't missed the fact that Hughe Rainwater and Vince Cole sat in the far corner watching over their boss and his wife. He also noticed young Billy Bonney leaning against the pillar across the street, keeping an eye on them. One thing was certain; Pablo Mendoza had suddenly become a very cautious man.

Chapter 19

Moses Carter spent several weeks scouting the Slash M range looking for tracks or any clue as to the whereabouts of the phantom rifleman. Again and again he combed the area where his boss had been shot and Randy Bean murdered to no avail. There was nothing to go on. At first he'd seen what he thought might be a trail, but the steady wind and spotty rain showers of the last few weeks wiped away any evidence of a trail. Then two days ago the tracks mysteriously reappeared. Soft indentations, but tracks nevertheless. Everything he saw told him the killer of Randy Bean was likely the same man who shot his boss. Then the trail disappeared again, a trail that came in from nowhere and then drying up to go absolutely nowhere. Not too many things could shake old Moses, but the way in which these tracks appeared and then disappeared had him conjuring images of Ole Bogy, the devil himself.

It was the only explanation he could conjure. He was dealing with the Devil. How could anything human command such power over an animal's ability to leave a mark on the land or not leave one, he wondered. He followed the ghost-like trail as far as he was able and then sat his horse dumbfounded.

He should run. He should get out now while the getting was good, but duty called and he was not a man who wanted anyone to think he might be afraid of anything. It looked as if the horse he was following sprouted a set of wings and flew away. Impossible, yet it was his only answer and a very uncomfortable conclusion for him. There was nothing out here except old cliff dwellings, and the former slave had been hesitant to enter them because he believed Indian spirits still dwelt there.

Making up his mind he turned his horse back along the trail where the cave dwellings overlooked the valley of dry bones. It was high up in the highest dwelling where he would wait, if he could overcome his own fear of the Devil.

Whoever the mystery rider was he appeared more than able to cover or conceal his mark on the land at will. Way out here in the middle of nowhere the only reason to conceal one's tracks was to conceal one's identity, a fact he could not possibly ignore.

The tracks came and went at times, almost as if the beast leaving the prints in the sand appeared and disappeared. His skin crawled as he processed the evidence before him. Who or what could muster such power over wind, sand, and rain? If Satan was the prince of darkness over this earth, then it could be him, but what of God? Rapidly he recounted all the things in his mind he knew about God, but one thing trumped every fact he remembered; God left for a while, he left to prepare a place for those who believe in him. If that was true, then the only explanation he could think of to explain the tracks he'd found, and those tracks he hadn't was the Devil.

He eased his horse in the direction of the cliff dwellings. These he noted were really underground living quarters. Wouldn't Satan reside in such a place? The closer he came to the cliff dwellings, the more he trembled with fear. Bones bleached white by years of sunlight accented the ground in front of the cavernous dwellings. Sweat trickled down his face. His horse stopped a mile short of the dwellings and stood still. Nudging his mount the horse refused to move. He thought to himself, Dis is sho' nuff a bad sign.

He dug his spurs in a little deeper but the horse refused to budge. Stepping down he pulled on the reins and the horse still refused command. Taking a long cloth out of his saddlebag he tied it over the animal's eyes and then the horse followed him. He knew he couldn't ride him blind, but at least the horse was willing to follow him.

Horse in tow, he walked in the direction of the ancient cliff dwellings, weaving in and out of the bones and cactus that covered the valley floor. He wondered if his horse wasn't the smarter of them. As he led the horse closer, he had the sudden premonition he was about to suffer great pain, but he shook it off and continued forward. He knew he must face such fears. He knew if it was the devil he would likely die, but he proceeded anyway. He could not let Ole Beelzebub win without even a fight.

With each step he became more cautious. With each breath he gathered his strength for the coming storm. With each tick of the clock, (yes he could hear his pocket watch ticking off the seconds), his fear grew to new proportions.

In certain situations fear begets strength and he was operating in the spiritual realm now. He had the strength of ten men pulsing through his veins and all it would take to trigger its use was an attack from some unknown predator, a rifle shot or a look at the devil himself. With each step his fear built and with each step his strength attained proportions he'd never encountered. He knew if he was not careful his soul would vacate his flesh and leave it lying in the hot desert sun.

Once he fought down his fear enough to enter the ancient dwellings, he discovered where his foe hadn't been so careful. Out on the flat lands and in the valley the man took extreme precautions to cover and hide his trail. When entering the cave dwellings, it was as if the phantom rider no longer feared a watchful eye, and let his guard down. In no time he found the old Spanish armor, the tools the man had been using to dig and many ancient weapons both of Indian and Spanish origin. Then he found some of the gold. At first only small flakes of it that seemed to originate from somewhere else, but the ore was present and suddenly he knew why the man would kill and kill again. He determined on examination of the new evidence this was an ordinary man, just a mortal human, but by any standard, a very canny one.

Gold fever was a fearsome thing if not kept in check, and he knew without looking further, the man had succumbed to the dreadful disease. Evidence lay about all over the inner cavern. There were gold pans used for panning gold, picks, shovels, and dynamite. There was further evidence in the form of work completed. One wall was exposed and this wall was itself lined with streaks of ore.

The phantom rifleman had found gold on the Slash M holdings, although located on a distant portion of the range. Why is it, Moses wondered, do men believe that gold is worth more than their soul?

So gold was the reason behind the killings and attempted murder of his boss. Leading his horse he made his way to the highest towering part of the dwellings and there he made camp. It was a dry camp but he waited, making no effort to cover his own fresh tracks, he sat down to wait for the unknown high grader.

The rider covered his trail up to a point, and that point had been the cave dwellings. Unlike the soft almost indistinguishable tracks he'd left out on the flats, here he'd left many, not trying to hide them at all. The unknown miner scraped, stamped, and walked all over inside the structures looking for more evidence of gold, and then he'd dug wherever he'd found sign of the ore. The unknown highbinder was likely of medium build, not small but not large or massive either. His boot style was different; instead of the usual pointed toe worn by the average cowboy, the toe was more rounded, much like the type of boot soldiers wore. As Moses lay back to rest in the a small corner of one of the higher up dwellings contemplating the facts about the man he was searching for, he heard a boot grate on gravel down below. The answer to the riddle was here.

Getting up from his resting place in a deliberate and quiet manner, the old timer eased himself over to the cliff's edge where he could look out and down through what was surely at one time a window. He saw nothing, yet he could see everything.

Amazingly he could see much of the Slash M holdings, only the ranch house was blocked from view by the rolling hills in the far off distance. Then he noticed the tracks.

From high up in the dwellings, the trails the man had been leaving were obvious. Why had he not considered it before? One thing was certain; he wouldn't have to wait long to confront the unknown stranger. The man was down below at this very moment and would no doubt see the trail Moses had left for him. Where had he been? He couldn't have been too far away, there hadn't been time. Was it the devil? Had he come from the center of the earth somewhere only to drag Moses back to the lake of fire? Had he left all the necessary evidence to convince Moses he was safe only to show up from the pit called hell anyway? Surely the intruder was a man.

Careful to make no noise, Moses eased himself back to his resting place fished out his Winchester, lay back down, pulling his big hat down over his face. He knew his hearing would be greater if he relaxed and closed his eyes. It was a practice he'd been engaging in since childhood. When he was a young slave back in Georgia, before his emancipation, he used to close his eyes and pick out or identify all the sounds within hearing. He would identify them or guess until he was sure he had them all correctly identified, but now the sounds were different.

Having lived out west many years, he'd found the sounds to be another variety, but he knew them just the same. He knew the sound of a mountain lion during mating season, a big horn sheep, even the difference between a brown bear and a grizzly. Now he was listening again and he knew he was being hunted, not by a wild animal but by his own kind.

If he'd never practiced listening, he would have never heard the clumsiness of a human. Man is a clumsy creature, his very clumsiness a warning to all animals, big and small to exit the area or lay still. Most men never gave it much thought but a man hunting has more eyes on him than he will ever know. The eyes of a field mouse, a rabbit, a fox, a hawk, or any number of birds, all of which could be watching him, yet the man would never know it, for they suddenly become quiet and unmoving, camouflaged by their surroundings.

Moses Carter was a dangerous man in his own right, simply because he knew how to walk among the animals without drawing their attention, without the clumsiness of most humans. He could out wait the best of Indian braves on any given day and had, in fact, done so many times. Today, Moses waited. He could wait patiently without moving, all the while listening intently for the manner of beast he knew would eventually come. He'd left his own tracks for just such a showdown. Only when the unknown drew near would he need to take action. Moses knew the situation was live or die but he was ready.

There was no sound but the high up wind and an eagle calling in the distance. Somewhere far off and on a distant hill, two big horn sheep were butting heads for territorial rights. Again the eagle called from somewhere over the valley floor, breaking the silence as a faint breeze drifted through the window of the open air room. He had a flash thought that he could be thrown bodily out the adjacent window to the valley far below, but he shrugged it off and waited.

A mouse scurried along the opposite wall and Moses opened his eyes to confirm his suspicion. A hawk answered the eagle high overhead. These were all the sounds he heard and then a grate on stone. It was in another room, maybe fifty yards away at most. The man stepped on the edge of a rock, and it had been forced out from under his boot by sheer weight. As the stone rattled down the passageway, Moses listened.

"Still wearing your boots is ya?" Moses taunted.

It made no difference if he spoke or not, the prospector knew where he was, but Moses knew he would be fortunate if the killer would answer. Now as the man killer drew nearer, Moses could make out each step. His movements were easy to follow. Moses lay patiently waiting, unmoving as the evil, (for man or beast it could only be evil), approached. The killer may have thought he was being quiet, but Moses was hearing and mentally cataloguing each step.

When the tone changed, Moses knew the killer was now in the adjacent room and he opened his eyes, lying perfectly still. His rifle was at the ready pointing in a straight line to the doorway between them. Then he saw the point of someone else's rifle slowly easing around the corner. As the rifle made its way around the stone entryway, Moses realized too late his opponent already knew where to look for him. Squeezing off a round at the emerging gun, Moses dove across the room to take cover behind a stone slab. Gathering his wits about him he again called out to the unknown enemy.

"Been a-waiting faw ya. I's know you'd come ta me if'n I left some sign." Somehow he had to get the man off balance. Yet, silence prevailed. No reply at all from the man who now knew it was a battle to the death.

"Ya been killing too many good and decent folk. Boss man says you got to go!"

Where was he? Moses knew time would be needed for his ears to readjust to the silence after firing a shot. The situation was not one he liked at all. His hearing proficiency had been temporarily diminished at a time when he needed it most. His senses were distorted from the hastily thrown gunshot and he knew it. Why couldn't man invent a weapon that when shot made no racket at all? It was going to take considerable time to refocus and time was something Moses knew he didn't have. He must know where the man was.

Where Moses lay offered good cover from rifle or pistol fire, but the assassin had not fired a shot. A ricochet was the only thing he worried about from his current position. Why didn't the man say something, or move? Anything would help.

What was that hissing sound? He heard it long before he recognized it. When he did recognize the sound for what it was, the room he was in exploded. Rocks tumbled down hitting Moses and knocking him unconscious.

As Moses lay beneath a huge slab of fallen rock, breathing heavily, the killer walked up and pumped two rounds into his back for good measure.

"You may have been waiting for me Moses, but I came prepared. I always do."

He turned his back on the Slash M rider and whistled his way out of the room. Moses Carter might still be breathing heavily but he was done for, and with the big boulder crushing his lower extremities, if he did live he would likely put a gun to his head and finish the job. There was no way Moses Carter was ever going to walk out of these caverns and the killer knew it. Then again, the chances of anyone finding him before he was a skeleton were mighty slim.

Later, in the heat of the day, Moses Carter's breath rasped out like the wounded, desperate animal he was. Still he'd not seen the killer. He was haunted by the fact someone was able to do what the man had done without his knowledge of character. Who was the man? He was in awful pain when he first awoke, but now all that was left was numbness. Lying face down he tried to gather himself off the floor. Something held him down. Hearing the digging and scraping going on down below, he knew it was the man who had done this to him.

Wrenching himself around for a look, he sprawled back on the floor in despair. He was wedged beneath a boulder he would never be able to move by himself. His rifle was still at hand. At least he still had a way to draw someone's attention. No doubt the killer figured him for dead, and knowing his situation, Moses understood why. He had at best forty-eight hours to live in his current condition, and things would get worse quick if he didn't get some help real soon.

How long had he been unconscious? The stranger was steadily working his illegal claim down below, digging and scratching with a pick and shovel. He said nothing, for it would not do to have the man believe he was still alive. He felt the blood caked on his back where he'd been shot. He knew his chances of living were next to nothing, yet he fought to live.

He lay there for what seemed like days, unmoving, not wanting the pain associated with movement. One leg was broken, crushed below the knee. He'd been able to work the other from beneath the edge of the large rock. His chest was on fire like nothing he'd ever thought a man could endure, and still he slipped in and out of consciousness.

He was still among the living. He was lying in a pool of his own blood, but he was alive. Taking his bandanna from around his neck he used the long piece to tie a tourniquet around his crushed leg, putting it just above his knee. Once the device was secured to his satisfaction he took out his knife and began to carve away the flesh from his leg, flesh he could no longer feel anyway. He blacked out twice and the second time he came to all was dark and quiet. In the solemn darkness and silence of the night he finished separating his lower leg at the knee, pulled himself free and sat back against the big stone slab that he'd originally used for cover.

Once again he drifted off in the foreboding pitch black room. When he came to, he looked at his condition in the early morning sunlight and was horrified. His wounds were no longer oozing precious fluid, but he was covered with dried blood and the caked on mud that stuck to his bloody clothes. He carried no illusions; he knew his number was up, only he wasn't going to die like a wounded and trapped animal. Not like this he wasn't, not by some two by twice sidewinder.

How long he'd been working to save his own life, he didn't know, but the man down below was gone. He'd pulled up stakes and headed for home. Wherever the man's home was it was not far enough away. No distance would ever be far enough away. He was now a man on a mission. No matter where the man lived Moses would find him and kill him. He would look him right in the eyes and shoot him dead. A hanging was too good for the likes of the man who had done such a thing to him.

The sound of horse's hooves awoke him from a deep slumber. Two, no, three horse's walking out in front of the cliff dwellings far below. Picking up his Winchester, he fired a shot into the air through the big opening of the room. The big buzzard that watched him from the ledge to see if he was going to die flew off with the man's first movement.

In fact it had been the buzzards' circling above the rim of the canyon that alerted the Slash M riders something was amiss. A few minutes only and he could hear the men coming through the ruins. "Where are you?" one of the men shouted.

"In here," he choked on his words and suddenly he was greeted by three Comancheros from the home ranch. What the Slash M riders saw leaning against the stone wall left them aghast.

Most men would have died, but Moses Carter wasn't most men. He had a new mission in life, a mission he never wanted, but not one he would shy away from either. He was going to find and kill the scoundrel who had done this to him.

Back in town, Jeb Blackwell was seething. While he'd been working his digger's claim for little bits of color here and there, Pablo Mendoza rode into town and deposited more gold than most men could dream of in a lifetime. He sat in his office with the door closed, nurturing a hot-blooded anger. All men have their personal illusions; some even nurse them into a quiet rage. Jeb Blackwell stood on that threshold, mad to the core, unable to think clearly. Eighty percent of the funds had been deposited in the Slash M account ending any thought he might have of foreclosing on the Mendoza homestead. The rest had been placed into a new account for Hughe Rainwater. In Jeb's mind, the only rational he could conceive for splitting the gold was both men found the cache below the border.

He was upset for several reasons. The deposit of such magnitude meant he would never own the Slash M. Consequently he would never have legal access to the gold he'd found. He'd always thought of himself as being the man who was supposed to be the richest in the territory. He knew now he would never be. Pablo Mendoza had too big of a head start. Riches for Jeb always seemed fleeting at best. The thought never dawned on him that all he had to do was manage his father's ranch assets and he'd quickly become a very wealthy man. The station of ranch owner was too far beneath him. To have to work the way his father had? The thought never occurred to him that the only reason he had his bank was because of the ranch his father built so long ago.

No matter what he attempted, nothing ever seemed to work out in his favor. Never mind the evil of such plans. The fact his father considered everything he owned also belonged to his son, and when he was gone the B & B Connected would become the sole property of Jeb Blackwell never seemed to surface as a reality in his mind. His father's ranch was something unclean and filthy, coarse and too rough of a life, a place to stay away from. He only wanted to forget he'd grown up on the place. Now he'd killed another man, and still his just inheritance eluded him. All those riches were in someone else's bank account.

David May stuck his head through the office door. "Time for me to lock up Mr. Blackwell," the young teller

said as he left the office and locked up the teller doors from the outside.

"Okay, I'll see you in the morning."

Sitting in his leather bound chair, he wondered what was it about such a statement he hated so much? Was it the insinuation he'd be right here, that nothing would change in the life of Jeb Blackwell? He wanted adventure, to rub shoulders with important people, the movers and the shakers. He wanted a new life, somewhere like San Francisco, but the old life had an iron clad grip on him and would not let go.

The teller locked the front doors and stepped out into the street leaving the bank and Jeb Blackwell in quiet solitude.

Sitting in his chair, stewing over the recent turn of events the answer suddenly dawned on him. The gold Pablo deposited was locked in the vault and there was nothing keeping him here. He could ride out to the ranch, borrow some good horse stock and ride out with all the treasure. With his knowledge of the west he could lay a trail that would be difficult to follow at best. He went to the teller's office, opened it up and walked back to the vault. Quickly he spun the combination dial and opened the vault door. For a short time he stood there, contemplating what he would do. It was a magnificent haul. The more he looked on the riches stored in his own vault the more he knew he would be somewhere else on the morrow.

He had access to the gold, the means to travel in a hurry, even with a heavily loaded, burdened down pack train. What about the guards Mendoza posted? Mendoza left men behind to watch the bank for just such an occasion. He would have to deal with the guards somehow. They would be outside walking circles this very minute. It would be two or three men, and he would need time to load the gold securely while they were out. Out? Of course, he would have to knock them out somehow, or kill them.

Little time was wasted making up his mind. It had been decided for him the moment he'd opened the vault and gazed on Mendoza's gold. The vault was stuffed to the point paper and coin money had to be kept elsewhere in the bank until the gold could be moved.

His original plans had been thwarted. Dean Reynolds, Three Finger Jack, and the rest of the hired guns failed him. Had they not been so inept and clumsy, none of this would have happened and he would be a big man on the Slash M this night. He would have been able to foreclose without difficulty and would have taken his time in filing his claim as there would have been no reason to hurry.

Now there would never be a legal claim, he would never own the Mendoza land and he would never dig for gold in the hills again. Randy Bean was pushing up daises along with Moses Carter and for what? The fact Pablo survived two assassination attempts was pure luck. As of now, no one could move anywhere near the Mendoza range without being observed by the Comancheros he'd employed. There could be no more attempts on the man's life.

The doctor wasn't giving Moses Carter much chance for recovery. "He's lost more blood than most men carry in their veins," he stated as he was about to leave the wounded man's room. Thinking Moses in too deep of a sleep to hear what he said, he added, "I don't give him more than two, maybe three days before he passes on."

"Doc," Moses chimed in from his bed, "I'll see dat man what done dis ta me in hell afore I enter dem pearly gates!"

"I'm sorry Moses, I didn't know you could hear me."

"I's can hear jus fine. Don't you be sending dat grim reaper after my body jus yet. I's got me a man ta kill first."

"Did you get a look at the man who did this to you?" Pablo asked.

"No I's didn't, but I'll know him soon enough."

"How do you figure?"

"He thinks I's dead. Got him a mining camp high up in the old Indian dwellings; he's been taking out gold from right under our nose."

"Do you have any idea who it might be?" Pablo asked.

"No sir, but I's tell you dis, he wears boots wit a round toe like what a soldier would wear, and he carries a brand spanking new Winchester .73 around wit him. I's only know because I carry de same rifle."

The doctor's brow wrinkled as he considered what Moses told them. He knew of only one man who wore a boot like that, only one man in a thousand.

"Don't you go telling old Moses just yet. I's needs time to recover, but when I's ready I's says so and den I'll go get him." He paused for breath, "Boss I got's ta kill dat man if its da last ting I do. Leav'n me like he done was just plain wicked. A man like him is as mean as I ever did see. Even with one leg I got's ta kill him."

"You stay here and rest," Doc said, taking Pablo by the sleeve. "Come with me."

As they walked down the hallway doc explained. "There's only one man in these parts that I can say wears books like that—Jeb Blackwell."

Pablo stopped mid-stride. "You're telling me Jeb Blackwell is behind this?"

"Well no, I..."

The new ranch owner didn't wait for he knew what had to be done. Once out on the front porch, Pablo gave immediate orders. "Miguel, I need five of your best men and your best tracker. We ride in ten minutes." Turning quickly Pablo added, "Doc, can you ride over and talk to Horace Blackwell?"

"What on earth for?"

"Jeb Blackwell has been killing people, and I think he is going to try and rob the bank."

"Why that's preposterous! I'll do no such thing. Jeb Blackwell is an upstanding member of the community."

"Listen Doc, he just tried to kill one of my best riders. He put a bullet in me, and he's killed others. We didn't have any idea who the killer might be until Moses spoke up."

"You're serious, aren't you?" Doctor Bradley said.

"We just deposited over nine hundred thousand in pure gold into his bank, Doc. He's been out here digging for gold on my ranch and all I can think is he has the combination to the vault. He doesn't even have to break in. I've never met the man, but if he's the only one with boots like Moses described, then he's the only one who's been blocking every move I make when it comes to money."

"But you have riders posted. You have the bank guarded."

"They're looking for anyone who might break in. They have no idea the bank could be robbed by the owner. Why would they? They wouldn't suspect him any more than you do."

"I see what you mean. I'll ride over and have a talk with Horace, but I still don't believe what you're saying. I'll inform him of your actions and suspicions, but that's all."

"Good, that's all I want of you. His old man should at least know what's happening. In the meantime, we've got to stop a bank robbery, and Doc, I won't do anything without Ranger Haslam's approval. I'll find him first and inform him concerning what we know and he'll make the decisions."

"Pablo, Horace will realize a great deal of comfort knowing you won't shoot first and ask questions later. I'll ride to the B & B as fast as my carriage will carry me."

"Thank you Doc, for everything," Shaking hands Doctor Bradley re-entered the house to collect his things. Pablo followed and both men went straight back to Moses.

"Moses, with the information you've given us I believe we already know who the killer is. I and some of the boys are going to ride into town to see he doesn't get away. What has me worried most is the gold we just deposited in Sonora Merchant Bank. If the man's been out here digging for high grade ore, he'll sure enough take everything we just deposited. We've got to stop him." Pausing he added. "We may already be too late."

"Boss man, I's notice money goes into dat bank, but don't come out so easy."

"It's Jeb Blackwell Moses, and he doesn't have to rob it like you think, he's got him a key."

Moses coughed before he could regain his composure. "Law'dy mercy! You best git. Old Moses ain't going nowhere a' tall. Ya'll stop him, or catch'm alive, but promise me boss you'll save his killing for when I's up and at'm again."

"I wouldn't want it any other way, but Ranger Haslam will be in charge of things. I'm just riding to protect the ranch's interest."

"G'wan wit you now and let old Moses dream of a lynching not his own."

Ten minutes later the Slash M riders headed for town.

Two hours later Doc Bradley pulled up to the front steps of the B & B to inform Horace of what was taking place. The old man greeted Doc at the front porch steps. On the way over, several facts about Jeb Blackwell came to the surface in Doc Bradley's mind. First, the man did have a brand new Winchester .73 repeating rifle. The exact caliber used on Moses Carter, Randy Bean, and Pablo Mendoza. He was never in town at the time of the shootings, so where had he been? Then he realized Jeb's hatred for anything to do with his father's ranch. He'd seen it for many years now, only he hadn't recognized the symptoms for what they were. Greed, just pure greed!

"To what do I owe the pleasure of this visit, Doc?"

"Horace, 'tis no good news I bring. Can we talk inside?"

"Certainly." Horace braced himself for the worst, having being afraid of his son dying first.

Once the men were seated comfortably, Horace could wait no longer. 'What is it Doc? What's happened?"

"The Slash M has uncovered some facts or evidence pointing to your son as being the man who shot Pablo Mendoza and now Moses Carter."

"Why that's crazy!" Horace objected waving off the accusation with his hands.

"Horace, I just came from the Mendoza ranch. They have good reason to suspect him. They're riding toward town at this very moment in order to prevent what they think will be an attempt by Jeb to rob his own bank."

"Now I know you're crazy! Why would the boy rob his own bank? Why, he doesn't need anything, Doc. He already has everything he could ever want."

"Does he? Horace, those men are riding to town to see Ranger Haslam. With what they've learned, and what Bob knows, there may be enough evidence to confirm what I'm telling you. If I were you, I'd saddle up and meet them in town, just to keep things fair and honest. You know, on the up and up."

"There's coffee on, and my house is yours," Horace said as he got up from his big chair by the fireplace. "You're right, if my boy is going to have any chance at all of a fair defense I've got to ride. Make yourself at home Doc," the old man added as he lifted his Stetson from the peg by the door and closed it behind him.

He knew everyone was making a mistake by suspecting his son. There was no way Jeb would be involved in the recent shootings and possible murders. Saddling his best horse he mounted up and headed for Sonora. It would be daybreak before he arrived, but if he was going to be of any help he had to make the ride. He rode alone, pondering on what he'd learned from Doc Bradley, but there was no way it could be true. Someone was obviously attempting to frame Jeb.

As he rode, it began to sprinkle and he pulled out his bearskin slicker, slipped the sou'wester over his head then replaced his hat. A cold wet night in the saddle was all the rancher had to look forward to. He'd found the bearskin to be so good at keeping him dry he'd never switched to the more modern version called a poncho. He was never keen on store bought goods except when their convenience could not be denied. Horace adjusted his hat brim to a lower position as the rain poured down, allowing the water to drain off effectively as he guided his horse toward Sonora. Lighting lit the sky to the north and a moment later thunder rolled over the hills. What was the meaning? Was it an omen? Maybe the storms of this life were patterned after the rolling thunder and driving rain. There was no letup in sight.

Chapter 20

At daybreak the rain tapered off. Along with the sunrise a mist began to evaporate from the rain soaked sand. Pablo Mendoza and his Comancheros guided their horses down Main Street. When they reached the bank they found the bank vault empty. Just as Pablo suspected his gold was gone. Bob Haslam was already sorting out the facts and didn't like what he was coming up with. Two of the guards Pablo left behind were sitting on the front steps of the bank, the third was dead, his throat slit.

"I take it you have an idea who did this," Pablo said.

"I do, and I don't like it. I don't like it one bit," Pony Bob said.

Several of the town's prominent citizens were present along with Dean Reynolds and Three Finger Jack. Some of the men were scuffing the ground with their boots yet listening to every word. Men were anxious to get after the culprit.

"Who did it?" Pablo wanted to know if Bob had come to the same conclusion.

"It appears Jeb Blackwell has robbed his own bank," the ranger stated as Horace rode up.

"That's impossible!" Horace said as he sat his mount.

"Horace, I have one dead man and two live witnesses. I can't deny those facts. As the man's father you have the right to believe what you want, but I have a job to do and right now I have very strong evidence pointing directly at your son. It will be up to the courts to decide if he's the guilty party."

Pablo noticed the new man standing behind Pony Bob, a man he had been seeing since his childhood back in St. Louis, a Pinkerton man came in on last evening's stage. He was well dressed as always and wore a colt revolver tucked crossways under his vest, an unusual position but an effective one for someone who wore a long black coat and wanted to get his gun into action fast. Why was the man here now and why did he keep eying the Slash M owner in such an odd manner?

"Now I've got to form a posse to ride after him and bring him back. I'll need some volunteers," Bob said.

"Me and my men will certainly go, although we'll have need of fresh horses after riding all night," Pablo said.

"I don't ride with Indians!" Dean Reynolds stated flatly.

"You can stay here Dean, because they're going," Pablo said.

"They're not going anywhere with me," the dispirited cowboy repeated.

"Dean, we're going after a criminal and these Indians know where all the water is. They can track like a hound dog and are less trouble than any man here. They're going whether you like it or not," Pablo said. "Besides, unless you can track a man after his tracks have been wiped out by rain, they're going."

"He's right Dean," Ranger Haslam added. "Let's quit wasting time and get mounted up. He has at least a six hour head start on us, and we're burning precious daylight."

"Bob, there's one thing you should know. Jeb tried to kill me and now Moses Carter. I believe he did kill Randy Bean. Moses is certain of it and all because he found gold on the Slash M." No sooner had the word gold escaped his lips and Pablo knew he'd made a mistake. Gold was a fever that when possessed a man knew no bounds. They were riding to retrieve what had been removed from the bank vault. Some of his Comancheros already felt betrayed because Hughe Rainwater intentionally lied to them at the border and rode after the elusive Mexican Army gold shipment. The Treasure del Diablo had been obscure for three hundred years and it was still proving difficult to pin down. Like the stories of old, anyone who managed to get their hands on the ore soon found more trouble than the gold was worth.

"Things are shaping up like I was beginning to suspect. Dean and Three Finger Jack, you two fellows were on the man's payroll," the ranger accused. The two men stiffened at his words. "Just what was he paying you men for anyway? I'm right curious to know."

Thinking fast, Three Finger Jack spoke up before Dean could say anything which might get them both strung up. ", all we ever did was deliver information to him."

"Do you expect me to believe that?" Bob's tone was harsh.

"Bob," Pablo said, "he could very well be telling the truth. If he was trying to sneak on and off of my range without being seen, he would want to know where everyone was."

Three Finger Jack had been looking at Huachuca, the Indian who removed his fingers, but suddenly he breathed a sigh of relief. "Thank you, Mr. Mendoza. You are proving to be a better man than I had you figured for."

"For the love of Mary, let's ride. Horace, are you going?" the ranger asked.

"I think I'd better stay here. He's my only son, Ranger Haslam. Will you do me the favor of trying to bring him back alive?"

"You've my word on it." Pony Bob turned to look at the town hostler. "Zeek, you fix the Mendoza outfit up with some fresh horses and we'll be ready to ride. By the way everyone, the man behind me is Saul Stewart. He's a Pinkerton agent. He'll be coming with us."

Pablo led his men down to the stable. At once they began to dismount and move their gear onto fresh horses. As Pablo moved his gear from one horse to another, he watched Horace Blackwell walk along the Sonora boardwalk with his head down. He wondered as he placed his saddlebags if this was what awaited him? Would he have son's to grow tall and strong beside him, only to turn on him and become the scourge of the community, a thorn in his side? Maybe being married and having children was an exercise in rebellion. It appeared the more some parents did for their children, the more they are despised no matter what they did.

He shook himself from his negative thoughts and cinched his saddle tight, yet the image would not leave him. What kind of children would he and Conchetta raise? Would they be rebellious or would they be respectful of their parents? Maybe it all hinged on the first born? But, what if the first born was all you had, like Horace Blackwell? As Pablo stepped into the saddle he made a note to himself, talk to Horace and ask questions. See where he thinks he went wrong and try not to repeat.

The Slash M riders rode up the street and stepped down. Pony Bob handed his reins to Toby his dog and left for a moment so they waited.

Pablo was keeping his eye on Three Finger Jack, who was eying the Indian who had Jack's fingers hanging around his neck. Three Finger Jack spit chewing tobacco in the general direction of the savage and Huachuca slipped his ten inch knife from his loin cloth and examined the blade for sharpness. Alternately he looked at the knife then back to Three Finger Jack. There was no mistake in his communication, though not a word was spoken. Another bit of chew in the Indian's direction and Three Finger Jack would become known as Lefty.

Pablo watched as Jack retreated to his horse and examined his gear. He pulled a fresh bandana out of his saddlebag and stuffed the old one deep inside. Then he tied the new kerchief around his neck and fluffed it just the way he liked. When he looked up the Indian was gone. Pablo saw him spin in all directions expecting a knife in his back at any moment.

Pablo chuckled. "Settle down, Jack. He went to get his horse," Pablo said.

Pony Bob's dog, reins dangling from his mouth, stared at Three Finger Jack as if wondering why the man was so jumpy. The Dalmatian's tongue hung out as he panted, soaking the lawman's reins, yet the dog watched the proceedings with the certainty of travel in his future. Usually he took his trips with Pony Bob, but today men and horses were prancing around preparing to ride. The Dalmatian wasn't about to miss whatever they were up to.

Pablo thought back over the history of the gold. It had been smelted into pure bars and was the stuff of legends. Cortez had fought the Aztec and stolen it from the southwestern Indians in Mexico during his trek in the early fifteen hundreds. On arriving in Mexico he burned his ships so there could be no retreat. This particular gold was the gold Montezuma, the Aztec emperor, hid from Hernando Cortez in a fit of rebellion. There are those who said the treasure of the Aztecs was never found, but the gold Hughe Rainwater recovered was evidence Cortez found at least a portion of their treasure.

Three hundred years had seen the treasure misplaced over and over again. Cortez never lived to spend a solitary dime realized from his conquest of the Aztec nation. He had the treasure, but he could not spend it. He spent the remainder of his entire life running from the Indian's assassination attempts, and his king who sent many expeditions after him in an attempt to have him brought to justice. Eventually he was returned to Spain, but his power was never restored and he died a lonely old man.

Then the gold vanished. Over many years tales of the treasure haunted Mexico, but each time the bullion surfaced it disappeared again with a new story to tell. And once again the treasure was missing.

The Treasure del Diablo it was called. The treasure no one could spend, and now the full breadth of its meaning was understood by Pablo. As he waited for Pony Bob to return, he wondered if he wasn't just the next in a long line of benefactors who would never live to see the gold put to use.

When he first learned of the gold as Bobby Joe Riggins, he didn't know what del Diablo meant. Now as

Pablo he understood the meaning clearly. The devil had been sewing trouble for him these many years. From the time he was orphaned as a little boy the devil had been trying to kill him. Now he was a grown man and nothing had changed. He'd learned one thing though, Satan could use anyone to get after you, up to and including your own loved ones. He could use a preacher, a child of God, or even a mother or father. He was the prince of this earth which meant he had every human form at his disposal, and that was something many folks tend to forget.

For the first time in his life he was really happy. As the rancher Pablo Mendoza he had power, he had a woman and he felt secure, yet other folks were always causing trouble for him. Jeb Blackwell was just one on a long list of troublemakers. Fate was forcing him to get the gold back. To let the man ride off with the treasure was not an option. He had to retrieve the stolen gold.

Without warning, his newfound security was anything but carved in stone. One stray bullet and the ranch would belong to someone else while he would be pushing up daisies. He looked around at the men who surrounded him and wondered which one might betray him. Miguel? What about Dean Reynolds or Three Finger Jack? Any one of them could pull a trigger. Instantly he was spooked. Exposed as never before, it was imperative he make this ride. His men would not respect him if he didn't go. He realized with clarity he was fairly trapped. He would have to put aside his fears and do what he must.

Just then Pony Bob returned from down the street. "I'll have to deputize you men in the name of the law. Everyone raise your right hand and repeat after me. I do solemnly swear..."

The men followed in unison. "To uphold the law of the Arizona Territory and to do my duty so help me God!" Taking a moment to look the men over the ranger gathered his reins from Toby and said, "Mount up."

The men stepped into their saddles and settled in for a long ride. There was no sense in running the horses for they would make better time than the mules Jeb stole. Once they cleared the buildings at the edge of town they settled into a steady cantor. These were men chiseled and molded by the unsympathetic land in which they lived. Their sense of evenhandedness was an eye for an eye, their demand for accountability a force within each of them, unswerving in their pursuit of justice. They lived in a land of desert and wilderness which set in motion their standard for courage and their code of ethics. The desert allows for no gentle mercy and the baron wilderness no milk of human kindness.

The Arizona territory had the potential to become a state within the Federal Union provided the territory could maintain a reasonable form of law and order. If Jeb were allowed to get away, the application for statehood would be set back several years and Arizona would continue being a territory. If the lawless were allowed to thrive, Arizona might never become a state. If the criminals were wary at all it was due in large part to the fact that everyone in Arizona carried a gun. The barber, the cook, the mercantile owner, and the cowhand were all veterans of the Civil War. Every inhabitant within five hundred miles matured handling guns and every man among them was prepared to use those weapons when no other option presented itself.

Pablo glanced at the tracks on the ground as they rode and suddenly realized he was not going to be back at the home ranch tonight. He'd hoped to have the ride over swiftly and be back at the ranch later in the evening, but as the trail led them on he realized their pursuit of the banker was not to prove so simple. First of all there was little to no trail, the rain had seen to it. The time necessary to capture the man, the direction of the trail, not even their choice of camp site would be left to them. Anything they might do would be dictated by the man they were after. Jeb Blackwell knew where he was headed, he knew where he would go and when, but the posse could not know. It was clear to him the man's aim was to demoralize and dispirit his pursers. By design Jeb was selecting the most dangerous terrain, the most awful path to lead the pack train, but even that took a while to find after the rain.

Now they were riding single file, twisting and turning in all directions. The hoof prints veered sharply south around a large shoulder of rock then straight back to the north headed for the larger mountain. They were no longer following the rain soaked tracks they'd followed earlier. Looking up at the mountain, they paused.

As they looked at the swollen terrain an uneasy feeling crept into the mind Pablo, and he was sure into each and every other man in the posse, it would not be long and Jeb would have them right where he wanted them, then what? How many of them would die?

Pablo's thoughts returned to Conchetta. She would be helping Maria prepare food for the men who remained on watch at the ranch. Would she wonder where he was? None of them expected this ride to last into the night, yet the sun lowered itself behind the mountains. No one desired a long grueling pursuit, maybe a brief gun battle, but not this. They looked for a campsite with water close by, cover and whatever they could use to their advantage. Jeb had seen to it they would have no comfort on this night. It was cold at this altitude. Glancing around, Pablo realized there would be no shelter from the wind either. There was no firewood for a fire and no smooth ground to bed down on.

"We'll make camp here," Pony Bob said.

Begrudgingly, the men dismounted. It was of no use to argue. Pony Bob was not a man who tolerated such gibberish. As Pablo unsaddled his horse, the thought occurred to him it could be a week before he returned home, might be longer—if he returned at all.

"Bob, you're still awful young," Pablo said.

"You must have been just a kid when you rode for the Pony Express," Jack said as he unsaddled his bronc.

"I was fourteen. Most of us were just kids, but I was glad for the job."

"And now?" Jack asked.

"I'm twenty-six, but don't let the age bother you none. I'm quite capable of handling the job."

"I know you are, I wasn't questioning your ability, just your age," Jack said as he dropped his saddle to the ground.

"What are you driving at Jack?"

"Nothing. I was just curious. Back before the war, I rode the leg from Grand Junction to Scofield."

"Well, I never saw you back then, but then you were in the Rocky Mountain region. I rode in the plains."

"Small world isn't it?" Jack said.

"Did you ever run into Nat Love while riding for the Pony Express?"

"The black boy what was the first rider who left from St. Joseph?"

"That's him, did you ever meet him?"

"I should hope to shout. That was one hombre who was better left alone," Jack said.

"I seen him down to Dodge City one time, took a bet for one thousand dollars that he could ride a particular bull from one end of town to the other. From the moment he settled down on the back of old Hurricane, that bull began to pitch a fit. Liked to killed two cowboys on either side of them before they got the chute opened. That bull went right down Main Street kicking and juking, bucking, and fighting. He entered the barber shop and tore it all to pieces, then the mercantile, and the west end stable, but Nat Love never flinched. He stayed on all the way out of town. He won the thousand, but had to pay half of it to fix the damage he'd caused."

"That sure would have been a sight to see."

"He never got credit from the newspapers for being the first Pony Express rider, but he never let it bother him. He was tough as nails and fast as a rattlesnake with that gun of his. I hear tell they made him a town ," Pony Bob said.

"Well now, I'm beginning to think there ain't no future in living outside the law," Jack said.

"With me and him wearing this badge, I think I'd re-evaluate my friends were I you."

The next morning they traced Jeb's footsteps, for he had dismounted in order to lead the animals across nearly impassable foothills eroded by time, wind, and rain. The unfolding landscape was sprinkled with Spanish bayonet while a cedar dabbed the lava rock terrain on occasion. Ahead of them were the first of many mountains. How many would they have to cross before they caught up with the banker?

Jeb was in no rush. His ability to take the longest route if it was easier on his animals was the same as most Indian's. He didn't appear to need water, but that was crazy. Everyone needed water, yet somehow Jeb didn't, nor did his animals. Either that or they somehow missed the water hole. Since leaving Sonora the skies cleared and the sun was once again baking the land like an oven.

Miguel topped out along the ridge after climbing all morning with Huachuca at his side. They drew up to give their horses a blow. The rest of the men topped out on the ridge and brought up short. Most of them were hard men, yet up until now they'd held fast to their own range involuntarily by the hand of Mother Nature. The limits of cattle and water along with the human need to see something started. None of them had ever ridden this far north.

It was Three Finger Jack who spoke, "Pony Bob, where do you reckon he's headed?"

"So far as I know there's nothing in this direction, nothing at all."

"The canyon is over to the northwest, he can't go that way. There just isn't any way to reach the other side, not without a bridge," Jack said.

The Dalmatian watched as the men looked over the terrain.

The saddleback ridge they navigated was seven miles long. Here and there they found where a mule's hoof left a scar on stone, but it took three hours to find where he'd left the ridge.

Huachuca chuckled. "White man like Indian, he no need run."

"Well, let's get after him," Pony Bob said as he started down the back side.

Pablo was surprised by his own change of thinking. He understood the need for law and order and he'd been dispensing his own brand of justice for a long time. Where no official law was on record it was generally up to the local citizens to maintain the peace. If the local folks held back, an area could be consumed by complete anarchy before anyone realized what was up. Pablo acknowledged the necessity of such collective thinking, yet the current situation was not at all one he was pleased with. Things were different than they were before he had anything. Now he had a ranch, a wife and a future. So much was different when you have nothing to risk or loose.

He held no ounce of enthusiasm for his current situation. He'd fallen head long into a domesticated lifestyle, tending to his own affairs, setting to supper with his young and beautiful wife, tasting the good cooking, feeling the comforts a home provided by the slow unwinding from a hard day's work. The welcome release of a soft warm bed that awaited him, and suddenly he missed things he'd never had.

One bullet, one bullet and he'd never see them again. With renewed awareness he guided his horse into position behind Pony Bob. If Jeb was to shoot at them he would likely not try to shoot the Arizona Ranger. He might try to shoot Pablo, but if the lawman was too close he would likely choose another target. This Pablo reasoned, although he needn't be worried, Jeb Blackwell was not worried about any of them, not yet.

Chapter 21

Afragmented and broken land revealed its shape as Jeb made his exit north, a majestic land with high peaks and low valleys carved by centuries of hard rain and ground sweltering heat, a land full of scattered escarpments, broken pillars of stone, and long rolling hills. A vacant land, yet a land crowded with baron formations reaching to the sky as if kneeling in worship before God himself.

For now he was riding in Arizona, but beyond the horizon and to the north sprawled the great land of Utah. Between him and San Francisco was a desert wasteland, this unholy land that stretched out before him was the most dangerous and least traveled stretch of waterless waste known to western men. He would have to trust to his skills, a good deal of luck, and creativity to remain a free man.

The Utah border was up ahead, but he was under no illusions. It was just a line on a map, a line that didn't reside in the minds of the men who would be in pursuit of him. If any one of them knew its location they would ignore such a boundary, for in their minds he'd crossed another boundary, one which maintained the difference between law and order, between what was right and wrong, between honesty and dishonesty. If they learned of, or suspected his involvement in the recent killings he could not know, but he wasn't going to wait around to find out. He took the gold and they would hunt him down for that alone. Never mind the killing of the man outside the bank.

Finding the mules that transported the gold originally had been a stroke of luck, for the animals had been used to the travel and stepped right back into their old pace. In only a short time he'd packed them and was riding north. The one guard, they would hang him for that alone, if they caught up with him. He'd not intended to kill any of them, but the last guard found him binding up the other two and paid the ultimate price.

He was under no illusions, save one. He actually believed he had the opportunity to get away with murder, theft and betrayal, for he'd betrayed the people of Sonora. There was perhaps no other behavior that would cause the good upstanding citizens of the west to rattle their hocks and mount their horses faster than betrayal. Murder they could deal with on a case by case basis, even theft was looked on with more favor than betrayal. He'd betrayed them all, and most of all he'd betrayed his father's trust.

Most of the men, if not all, who followed him were his neighbors and he knew them well. They were not the kind of men who would give up after a light chase. They would follow him to the gates of hell and back if necessary provided he let them, because that was where he was headed. He'd lived among them, grown up with some of them, and fought alongside them. He would know most of them by name, for they'd built homes, a town and the foundation of civilization yet he'd systematically dismantled it with several criminal acts. Then he remembered the Comancheros. What if it was Mendoza's men? He knew none of them.

He knew he had to flee or fight, yet he did not wish to fight these men. Some he shared memories with, most would have families to go home to, yet he must be prepared to kill. He had no hostility toward them having obtained what he thought he deserved; now he just wanted to be left alone.

For three days the men searched for sign of tracks, but it was the Indian Hauchuca who found them. He fired his rifle and the other men came running. It was a ghost of a trail, not nearly enough to convince the others he'd found anything, yet they listened to his advice and followed. On their own they had found nothing, so there was little argument. It began to look as if Huachuca had not found anything either, but three hours later they came on tracks too obvious to be mistaken.

"Where's he headed?" Bob asked no one in particular.

"Straight to hell, and gentlemen I do mean hell." Hughe Rainwater said.

"Get to the point Hughe, what are you really saying?"

"He's headed for the Utah line, and gentlemen from here to there, you'll find nothing but Hell on Earth. Why there ain't enough water in that part of the desert to keep a June bug alive and we're gonna play hob getting water for us and our horses."

"Bob, Jeb has that big buckskin and twenty mules and no doubt he's packing water along with the gold. They ain't going to need nowhere near as much water as we are. We'd best look at the hand he's dealing us before we bet on riding in there after him with this bunch," Three Finger Jack said.

"You're right, we're asking for trouble if we ride in there with this many men," the ranger agreed. "The desert would kill half of us for him. We'd better trim our ranks. Pablo, you and your men can turn back, but I would like to keep Hauchuca with me. He's proven the best tracker in these parts now that Moses is all stove up."

"I'm not turning back. My men can go, but I'm staying on," Pablo said.

"Now look..."

"You heard me, Bob. I'm not going to fight with you about it. Huachuca can remain with us and the rest of my men can go home."

"Okay, but only five of us go on from here and I'll name the other two. Three Finger Jack if you don't mind being called such, I want you and Hughe Rainwater along. Saul, you're in charge until I get back. You'll remain deputized while the rest of the men stand down. Make sure these men get home safely will you?"

"I'll see to it."

"Those who can spare your water, leave it with us, and any spare canteens, or water bags. We're going to need them," Bob said.

Three hours later, Hughe shook his head and addressed the others. "We've bought ourselves a pack of trouble," paraphrasing exactly what Hauchuca had been thinking. "He's covering a lot of ground and he's saving his horse at the same time, and he's caring for those mules."

"Are we gaining any ground?" Bob asked.

Huachuca and Hughe shook their heads no in unison. Dust hung in the air around them so Bob removed his hat and wiped his brow, looking around. The heat of the sun was bearing down on them, cooking their shoulders beneath their clothes. Heat waves rose from the desert floor like dancing curtains offering the promise of water where there was none.

The trail stretched out before them swerving only at a clump of rocks or to skirt a thorn riddled plant, weaving itself into the distance then fading from sight, mingling with the desert heat waves the sun provided. Pony Bob and four other men pressed on. With worried caution, Bob concerned himself with what the near future held in store for them. Dust swirled around and over the posse.

Pablo pulled his now dusty bandanna over his nose and mouth, the others followed suit. Reaching down he placed his hand on his canteen making sure he still had it, then he reached to the other side of his saddle and patted the water bag he'd acquired from Miguel. He knew not to drink yet, but he wanted the feeling of security just knowing the water was available. "Not that long ago," he mumbled to himself.

After three days of brutal heat, following only a slight trail they were nearing the Grand Canyon. As the men rode steadily onward it became clear to them, this was not going to be an easy ride. And then, with no warning they rode up to the cliff's edge.

Seven hundred feet below they could see the man leading the mules more than a mile away, but how had he gotten them there? The tracks lead right up to the edge of the cliff and then disappeared. There had to be some sort of sign, some tracks wiped out, something, yet there was nothing.

"Now how in Sam Hill did he get down there?" Bob asked.

Huachuca was already off of his horse and scouting the nearby ground to the left. On the right Hughe Rainwater was doing the same. The other three men sat their horses in amazement. Stunned admiration described their condition best. Both Three Finger Jack and Pablo were speechless.

After the ranger's question, no one had answered, for there was no answer. Eventually each of the remaining men dismounted and pondered the situation themselves. Each studied the lay of the land, the tracks he'd left behind and the breadth of his own knowledge and none could explain the appearance of Jeb Blackwell down below the cliffs, in the canyon surrounded by water, life giving water, and plants.

Hughe returned after about ten minutes and offered no explanation. Another thirty minutes passed and Huachuca returned and motioned for them to follow. He led them until he came to a point where the rock split and a steep trail presented itself. It was a game trail of the likes to scare any normal man right out of his skin. They could see where Jeb had picketed the mules, and the tracks made things quite obvious. He'd taken the animals down as one long train, certain of his footing. Had he been here before?

The trail was that of a mountain goat or a big horn sheep. No other animal in its right mind would try to descend such a hair-raising path.

"The question is does the complete trail still exist?" Hughe asked. "If a man got halfway down the trail and found it sabotaged he would never be able to turn his horse around and come back up, hence he would have to send a good horse to its death and then return on foot."

"You stay. Huachuca show you how."

Taking a long piece of cloth from his lance he tied it around the horse's head to cover his eyes, and then walked the horse in circles to confuse its bearing, three to the left and then three to the right and started for the ledge. Like a mirage, man and horse disappeared over the cliff. All the other four could do was wait.

Three hours passed when they heard the shot. Looking over the side they could see Hauchuca waving at them to come on down. Pony Bob had been hoping in secret the trail would be impassable, hoping for a turn of events, anything to prevent them from risking their lives on the side of such a cliff, but it wasn't to be. He waved back and walked his horse in the throes of despair at having to traverse such a wicked and dangerous trail.

"I'll go first," Three Finger Jack volunteered. Bob followed a few minutes later, then Pablo and finally Hughe brought up the rear.

"You'll have a hair-raising experience to tell your grandkids," Bob said when Pablo reached the bottom.

"If I live to have kids."

"You're the one who insisted on coming," Bob said playfully. They watched as Hughe descended the last of the switchbacks.

"Don't remind me."

Once Hughe caught up to them they waded to the edge of the river and let their horses drink, then mounted and rode out. The posse gained ground unexpectedly, yet they started out easy to let their horses get their feet back under them. For several hours the weary men followed a now easy to read trail.

"What I can't figure out is how he covered up the tracks he made up on the cliff and how it looked like he'd ridden right out into thin air," Three Finger Jack said.

"We're all trying to figure out how he did it," Pablo answered. "He's leading twenty mules and those tracks just disappeared."

"We'll ask him once we capture him," Bob said.

"What if he don't want to be captured?" Hughe asked.

"If we have to shoot him, make it somewhere it won't kill," Bob said looking right at Three Finger Jack. "I'm still not convinced you're so innocent in all this."

"I'll admit I've been caught with my hand in the cookie jar a time or two, but I'm not really a bad man. Randy and I were friends for a long time. Now I might not be the smartest fellow on the range, but a friend is a friend, and Randy grew up not two miles from me in Knob Lick, Missouri. We were like brothers and I knew a long time ago when he went bad on me. I just couldn't bring myself to abandon a lifelong friend.

"What scrambled my brain is, if I'd ridden out with him the night he left, I'd be lying in a grave right alongside him. Now, that's more explaining than I've done in a long time. Don't expect no more," Three Finger Jack said as he spurred his horse ahead of the others.

"I must have touched a nerve," Bob said.

Pablo laughed, "I'd say so."

Huachuca rode up well ahead of the others and now with Three Finger Jack in tow they were returning. Jack had only been gone a moment. "Indian has something he wants to tell ya'll."

"White man disappear. Trail disappear. No sign anywhere. Getting dark, we camp here," the Indian motioned toward the ground.

The men sat their horses looking at each other wondering how the man could have just disappeared with twenty mules for the second time in less than two days.

"The next time we see him we'd better ride straight in after him or we may never catch him," Hughe advised.

Pony Bob looked straight at Hughe. "Might I remind you what we did today?"

"No, you needn't remind me."

"I sure hope things go better tomorrow," Three Finger Jack added.

In reflective silence the men dismounted and untied their blanket rolls. Spreading them out on the hard ground they made them as comfortable as possible and nestled into them for the night.

When morning dawned the Indian was already gone, looking for a trail they could pick up again. Returning to camp, he found bacon and hot coffee ready. He didn't say a word but took out his cup and plate and accepted his portion. Knowing the white man's way, he kept silent wanting to agitate his counterparts as much as possible before telling them what he'd found. His own personal amusement was something he'd learned from the Comanchero and more and more he was finding ways to exploit this new phenomenon to his personal satisfaction.

"Are you going to say anything, Huachuca? Or does the cat have your tongue?" Hughe asked.

"Cat, what cat?"

"It's a figure of speech."

"Figures and speech two different things."

"Are you kidding me?"

"No. No squaw, no kid."

"Hold on Hughe, I think the Indian's playing with you."

"White man cross river and back downstream he go."

"Are you saying we've gone right past him somehow?"

"No somehow. We rode right by him."

"Where is he now?" Bob asked.

"Man with many mules ride out of canyon."

"Well, where did he get to?" Bob patience floundered.

"Not know, him vanish like buffalo on the Great Plains."

The men continued to rest against their saddles, sipping coffee and frying up bacon, not inclined to begin another day with no idea what to look for. Each of them pondered what the Indian said and none of them liked what they were faced with.

"I guess we'd better get a move on," Bob finally announced, "otherwise we'll never catch him."

It was mid-afternoon when they finally found the spot where the mule train departed the deep cut bottom of the canyon, three miles past where they'd entered and on the other side. The man left no visible trail to announce his presence in the lower recesses. The best anyone could tell the man simply disappeared. It was Pablo who had found the opening into the cave. He fired one shot into the air and waited. When the others rode up they were a grimed-faced lot.

Pablo pointed at the opening. "He went through here." Pablo said.

"Well, let's get after him."

"Hold on, Bob. That's an enclosed space we're riding into. Don't forget what he did to Moses. We're going to need some way to light our path. We can't go riding in there blind, he might be laying for us."

"He's a man who wants to live. No fool in his right mind would start a gunfight in a cave where he could cause a cave-in and bury himself alive. He won't be in there," Bob said as he dismounted.

"Bob, you don't know it yet, but the man threw dynamite at Moses in an enclosed room much like this cave. I wouldn't be in such an all-fired hurry to go riding in there after him. If we corner Jeb in there what's to stop him from doing the same to us?"

"Your concern is duly noted." Taking his horse by the reins Bob entered the tunnel. No one had a light to offer, except a match every once in a while. Hughe happened to carry them to light his tobacco; otherwise they would have had no respite from the darkness.

The night was pitch-black when the posse made their exodus into the cool night air. No one commented, no one moved for it was obvious to them all they weren't going to follow the banker on such a night as this. A raging storm was off to the west, but headed for them at breakneck speed. The wind gusts were already filling the air with the smell of rain.

"Let's spread out and get some fuel for a fire if we can and we'll spend the night back here inside the cave where we can stay dry."

As a well-oiled unit they fanned out to gather what they could before the storm arrived. Anything that might burn was scarce, but they did manage a few dead twigs from some scrub brush. Had it not been for the experienced Hughe gathering his own wood for a fire they would not have been warm in the cave at all, but his wood scavenging prowess saved them. The men warmed their food over the fire but said nothing. They knew what the storm would do to any sign left by the banker. His trail would be completely obliterated by the raging storm, as if they didn't already have enough trouble following the bits and pieces he left behind. Each man feared what they would find in the morning when they awoke and rode out of their natural cave shelter, which they suspected would be absolutely nothing. When they did ride out their worst fears were realized.

"What do we do now?" Pablo asked.

"How many hours of a head start do you figure he has?" Bob asked.

"At least ten, if he stopped and rested last night, if not, it could be more," Hughe said.

"We'll ride the same direction he was headed before the storm, and if we don't cut his trail late today we'll have to spread out and look for it."

"I sure hope luck is with us, because that could take days," Three Finger Jack said.

"Let's ride, gentlemen."

The men turned their horses into the wind and headed northwest. They were four hours into the heat of day when they saw the trail and it was fresh tracks made after the storm.

"We've got him," Bob announced, and the posse picked up its pace

Unexpectedly they changed course. They'd been riding northwest but were now headed due west directly into the path of the sun. The trail swerved sharply and Pony Bob swore.

Pablo rode up beside him and stared down at the ground. The men found themselves looking into a draw now only a crack, seeping water. The pool or what used to be one was now only a trickle of water dripping down into the bowl shaped rock. It was just a trickle, but it was water. Where there had been a small pool about three feet in circumference and a foot or so deep there was now only a few drops. Each man knew it would be a while before the pool would refill itself to the level of water Jeb found when he happened on the place. If not for the previous night's rain, there would be no water at all. Then they saw the note sticking from beneath a rock.

Stepping down from his horse, Bob took it out from under the paperweight and unfolded the gritty piece of paper. He read out loud. "You may as well rest your horses and make camp. This is the only water source you'll find for the next sixty miles and should take the rest of today and all night tonight to produce enough water for you to carry on."

Jack grabbed the note from Bob and read for himself. "He's taunting us."

Bob looked at the inept trickle of water. "Maybe, but he's right. Let's make camp fella's, we're going to be here for a while," Hughe said.

Dropping from their saddles the men made dry camp in the shade of the surrounding rocks and waited. They napped, rested their mounts, and studied their dilemma. Well after dark the men let their horses drink and then filled their canteens. At sunup they refilled their canteens and water bags and let their horses drink again. They mounted up and took one last look at the dripping water then headed out on the open desert. No one felt like talking. The note Jeb left had been an insult to them all, especially Hauchuca, even if the banker had been correct in his observation.

These men believed they would ride the rogue banker down in short order, yet nearly a week into the chase, a majority of the posse was no longer with them and those who were left were no longer sure of themselves.

After two hours of riding the men found themselves right back where they'd started. They were no less than three hundred yards from where they'd made camp the previous night and looking down at where Jeb Blackwell had stayed. Studying his campsite gave them no comfort.

"Men, this ain't no-how, no way going to be as easy as I thought it would be when we first started. If any of you want to pack it in, you're welcome. I'm the only one here who has to go on," Bob admitted.

"I reckon we're staying," Pablo said, "but, we might as well water our stock again while we're close to water."

When they reached the small trickle of spring water that's all they found.

The men faced the empty pool with the knowledge Jeb had recently watered his mule train while they were out tracing his steps trying to figure out where he went. To a man they felt as if they'd been taken advantage of and made a fool of.

Compressed under the same rock was another note. Stepping down Bob retrieved the piece of paper and read aloud one more time. "Three Finger Jack, your horse is losing a shoe. Best turn back if you want to survive."

"I've been thinking the same thing," Hughe said.

"White man has good eyes," Huachuca said. "No Indian can see that good."

"He's got a set of field glasses, that's why he can see Jack's horse from where he is. Randy Bean used to travel with a set left over from the war. I found them on him when I discovered him," Bob said to Pablo.

"Bob, we'd better do some figuring and do it fast because up to now this thing has been a little one sided, and we keep coming up on the short end of things. We might live longer if we turn around and go back. The Slash M is paid off. We know there is more gold on my ranch, plus there are plenty of cattle. I'm in good enough shape to last a while with or without the treasure."

"Are you saying we should give up?" Pony Bob was surprised.

"Not necessarily. Look, we don't need to get ourselves killed for no reason. At the same time he can't be more than an hour or two ahead of us, if that. Either we run him down now, or throw in the towel. We need to make a decision."

"If any of you want to bow out now's the time. The next couple of hours will be the most dangerous we've encountered so far. Nobody will hold it against you," Bob said.

No one said a word. The men looked to Pony Bob for his reply, for their silence was answer enough. "All right then, let's ride. If one or more of us get hurt or separated for any reason make your way back to this water hole."

Touching spurs to their horses the five men rode out of the draw and pushed their mounts. They'd been riding for fifteen minutes when a bullet lifted Hauchuca from the back of his horse. He'd been the easiest to identify because he was the only rider among them who did not resemble an honest to goodness cowboy.

No one saw where the bullet came from but they heard the report of the rifle while the Indian was still yet in the air. The outlaw banker had laid an ambush for them. The remaining lawmen dove for cover, and scrambled to get behind the large rocks scattered across the desert floor.

"Where is he?" Bob yelled. No one answered so he asked again.

"Did anyone see where he was shooting from?"

Still there was no answer. None of them wanted to provide Jeb a target to hone in on. They waited for what seemed like hours but it in reality was less than thirty minutes. Another shot rang out and Jack's horse went down. Then another and Pablo's horse hit the ground graveyard dead. Another bullet took Bob's appaloosa to the ground just as Hughe was reaching for his mount to pull it to safety. Huachuca's horse had run off a good distance and was out of reach of any gunfire. Hughe managed to get his behind the big slab of jagged rock before Jeb could kill it.

"What in the devil's name are you doing?" Bob shouted across the large ravine that presented itself as a gulf too wide to cross from where Jeb had the lawmen pinned down.

"I'm setting you afoot," came the banker's reply. "Besides, there's no law against shooting a horse, just for stealing them," Jeb shouted.

"Did anybody see where he is?" Bob yelled. Then he saw the Indian. The red man was making his way in the direction of a clump of rocks partially hidden from view by bushes. There was a buildup of tumble weeds off to one side.

"Pablo, Huachuca is okay. I can see him," Bob whispered.

Pablo did some moving of his own. Three Finger Jack and Hughe had the same idea. Pony Bob Haslam was pinned down right where he was, but the others were free to advance using brush and rock formations for cover. Figuring he'd killed the Indian with his first shot, Jeb paid attention to the other four men in the posse, letting his concentration on the Indian lapse.

Pablo moved up near Pony Bob, but in his own hiding place where he could still maneuver. The Slash M owner tried to get Bob's attention and a bullet clipped a rock near his head. He then lay perfectly still. Suddenly there was a volley of fire from both sides; a sudden exchange that tapered into dead silence.

Bob was no longer in the mood for talking, but in his current position he couldn't very well see what was going on. Thank God there was a bunch of veterans with him, men who knew how to fight and how to maneuver, otherwise he would be in a much worse situation.

"Jeb, you might as well give up. I promise you'll get a fair trial," Bob yelled across the ravine. "There doesn't have to be any more bloodshed."

Looking back, Bob wondered where the Indian had gotten to. He could no longer see Three Finger Jack and when he turned back to look the other way, Pablo was no longer visible. It seemed everyone was able to advance but him.

It was Three Finger Jack who stepped up behind Jeb first. "Howdy Jeb!"

The gunman wheeled around as if he'd been stung by a bee and Three Finger Jack shot him in the shoulder just before he could bring his rifle to bear on Jack himself. The banker slammed back against the rock he'd been using for cover and slumped to a sitting position, holding his wounded shoulder, his Winchester slung wide. He took his hand away from his wound and tried to pull a six shooter from its holster, but Three Finger Jack slapped it away and then retrieved his last firearm.

"What are you doing, Jeb? You know you're going to hang. I should kill you right now for what you did to Randy, but I guess Randy had it coming."

"I..." he coughed violently, then said, "...wanted a new life, far away in San Francisco or some exotic place." The banker was breathing heavier and sweating now.

"Well, looks like you got what you wanted only the exotic place is going to be prison."

"I never wanted the old man's ranch. That was his idea of a good life. I wanted a home on the beach somewhere. Not some dirty, smelly cow ranch."

"You sure played hob."

Huachuca walked up and sat down across from Jeb.

"You keep that Indian away from me." Jeb demanded. "I've seen what he can do."

"Oh, you mean like removing someone's fingers?" Three Finger Jack said as he raised his three fingered hand, and waved it in front of Jeb. "I think we ought to let him guard the jail just for the fun of it."

The ranger, Pablo, and Hughe walked up as the two men were conversing.

"I guess you got your gold back," Bob told Pablo. "Can he make the trip back?"

Jack pushed Jeb's shoulder with the rifle barrel. "He's not hurt. We'll have to travel slowly anyway since some of us have to ride these Missouri mules to get home."

Chapter 22

The entire territory of Arizona was a cauldron of intrigue within days. Everybody who knew anybody and wanted to listen had a full accounting of the events of recent weeks, reshaping the lives of many who lived in Arizona. All knew the name of Pablo Mendoza, Bob Haslam the Arizona Ranger, and Three Finger Jack. The folks in and around Arizona also knew well the names of Hughe Rainwater, Hauchuca, Billy the Kid, and finally the name of Jeb Blackwell. The story of Jeb leaving Moses Carter for dead lost nothing in the telling and was told everywhere men gathered. Men were appalled, and women were horrified at the cruel and evil ways of Jeb Blackwell. They heard how he'd robbed his own bank and murdered perfectly good horses while trying to escape the posse.

They knew he'd been captured and was awaiting trial for murder, bank robbery, and fraud. They knew about the lost Mexican gold shipment being recovered, and they knew also the Mendoza ranch was better left alone. Better left alone had now come home to roost. This was the kind of story that convinced drifters of little means to become part of a town they had no business in. A chance to witness such events first hand was all they wanted and the town of Sonora was filling up with strangers eager to see the trial and eventual hanging.

Several attorneys were sparing for the opportunity to represent the condemned while on the government's dole, others to represent the territory of Arizona itself. Miners began to arrive, yet they were unable to cross Slash M range for they would be captured and brought right back to town.

The people in and around Sonora watched with reverence and curiosity whenever the Mendoza's rode into Sonora. Whether it was the couple themselves, or the Comancheros returning lost placer miners, or coming to town for a break, the Slash M drew the watchful eye of outsiders who only wished they could have been part of the story.

Two and a half weeks passed since Jeb's incarceration, and on this day his cell would not hold him. The discontent banker had been studying the ceiling long enough. The roof was sturdy, but the mason work just below it had been repaired several times. If there was a weak spot the repair work would be it. Obviously there had been several escape attempts, had they been successful, or were they attempts only? The wall would be weak at such a point and Jeb wasted no time once the ranger left the building. As soon as the office was vacant he went to work chipping away at the wall with a piece of metal he'd managed to remove from the bed in his cell. Within minutes he was seeing the stars in the distance through the hole he'd created. Suddenly the weak spot in the repairs revealed itself and Jeb gave a good shove to the portion of wall he'd been scraping away at. The back wall opened up and suddenly Jeb found himself standing on the outskirts of town and once through the opening he wasted no time in stealing a horse and hightailing it out of town.

Two hours lapsed before anyone knew Jeb was gone and a posse at that particular moment was not even a thought in anyone's mind. Bob Haslam lost a prisoner, but he would get the man back. At least that's how things were in his mind.

Since locking him up, the Slash M had been operating under normal circumstances for the first time in months. They did have one additional rider by the name of Three Finger Jack, and the fact he was missing two fingers made no difference in his work ability, he was as good as the ranch had. Three Finger Jack and Pablo were actually becoming inseparable friends. Jack was becoming respectable after having negotiated a fair deal with the new ranch owner. Wherever the ranch owner went, Three Finger Jack could be seen at his side, and nothing could have rankled Dean Reynolds more. Dean knew his play was through, but he refused to leave town.

Things were moving along briskly on the Mendoza ranch and Pablo's men could have no way of knowing Jeb escaped the jail. Three Finger Jack and Pablo were over by the newly formed lake having a discussion with the owner of the B & B Connected when the ranger rode up to inform them of Jeb's escape.

"Howdy Bob, what's new?" Pablo asked.

"Jeb managed to break jail last night. I've followed him onto your range, and I believe he was headed for your house or maybe somewhere near it. He must have seen you up here and turned the other direction. I thought it best to come and tell you. I'm going after him wherever he's headed."

"The women are alone with Moses," Pablo said, and spurred his horse to a dead run.

Not one of the men hesitated following Pablo's example in unison. Four riders headed for the ranch house at breakneck speed while the rest of the cowboys were culling the herds. The distance was a good seven miles and no one need tell them what could happen.

The men were still two hundred yards away when the gunshots at the ranch compound cut through the air like a knife. Jeb was coming out the front door as the four riders came tearing through the courtyard entrance at an all-out run. No one needed to tell him the kind of trouble he was in for. He was still holding his gun belt in his hands as he dove back into the house through the closed screen door.

Bullets chipped away at the door facing, sending splinters of wood around him as he made a panicked dive for cover. Conchetta still sat in the corner of the front room curled into a ball, her dress in shreds and her face bruised and battered; sobbing from the advances she'd just endured at his hands. Anna lay sprawled on the kitchen floor out of view from the now helpless and shocked Conchetta.

Scrambling back to the nearest window Jeb examined his options, and looked at Conchetta with malice. God she was pretty. Too bad she belonged to Pablo.

"Get over here," he ordered.

Still reeling from her recent abuse, the girl failed to respond; to hear anything her abuser said to her. So withdrawn inside of her protective cocoon no words registered in the brain of the young wife of Pablo Mendoza, not from the man facing her from across the room.

"I said get over here," he repeated.

Still Conchetta failed to respond, no movement except to curl up tighter in the corner, allowing only for the tears which she now shed.

"Jeb let me come in and talk to you!" Horace yelled at his son.

"I don't have anything to say to you, old man."

"I'm coming in any way," Horace yelled back.

Footsteps sounded on the stairs and Horace Blackwell pushed through the torn screen door to face his son. "Good God almighty son. What in God's name are you doing?" he asked as he looked on the carnage his son had caused.

"I'm going out in a blaze of glory and I'm going to take as many of them with me as I can," he hesitated, "This ranch, the gold, all of it should have been mine. If I can't have it, neither can Pablo Mendoza!" The young man shouted at his father.

Horace turned to look at Conchetta, a picture of fragile and torn innocence, a shattered young girl. As he stared at her, he realized his right hand was out of sight from his son's scrutiny. Jeb would never suspect his own father would turn on him, of that much Horace was certain, for he'd given the young man everything, everything except a conscience. He was also certain things could not be allowed to continue. Slipping his well-worn revolver from the aged leather holster with his right hand the old man turned to face his son and started shooting. One, two, three, four, five, click, click, click...

Staring at his father wild-eyed as blood choked off his breath, Jeb tried to shape his words but they would not come. He tried to raise his pistol but it slipped from his fingers as he lifted it to bear on his own father. One of the bullets caught his forearm and left it mangled. The dying man finally summoned a breath and said his last words, "But, you're my father."

Just then a shotgun boomed from inside the hallway and Moses Carter hobbled forward.

"I's sorry, Mr. Blackwell. He'd no call," he stated.

"It's all right, Moses. He was a bad one. I thought I could change him, but I was wrong."

Ignoring his lifeless son, Horace called out to the others and holstered his weapon. Walking over to Conchetta, he reached down to help her up. Within seconds Pablo was beside him and picked his young bride up and carried her down the hallway to the master bedroom that they'd been sharing as husband and wife since saying their vows that day with Pio and Anna. He did everything he could think of to make her comfortable and then sat down beside her.

Three Finger Jack tapped on the door and stuck his head inside. "Boss, he's dead and gone. Is there anything I can do for you or the little lady, anything to make you more comfortable?"

"Go get Doc Bradley, Jack. I don't know where he is, but I want him here as fast as a horse can fly."

"I'm on my way," Three Finger Jack said as he closed the door behind him.

With tears welling in her big green eyes, Conchetta looked over at the man who was her husband for the rest of their lives. "Pablo, please forgive me, I could not stop him, he was so swift. I...he had a gun. I..."

Touching her cheek he brushed away a tear and tried to comfort her with words. "It wasn't your fault. There's nothing to forgive. I should have never left the hacienda unguarded. You should have never been unguarded."

"What if," she paused, "I'm afraid, what if I'm pregnant?"

"What?"

"What if I'm pregnant?" she repeated.

Pablo now understood how far things had gone. "My dear Conchetta if you're not already pregnant I would be in shock. Why that man doesn't have a chance," he promised. "There is no way you could be pregnant by him, only I can be the father. The way we've been going at it. Are you kidding me? Look at me, I can't even walk straight my back hurts so much from making love to you."

Conchetta struggled to laugh for she knew Pablo must be correct, but her laughter was drowned by the tears and torment of the moment.

"Remember my dear, abuse is only abuse as long as it's going on. The moment it ceases it becomes a blessing. I don't know how, I wasn't here when God put everything in place, but I do know you are now blessed. All we have to do is find where your blessing is hidden." He smiled and squeezed her hand planting a kiss on her cheek.

Two hours later the others were still in the front room cleaning up the mess when they heard the laughter coming from the bedroom, an almost insane tone making its way down the hall. They paused for a moment and then continued their work in earnest.

The Ranger tried to smile. "They do say laughter is the best medicine."

Just then Saul Stewart the Pinkerton man walked into the house.

"Are Pablo and his wife okay?" The agent asked.

"They're going to be fine. That's them you hear laughing in the back bedroom," Bob announced.

"I need to speak to Pablo. Do you think he'll mind?"

"Can't it wait?"

"I've waited too long already," the detective said as he turned and headed down the hallway.

There was a tap at the door and Pablo got up to open it.

"May I come in, sir?"

"Why not, everyone else is."

"For that I am truly sorry sir, but I have news that I must impart to you."

"Come in and close the door." Walking back to Conchetta sitting up in bed, Pablo turned back to face the strange man. "What is it?"

"I was hired by Pratt and Pratt out of St. Louis Missouri to find two brothers. One of them grew up on the streets of St. Louis, the other was raised by the Mendoza family; that would be you, sir.

Suddenly Bobby Joe understood. The man he'd buried in Mexico had been his brother, a brother he would never get to know.

"The birth names of the men I sought were Eugene and Robert Westmoreland. They were members of an elite old English family born to the postmaster and his wife in Hermann, Missouri before the outbreak of war. You sir, were given the name of Mendoza on your adoption in your first year, your mother having followed your father in death when you were born. Your brother Robert was adopted by a family from New Madrid, Missouri and given the name of Bobby Joe Riggins. I do believe he has become somewhat of a noted gunman,

322

although it appears always on the side of right. I seem to have lost track of young Bobby Joe, just as I have found you. You sir, took some finding."

"Why are you telling me this? Why does any of this matter now?"

"Because sir, you and your brother have inherited a grand estate; an estate like no other. It is to belong to one or the other of you, if you claim it on time. And sir, it does come with a rather large sum of money."

Pablo began to laugh while Conchetta sat in bed perplexed, paralyzed by recent events.

A puzzled look came across Saul's face as he tried to comprehend the laughter. "What is so funny, sir?"

"Who's lying in wait to ambush me?"

"I don't understand the question, sir." The Pinkerton agent was truly perplexed.

"Who doesn't want me to show up?"

"Why, I have no idea what you're referring to."

"Exactly! Mister the dust around here hasn't even settled yet and you want us to start all over again? Thanks, but no thanks. I'm a little tired of having a target painted on my chest."

Grabbing the fellow by the arm, Pablo escorted him to the door and just as he ripped it open the man erupted. "But sir, you must do something with the money."

Pausing Robert Westmoreland as he now understood himself to really be said, "How much money is it?"

"Seven million dollars."

"And it has to be claimed?"

"Yes sir. You must state your claim."

"Mr. Stewart, there are no less than twenty-four orphanages in the French settlement known as St. Louis.

My wife and I have little need of any more money. Can you arrange to have one hundred thousand dollars a year divided among them? They fed me more than once when I was growing up as a youngster."

"But sir, you grew up in Laredo, Texas."

"If you say so," Pablo replied.

"You mean..." Saul began.

"I wouldn't try to figure it out at this very moment. Let's just say that you have located the right family."

"I see. It will take me a few days to make the necessary arrangements, but I can do so. You'll have to sign papers, of course."

"Of course," Pablo said.

Saul continued to stare at the young couple then slowly backed out the doorway and made his way down the hall. There was no answer he could think of, yet he understood exactly who he'd been speaking to. The young rancher had been Bobby Joe Riggins, or more aptly put, Robert Westmoreland the Third. As the Pinkerton man stepped into his saddle he shook his head in disbelief and rode away.

"Well, at least one of them survived," he told himself as he rode out of the ranch compound. "So, Pablo Mendoza it is."

324

About the Author

John T. Wayne graduated from Hermann, High School in Hermann, Missouri in 1976. By mid-summer he had joined the United States Marines where he turned eighteen in boot camp. He learned quickly to shoot and became an expert marksman with both the rifle and pistol. He was trained as a radio operator and communications expert, whose life expectancy in a combat situation is approximately eight seconds.

He was sent to Okinawa, Japan in December of 1976 where he spent two and a half years. While on the island he developed a passion for reading Louis L'Amour novels. His love for a good western was fueled by the stores written by the most published author of the time. Of course, those westerns would not have happened without the Civil War, so John dove in and studied the War Between the States.

As a former Marine he attended the University of Oregon on his G.I. Bill. While doing so he lost his daughter Kimberly to cancer. It was then he started writing his stories. At first he wrote just to keep his mind straight. Then as time went on, "I figured if I was going to be writing so much, I might as well write a novel. The only thing I knew anything about was what life could do to a man, and the Old West."

His books are the result of many years of study, and many years of working on his writing style. We hope you like them.

List of men killed in the Civil War

In my research, I have had to swallow some bitter pills about what it really means to be an American. When I realized that every state in the Union was a sovereign entity prior to the Civil War, and that the Federal Government had no power to tell them what to do, it sheds a new light on the subject of state's rights. When the war was over, every Yankee Doodle Dandy in the north and every Swinging Dixie in the south handed their freedom and sovereignty over to the Federal Government. That means every state in the Union lost, not just the south. The men listed below died that we might remain free. Had the north known in the end they would be handing their freedom and sovereignty over to the Feds, they would likely have never picked up a rifle.

CSA

Capt. Matthew Gray 1st TN Reg
Pvt. John H. Perciful 1st AR Cav.
Sgt. William Henry Atkins 50th Reg. TN
Sgt. L.E. Williams 4th Artillery MD
Cpl. John Archer Hurt 47th TN Infantry
Cpl. Hezekiah Westbrook 77th Mounted Cav.
Pvt. J.H. Hester 12th Kentucky Cav.

CPSIA information can be obtained
at www.ICGtesting.com
Printed in the USA
FFOW03n1529181117
43546601-42301FF